CW01160090

Hairy, Scary, Lumpy, Bumpy, Woof

More Critters who Adopted the Williams Family

Stories and Artwork by Jennifer Foreman de Grassi Williams

Watercolors by Bobbi Kelly

The Williams Family Animal Tales of Tails — Volume No 2

Copyright © 2020 Jennifer Williams
All rights reserved.
ISBN-13:

Kindly dedicated to my beautiful Mother who would say "do no harm".

With Empathy for all creatures we share this Earth, and especially those I've had the privilege of knowing/loving/helping more than most humans I've met~

Lovingly written for my own children whom I've dedicated most everything positive I've accomplished in my life until now~ but passing the torch to my quirky, adorable, clever, fun-loving, sweet, sensitive, artistic, and kind grandchildren~ those little tricksters: Norah, Harper, Sonja, Reed, and leaving this space for the grandbabies yet to be:

_____

Kirk (TLOML)

Joey (My "see-stir")

Contents

The Williams Family and an Iguana Named Diego ....

The Williams Family and MJ the Red Knee Tarantula ....

The Williams Family and Sunshine the Yellow-bellied Marmot.........

The Williams Family Saves Moose the Kangaroo Mouse..................

The Williams Family Fosters Rabbits, Parakeets, and Snails............

The Williams Family Nurtures Squirrels ....

The Williams Family and Two Dogs...

Button, Buddy, Bunty and Boo are the four remarkable Williams children who were faced with growing up in a house filled with all assorted animal friends… some cuddly and soft, and others that had big teeth. These sentient creatures taught the four B's many lessons about life, love, caring, sharing, acceptance, sensitivity, perseverance, trust, adventure, dedication, duty, responsibility, empathy, respect, embracing the unusual, and setting something free.

The lessons learned, as hoped by their parents, are that all things deserve to be loved and treated with respect. No doubt the four B's will share childhood memories with their own children and continue to be mindful of the footprints they leave in the world, and never forget that if animals could talk they would probably speak of all life as being one big family. Lucky me that I had a Mother who modeled 'do no harm'. While she was not an animal person in all reality, she did go along with my many, many animal adventures as a young girl. I grew up during a time when there were no pet stores I ever knew. And yet my love for all animals was such an innate part of my being, that I seemed to be 'positioned' to find many, or have them turn up in the places I'd hike, bike, run, or hide. They seemed to find me, follow me, or just be there. Once I turned over a rock and there was a snake on a dollar bill, but wedged in such a way that he was trapped with his riches. Another snake needed rescuing from an area of picnickers, and sitting on my lap decided to deliver her dozens of babies right there. (Oh, and the two winter 'rescue' snakes that disappeared into our home and showed up 6 months later, quite thirsty and hungry!)

My mother brought me a day old kitten, the only survivor on the road in a busy industrial area of Oakland, my first experience at night feedings with an eye dropper...and only the beginning of many encounters, and dozens of kittens/cats I continue to rescue and bring home! My mother helped me navigate my intense feelings of responsibility and sensitivity as I had intricate funerals for the animals I helped and lost, and shed more tears than I can count. I cared for an injured hawk that flew down our chimney, raised alligator lizards that would have loved taking my fingers for finger food, brought home box turtles from the creek who sunned themselves in the road, ran like the wind with tadpoles gasping for their last breath in the dried rain puddles by the horse stables, some nearly frogs, and continually relocated the garden snails that were in harm's way. I'll never forget the gasps from women at my mother's tea party as I carried a mole in the crease of my elbow to show them what a red-tailed hawk was about to eat, or the wounded Cooper's hawk hit by a car that people were afraid to rescue and looked right into my soul as only a bird of prey can do, the dozens of squirrels pulled from the road needing rebab after being struck by a car, or the multiples of injured birds who flew into windows or escaped something with fangs. A Western desert tortoise needing mouth to mouth after drowning in a pond came back to life with my mouth to his beak. Tortoises and turtles found their way to my home by neighbors and students who had no idea their stories. There was no hesitation in capturing the bats I brought home from the rafters of the high school who were not being treated very kindly by students, or the baby rattlesnakes who needed removing from a student's locker, and the rock chuck left for dead on the highway. I never really looked at the potential peril of rescuing/saving, though my husband thinks it is a real possibility I'll die trying to save something, or at least end up in the emergency room (like the time

Stewy the squirrel attacked me).

My belief is that some of us have been destined, since birth, to be tasked with an empathy that won't allow you to look or walk away. We take in a plethora of things we probably shouldn't, give to organizations around the world to help with animals we will never see, like elephants, dolphins, gorillas, chimps, whales, sea turtles, tigers, seals, polar bears, wild dogs and cats, etc. We try to educate people about the food and clothing industry, and take lots of risks to save an animal in peril. Teaching allowed me a positive platform to engage students in kindness, and to mentor and model the kind behavior so deserving of sentient beings, and other creepy crawly things. Many times I brought animals into my classroom, like baby sheep, pigs, turtles, mice, or a day old squirrel that needed to be fed. Writing children's books has taken me back into classrooms to read and share stories about the importance of all creatures in our circle of life...we being only one minute part of that circle. I want to know that I've tried my very best to share this Earth with all living things, as equals, and to never take for granted that each living thing has an importance to our well-being and very survival. I always say that

Just because an animal cannot speak in a language we understand doesn't mean they aren't at least as smart as we are. Because we are in a hurry doesn't mean we should flush a spider down the toilet instead of taking the time to carefully take it outside. Just because a person likes meat, doesn't mean we shouldn't allow the animals eaten a happy, uncaged life with a kind and humane death. And because we can own pets, doesn't mean we should treat them any less kindly than a child we love.

I think of all creatures as this Emily Dickenson quote:

If I can stop one heart from breaking,

I shall not live in vain;

If I can ease one life the aching,

Or cool one pain,

Or help one fainting robin unto his nest again,

I shall not live in vain.

The Williams Family and an Iguana Named Diego

A lesson in unconditional love and acceptance no matter the 'scale'

Story and Artwork by

Jennifer Foreman de Grassi Williams

Dedicated to my treasured granddaughters, and my family and friends whose arms open wide to embrace all living beings ~ sentient beings ~ who by no fault of their own, have been taken from their native environments and forced to survive in unnatural habitats.

Thank you to everyone who has tried, and maybe failed, to give an exotic a better life, and never entertained the thought of discarding it, like garbage, into a creek or desert, or worse.

Thank you to all who truly get that sentient beings think and feel, give unconditional love, even if treated poorly, and look to us to be their caregivers.

Thank you to Dr. Alicia Konsella DVM, for always caring that the animal facts are presented accurately so that the quality of an animal's life is the best it can be, and to Reptile Organizations that don't take more from nature, but help nature heal from our taking.

Thank you Bobbi.

Story number 1 is about our very own pet dragon, an Iguana named Diego. It is funny how animals end up in a household. Sometimes there is a grand scheme and lots of planning, and other times, by luck or chance, an opportunity happens. I wasn't looking to have an Iguana, though I always admired their very prehistoric good looks. There happened to be an ad, in which someone was looking to rehome their very large Iguana, because the husband had his pet banished to the garage. The man liked his Iguana, and had him since he was 6" long. The now 4 foot lizard intimidated his wife. Anyone who knows an Iguana realizes that they can stare at you without blinking an eye. His wife found this unnerving as she never could figure what Diego was really thinking. As a matter of fact, I was sent to the garage to meet Diego by myself, and there he was looking at me from behind his giant glass aquarium. For me, it was instant curiosity, admiration and love. I really didn't know much about Iguanas, but knew I would do my homework. Life with Diego was always interesting. Yes, he had a large cage in which he could retreat, drink, eat, sleep, defecate, and climb on wooden limbs. Most days the door was open so he could look out of a window, sun himself if desired, or even climb down and explore the house. Our cats never seemed bothered by Diego, but looked at him quizzically, as only cats can do. Diego would glance once when passing one, but never acted like he felt threatened by his new roommates. There seemed to be a very mutual respect, and that would be a lesson for all of us no matter how different we might seem. Love was unconditional, and each day seemed a new adventure of trying to find where Diego was hiding, or trying to guess his thought process as he rested and stared at you. My mantra was just to observe, behold, and never try to control. Life with what nature had allowed us to experience in his handsomely primitive beauty, was also witness to how he could weave his innate and instinctive behaviors into our lives.

Diego

A dinosaur creature came to live at our house,

It seems funny now how this all came to be;

A friend who first had him just couldn't quite see,

That to us he was beautiful, scaly and prickly.

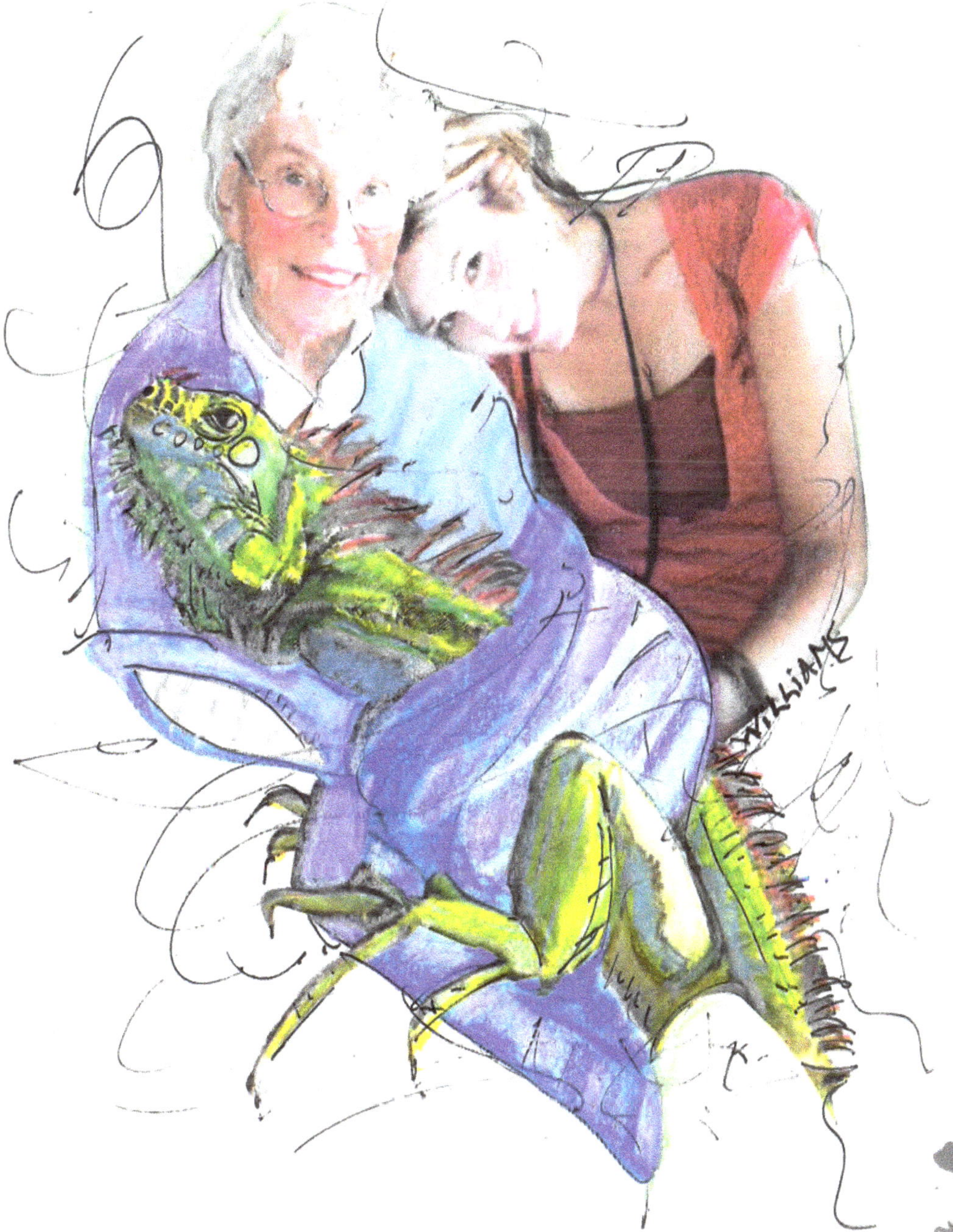
WILLIAMS

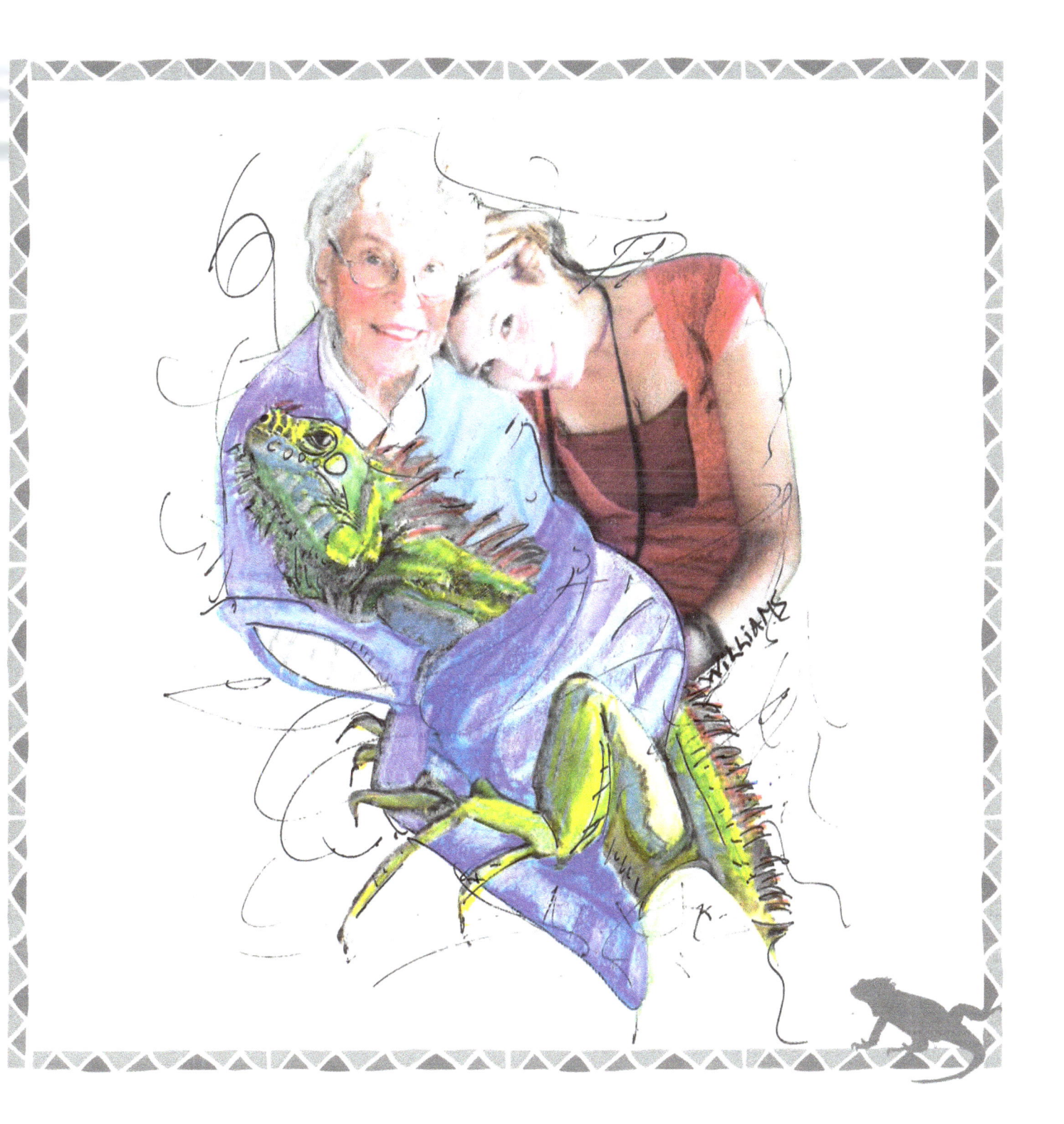

Swimming in an ocean in a big foreign land,

Was the first time that Mommy had seen an Iguana;

She jumped in the water thinking he might be drowning,

But this is quite common in the towns south of Tijuana.

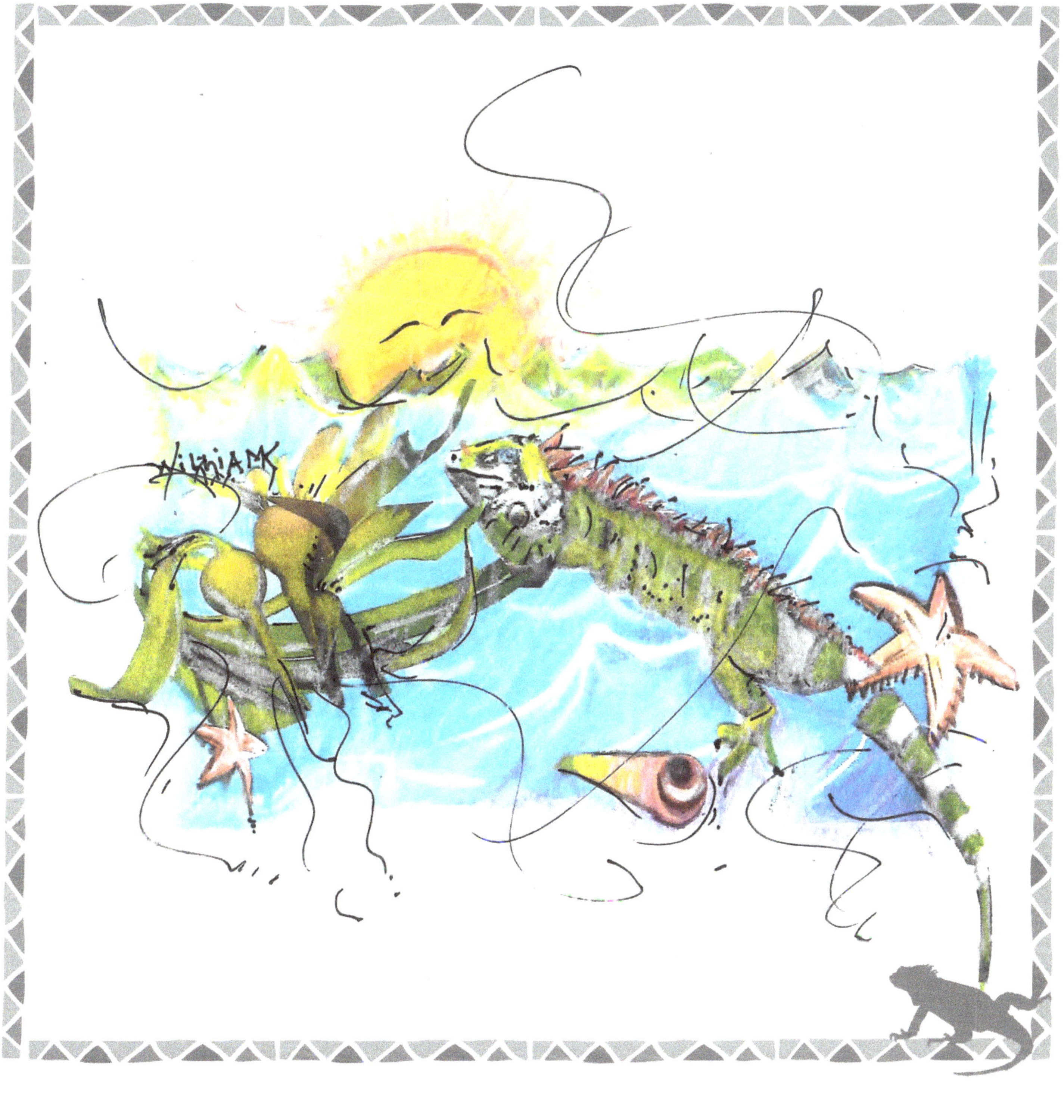

Diego had colors that would change with the cold,

While mostly he sparkled like a hundred rainbows;

He'd sit in the warm sun and how colorful he'd be,

From the spines on his head to the tip of his toes.

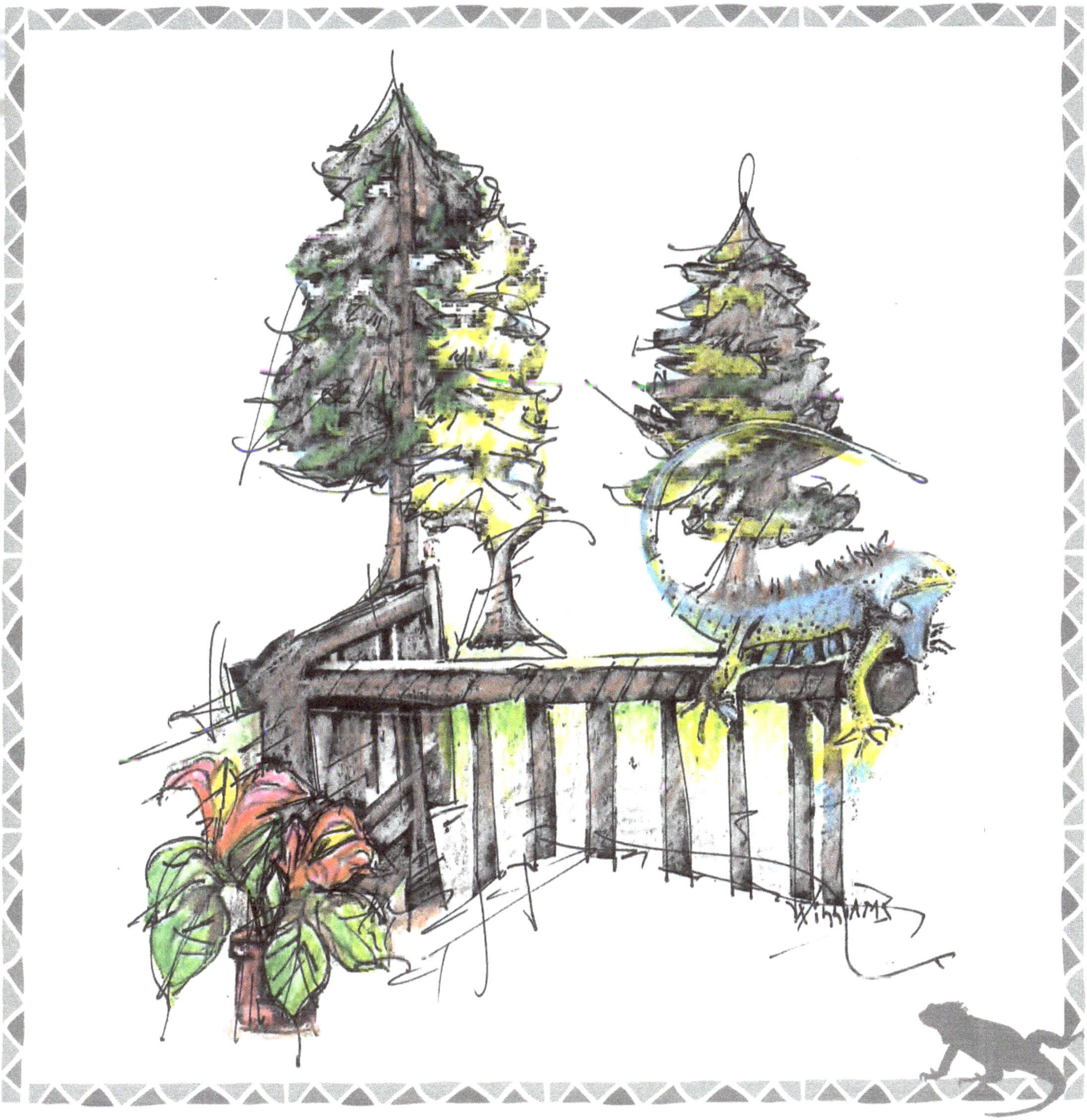
WILLIAMS

Sometimes never blinking as he sat by your side,

So cute was this guy and how still he could be;

But oh he was thinking of where he'd go next,

Would he creep slowly or run fast up a tree?

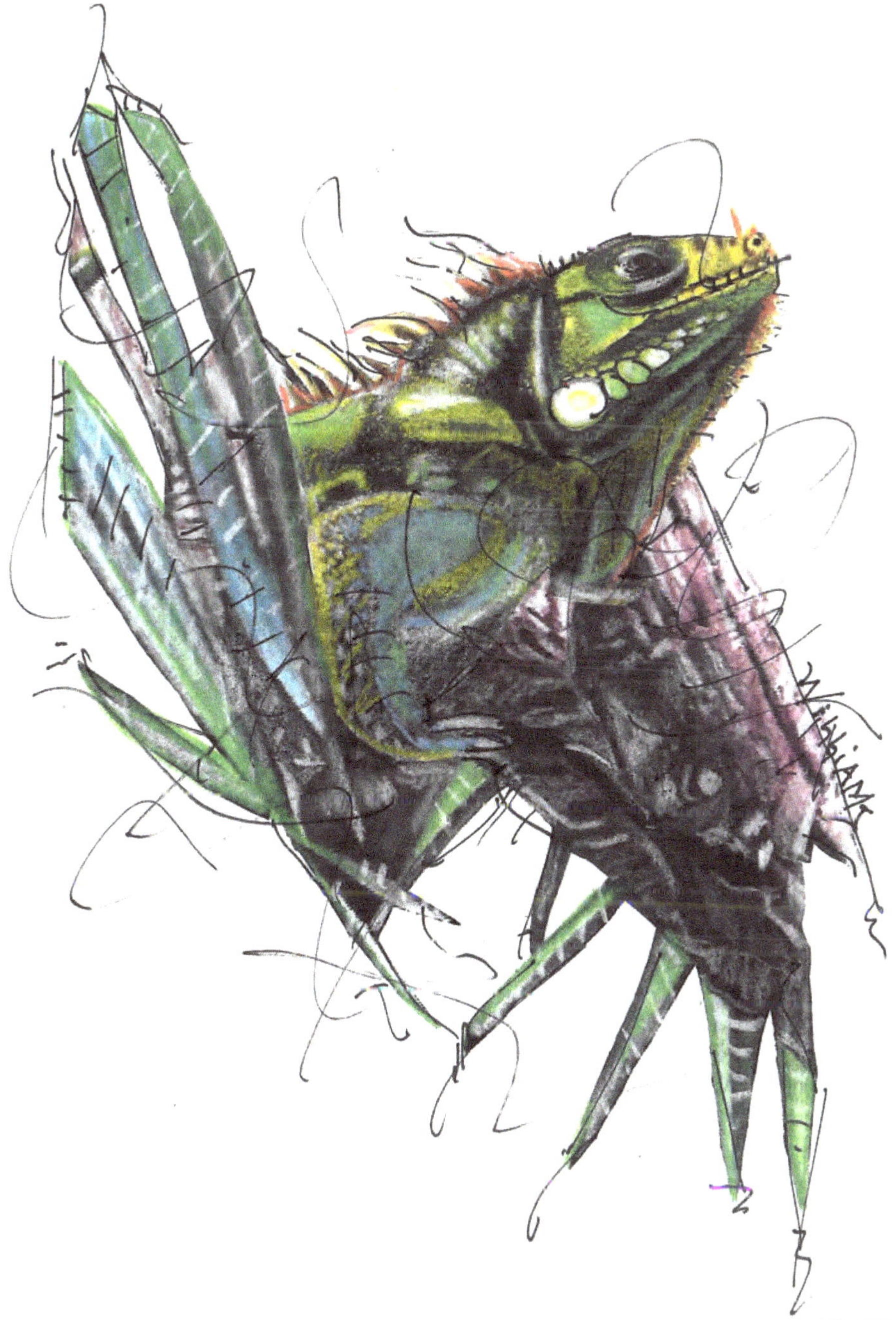

Curious guy would find places to hide,

So each day made us wonder and totally laugh;

Where he would go you might only see his tail,

Or water on the floor as he crawled in the bath.

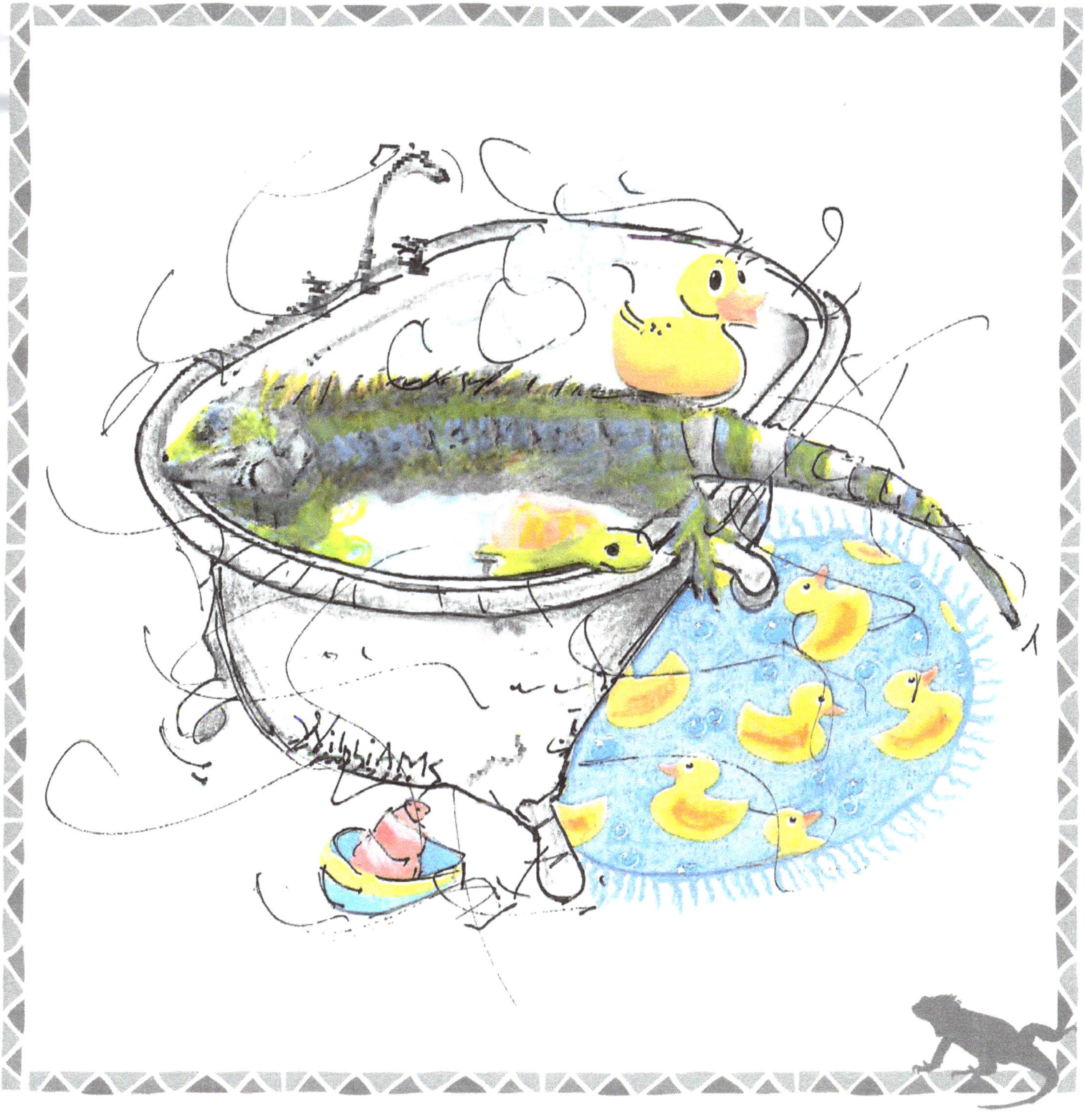

On a shelf in the closet or on top of our clothes,

Our buddy Diego surprised us in spaces;

I know that he tried on our scarves and big hats,

And hid things from us in unusual places.

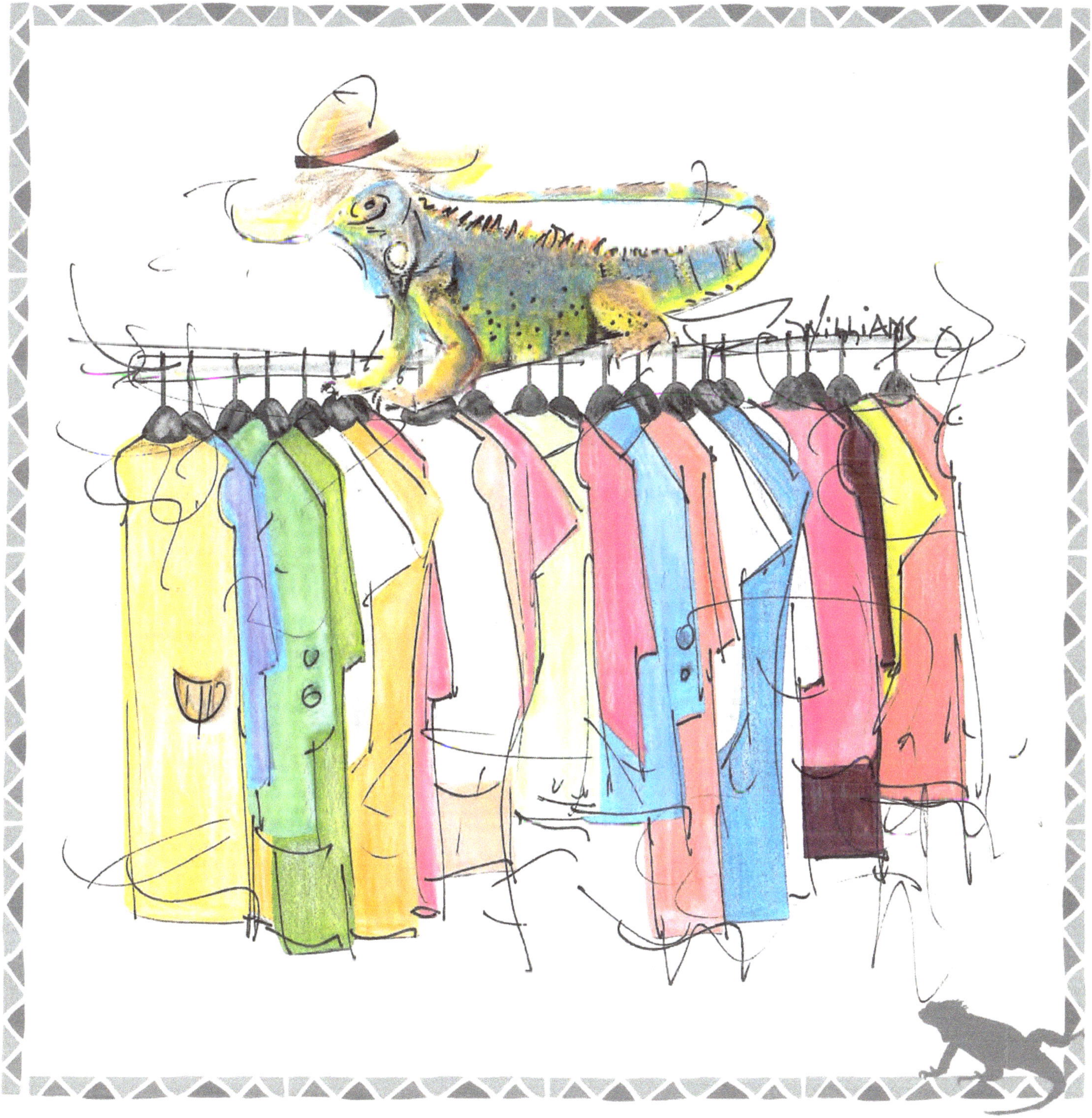
WILLIAMS

Mom loved the feel and texture
of his skin,

And thought it was cute when
he'd climb on her head;

She'd tell him they were going to a
Rainforest to live,

Though they ended up playing in
the garden instead.

Williams

Nasturtiums were yummy and Diego loved them best,

But they also created a great camouflage;

In them he could hide his big sweater and hat,

Because silly old sweater had a big Santa Claus.

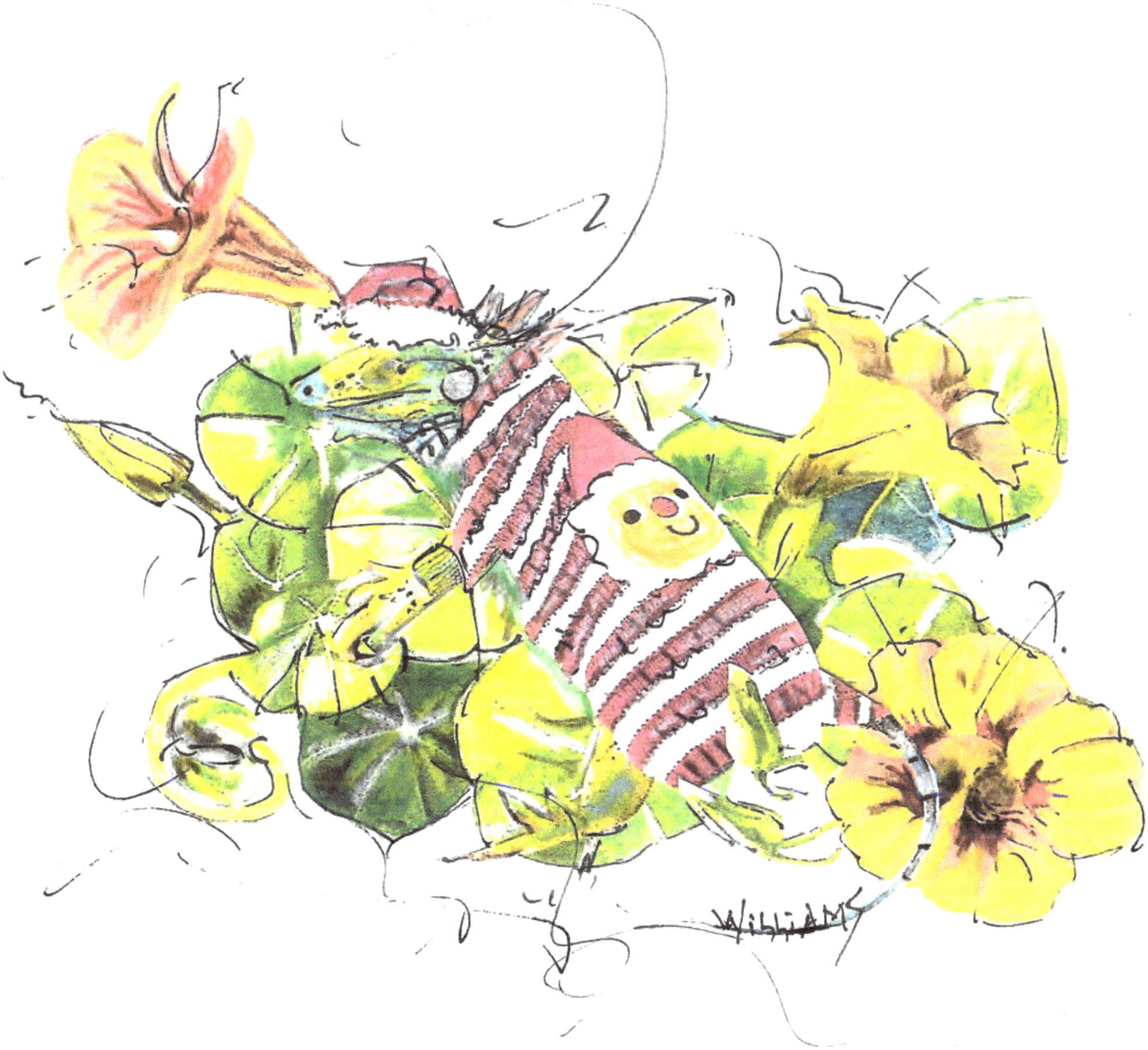
WilliAMS

A lizard like Diego would never eat meat,

And kept himself healthy with kale, and flowers;

Searching in the garden for green turnip tops,

Strawberries, and squash he'd eat for hours and hours.

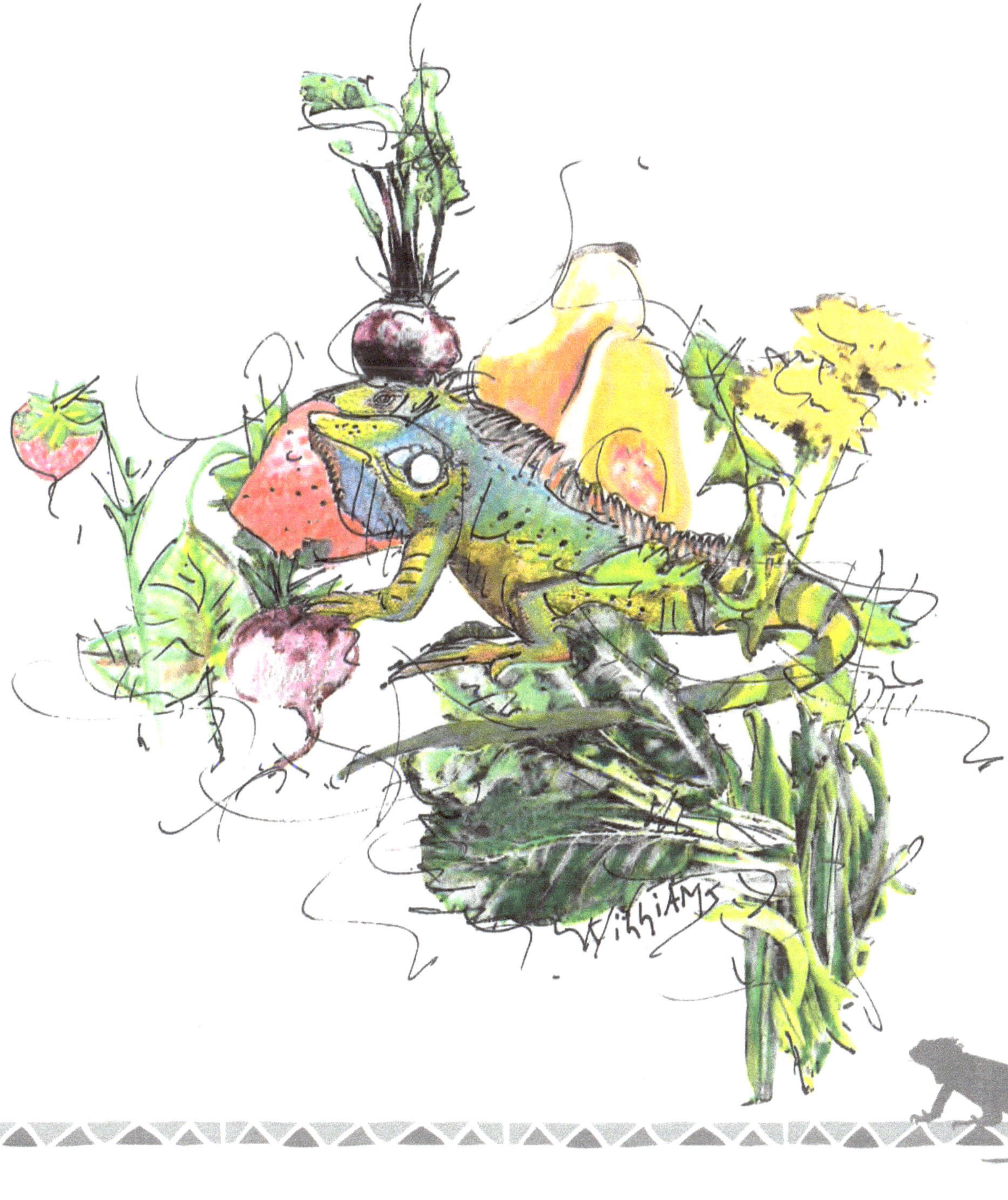
WilliAMS

Grapes whether purple or green were like candy,

He'd gobble them cuz they were good in his diet;

We all loved to feed him and watch as he gobbled,

And we'd chew one sometimes just to say that we tried it.

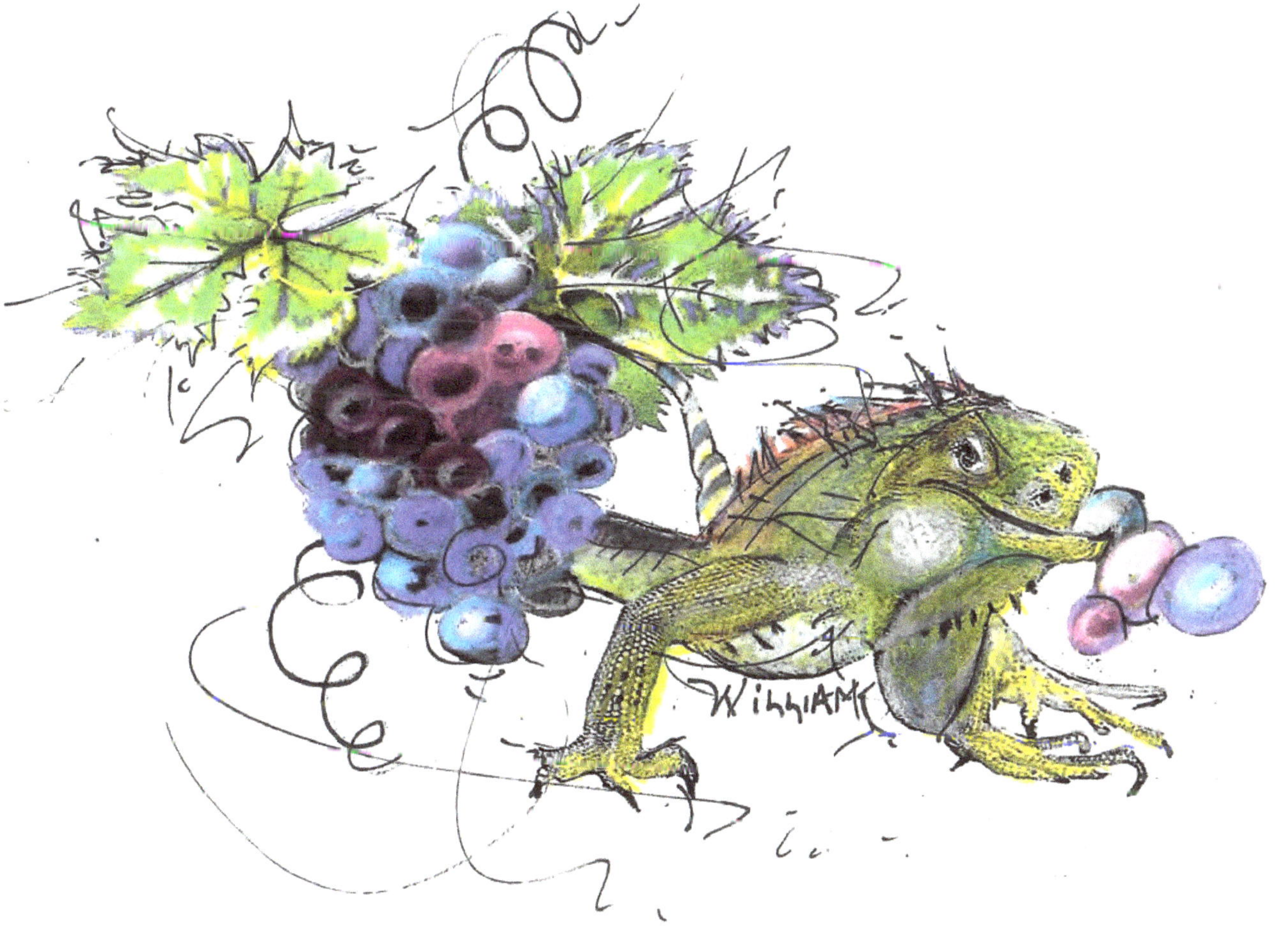
WilliAM

Diego had friends like the kitties in our house,

On the floor you would find him or by them in bed;

He really wasn't fond of a dog, rat or fox,

But he really liked sleeping next to Andy's furry head.

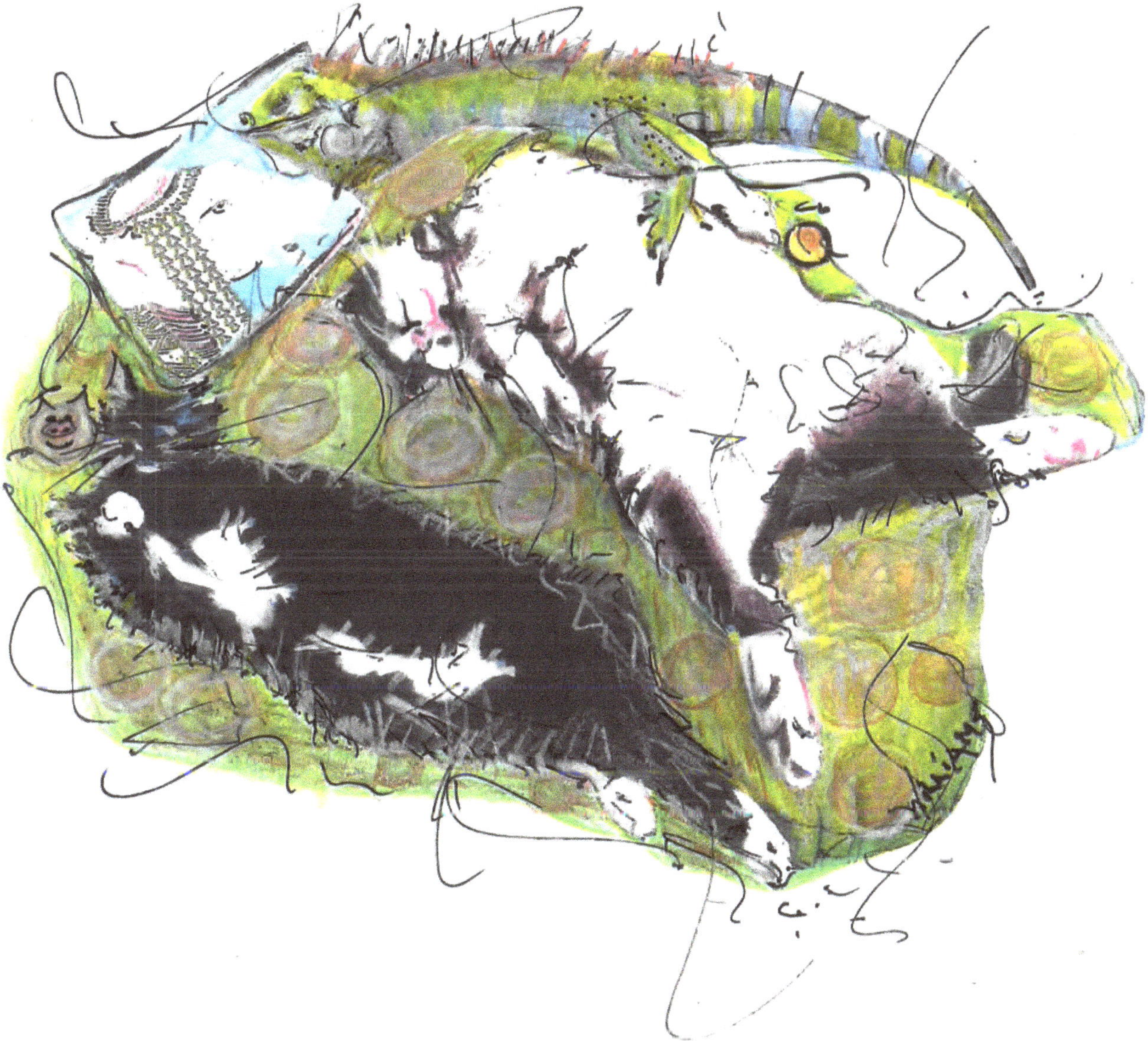

Grandma loved him lots, but dear Jo just wasn't sure,

That loving unconditionally was what he taught us best;

A picture spoke a thousand words upon the family bed,

Grandma, Jo, and kitties too, plus Diego made us blessed.

The End

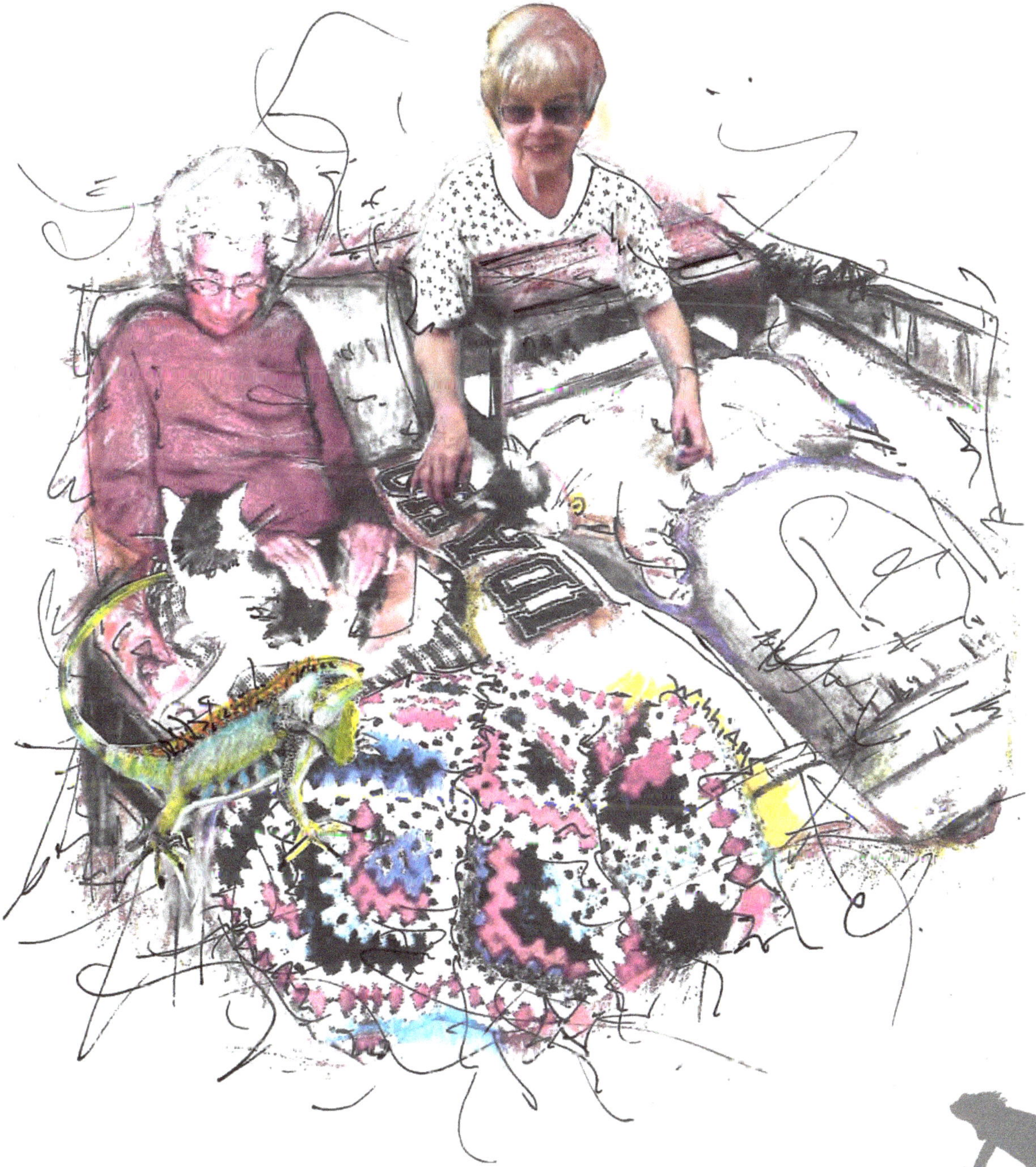

Green Iguana Facts:

1. Pet Iguanas are the largest lizards in America. They can measure between 5-7' and can weigh 20 pounds.

2. Pet Iguanas can live to be 20 years old.

3. Pet Iguanas need plenty of space. Start with a small enclosure when the Iguana is young, but be prepared to expand as the Iguana grows. The enclosure should be twice their length and as wide as the Iguana is long. You may even consider no cage as your Iguana grows and acclimates to the environment.

4. Pet Iguanas require a heated area as they are cold-blooded. They need to stay warm as a cold Iguana will become sick very quickly.

5. Pet Iguanas thrive in temperatures between 80-88 degrees Fahrenheit. Cooler temperatures at night are okay.

6. Pet Iguanas will need UV lighting to help build strong bones and promote metabolism. These lights should be changed every 3 months.

7. Pet Iguanas need a basking area to sit under that is over 100 degrees. They also need an area to escape the heat, if desired.

8. Pet Iguanas need a distinct day and night, as sleep is important to them.

9. Pet Iguanas are vegetarian and require fresh vegetables and some fruit, sprinkled with calcium to reduce the risk of metabolic bone disease and fractures. Do not supplement their diets with cat food as meat-based foods are too high in protein, and could compromise their kidneys, causing renal failure.

10. Pet Iguanas like dandelions and raw vegetables like collard greens, green beans, turnip tops, and yellow squash, with fruits as a once a week treat. Spinach, rhubarb, and carrot tops can rob the Iguana of calcium.

11. Pet Iguana youngsters need their food cut into small pieces to avoid any chance of a blockage.

12. Pet Iguanas can also be given some moistened commercial foods specific to them. Chronic dehydration is a very common cause of kidney disease, and Iguanas seem to be more prone to this in drier climates.

13. Pet Iguanas are known for being engaging, especially if raised as a youngster. However, males can become aggressive (including with people) at reproductive maturity (usually between 3-4 years of age).

14. Pet Iguanas will seek out the company of their caregivers and may even follow you around like a dog, if you begin socializing them as youngsters. The benefit is a friendly reptile that won't bite.

15. Pet Iguanas may carry salmonella. It is imperative, when holding any reptile, that you wash your hands after any contact.

16. Pet Iguanas are naturally tree dwellers and will need vertical space also. They love to climb tree trunks, clothes in a closet to rest across the top bar, and may even climb to the top of shelves and cabinets. Placing strong branches that criss-cross the cage interior is a good idea.

17. Pet Iguanas need substrate that won't hurt them if eaten, like paper, reptile carpet, or even linoleum.

18. Pet Iguanas can suffer health issues, which are mostly created by poor caregiving. Heat mats and hot rocks can create burns because Iguanas sense the heat through the parietal eye in their head and not their belly.

*Green Iguanas are very popular as pets. They come from the warm and humid rainforests of South America.

*80% humidity can be created by placing a large water bowl on the surface of the enclosure for evaporation purposes, and misting your pet with a spray bottle a few times a day. An additional bowl of water should be added for drinking purposes, though Iguanas get most of the water they need from the food they eat.

*Iguanas love to bathe and defecate in their water. Changing all water daily is a good idea.

*Iguanas can swim and love a small amount of water in a bath tub.

*If an Iguana loses its tail, a new one will usually grow.

*An Iguana is a beautiful and exotic animal and needs the commitment of time (at least 20 years), space, and love. Sadly, most Iguana premature deaths are caused by poor caregiving for what was probably an impulse pet to uninformed consumers.

https://www.vetbabble.com/reptiles/Iguana-care/

Grandma feeding grapes to Diego.

The Williams Family and MJ the Red Knee Tarantula

Encouraging kindness and respect for all animals in nature,
even if they are hairy and scary

Story by Jennifer Foreman de Grassi Williams

Watercolors by Bobbi Kelly

Lovingly dedicated to:

My children first, and then my beautiful granddaughters, because a friend told me that if she had known how wonderful grandchildren were she would have bypassed her kids.
Not me!!!

My thousands of students, especially those who felt different~ thankful you were.

A big thank you to Dr. Nick Ledesma who has kept many tarantulas, other arachnids, and invertebrates over the years and has verfied the tarantula facts in this book.

My Mom because her genetics helped me write my feelings.

My husband who married me anyway.

Story number 2 is about a red knee tarantula we named MJ, for Michael Jordan, because tarantulas are notorious jumpers! A friend's mother asked if we could take him. She could never say no to a request from her children; but when they tired of a new pet, she knew we would never turn anything away. So there she stood, at our door, holding MJ in one of those tiny fish bowls (like the ones you have to purchase because your child won a goldfish at the fair), and poor guy was eight eyes to eight legs to hairy bottom in the bowl. I wondered when he had eaten last, or if he had shelter or hydration. I have had many experiences interacting with, and observing, all kinds of spiders growing up in the Oakland foothills, and kept a beautiful spider with her egg sac in my dorm room at San Jose State to study one semester for an Entomology class (much to the dismay of my roommates). I marveled at the massive tarantula migrations we experienced driving through Texas. My animal loving, empathetic side kicked in and my mind raced with so many questions when I stood at my door knowing I had taken on something I knew very little about. Was he docile enough to hold? Would he jump at me, or simply crawl up my hand? Would I panic and try to shake him off of my arm if he started crawling toward my face? Would he escape into our home (like the snakes we rescued) and not be found, or discovered in the dark of the night at the top of my pillow? Would he continue to grow and maybe escape like the movie "Tarantula" I saw as a child in 1955, and become a "creeping, crawling, monster"?

MJ

It is amazing how spiders, (perhaps more than any other living wonder of nature, except snakes), can give a person a very active imagination. I did my research and spent time creating a safe and healthy environment for him, escape proof, to put my family at ease. MJ was a curiosity for everyone who came to see him, and certainly a beautiful guy that taught us so much about the respect all living things deserve, and that they never ask to be taken from the wild. Red knee tarantulas are considered near threatened by climate change, local farming, and the pet trade. In the United States only captive grown spiders are allowed to be sold. As friends were introduced to MJ, the newest rescue at our home, I can hear myself repeating, "Be kind. Be kind."

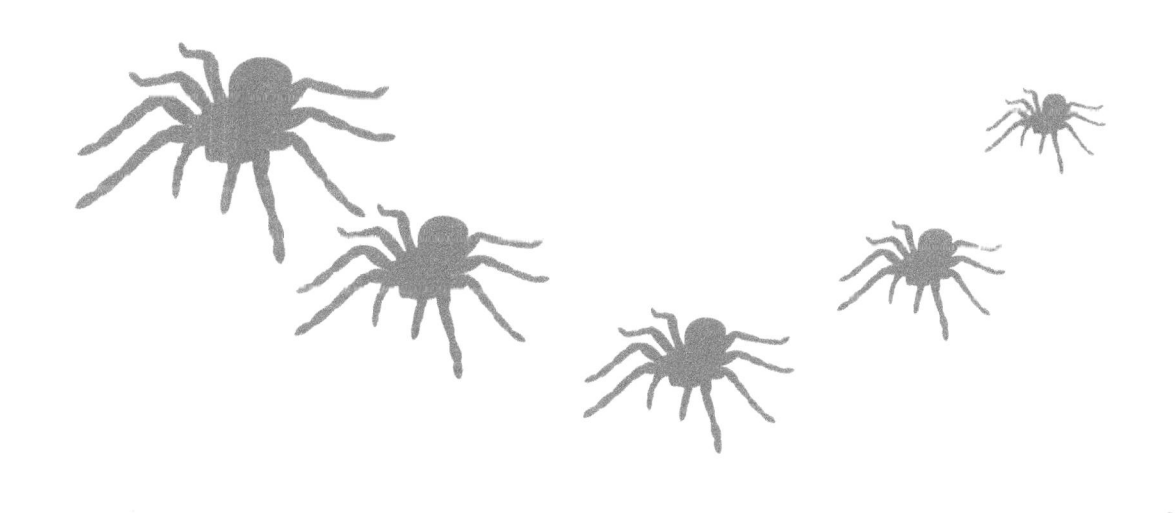

Something hairy, kind of scary,
with eight legs is hiding,

From underneath a big sombrero
on a sunny day;

I see some orange, maybe red, and
eyes that look at me,

I should be scared, but I am not,
she may just want to play.

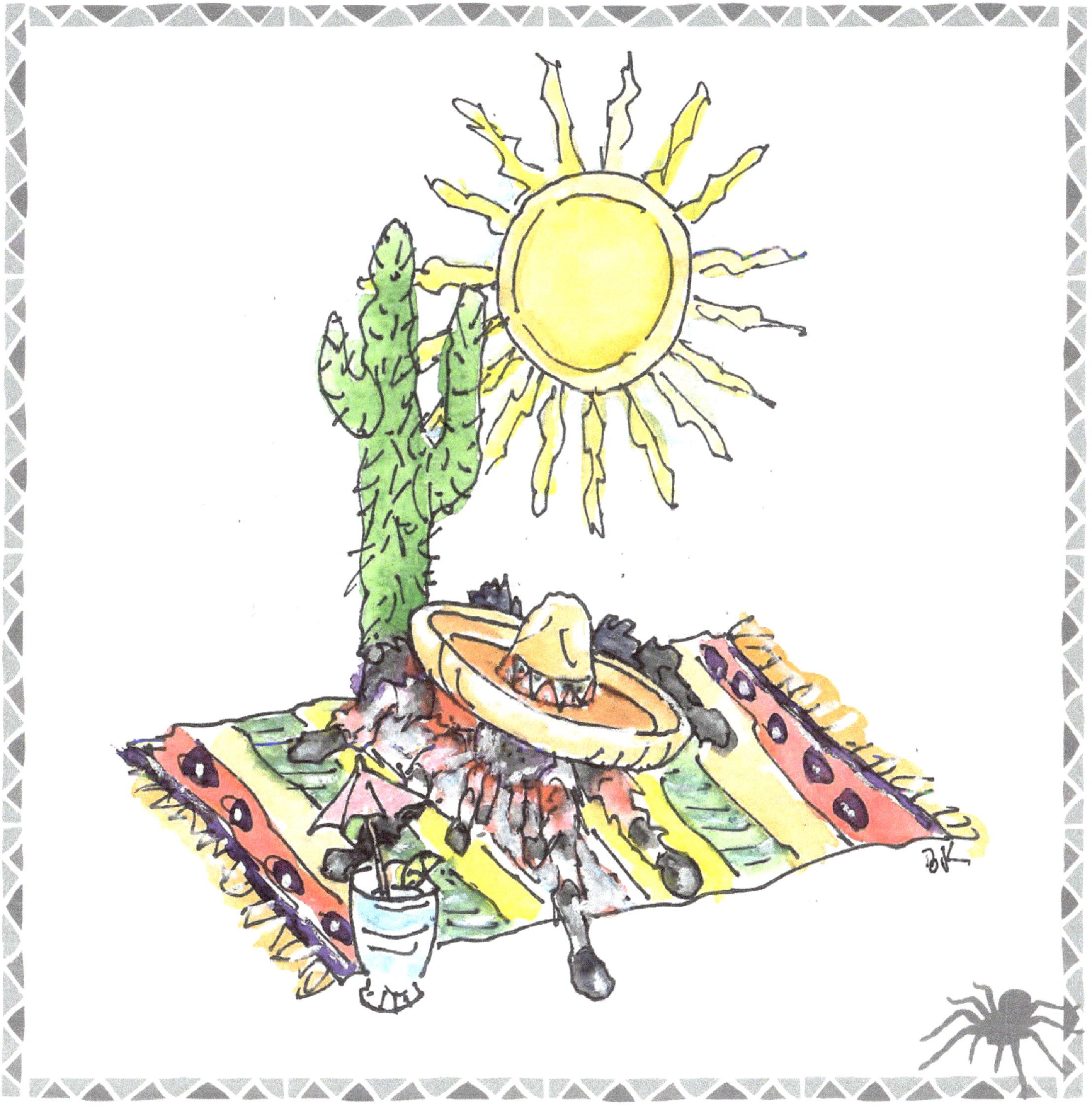

Inside an old clay pot she sleeps because she feels safe,

Tarantula is what she is and big just like her name;

She likes to hide and burrow as she would out in the wild,

But here she feels safe and warm and acts so very tame.

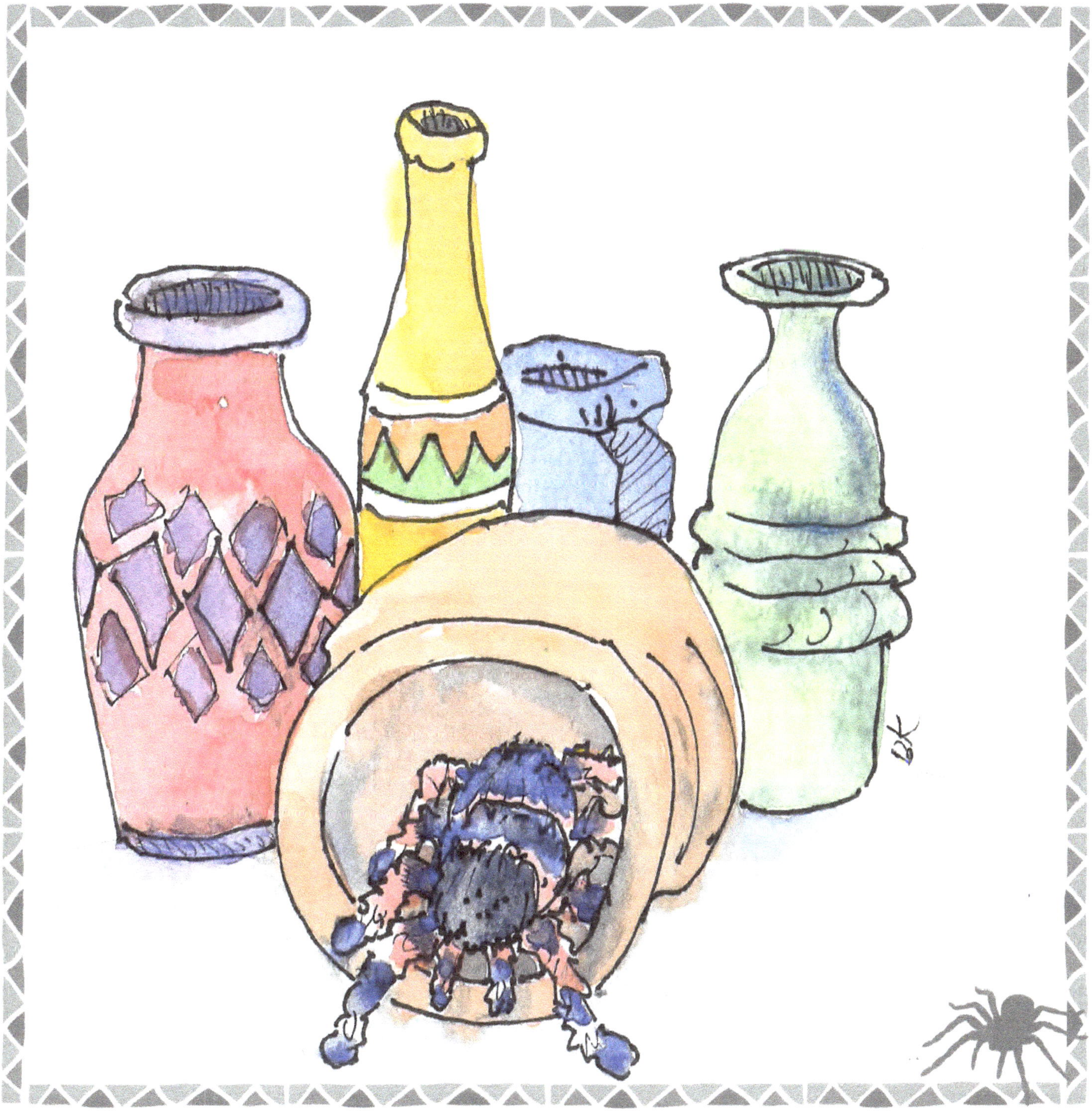

It may look odd or funny if she sits upon your arm,

Or rests on top your shoulder to see with her eight eyes;

She has no need to bite or kick the hairs from on her legs,

As long as she is never hurt or by accident surprised.

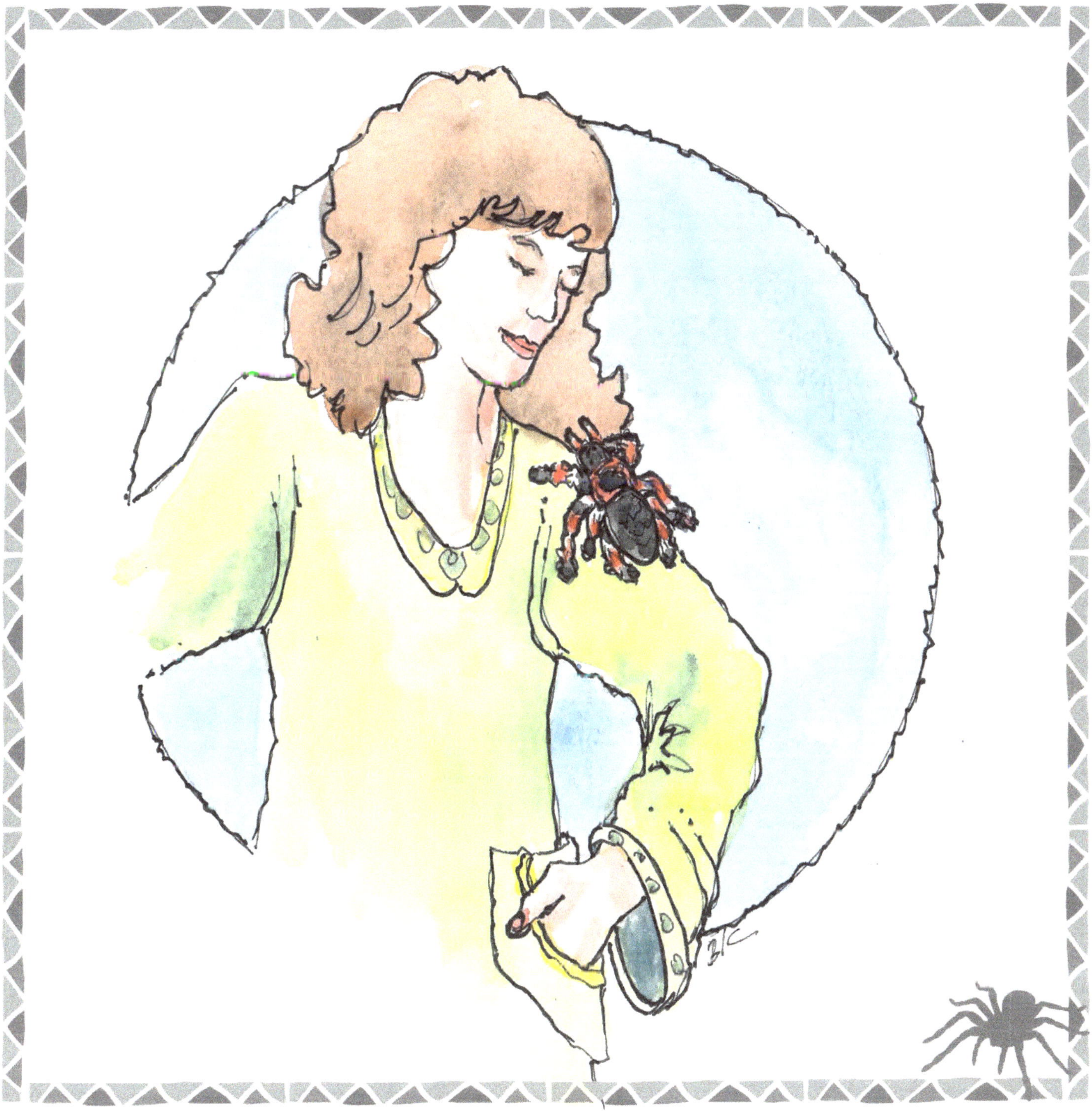

I must admit and certainly my family would agree,

That if you see her in your room you might just wonder why;

The chances are she only wants to crawl up on your bed,

And wait there on your pillow which is her way to say "hi".

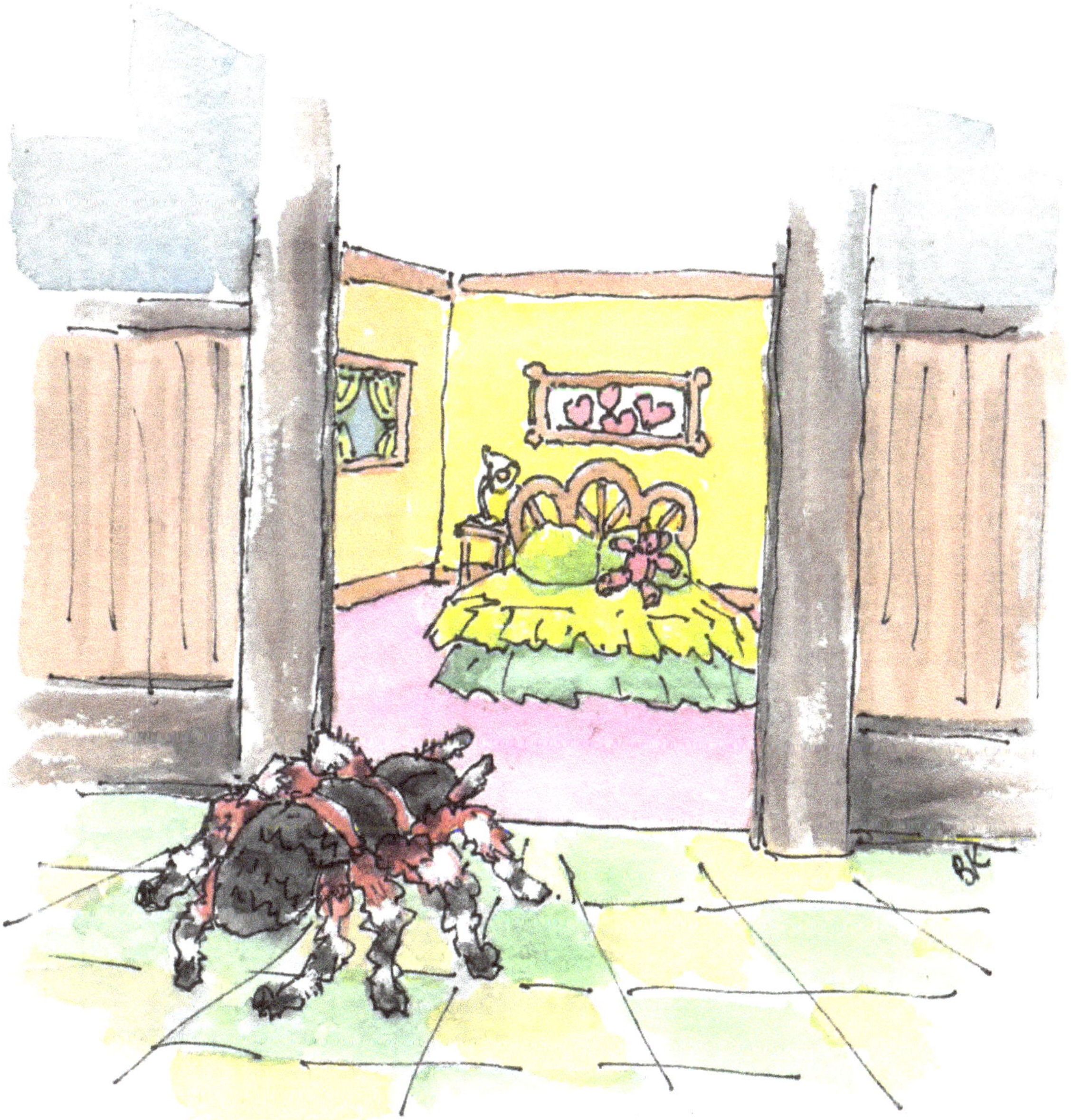

MJ can see back and front at nearly the same time,

But still her eyes are kind of weak and just don't see that well;

A spider has so many legs that help her do so much,

She uses hairs on her long legs to feel, and taste, and smell.

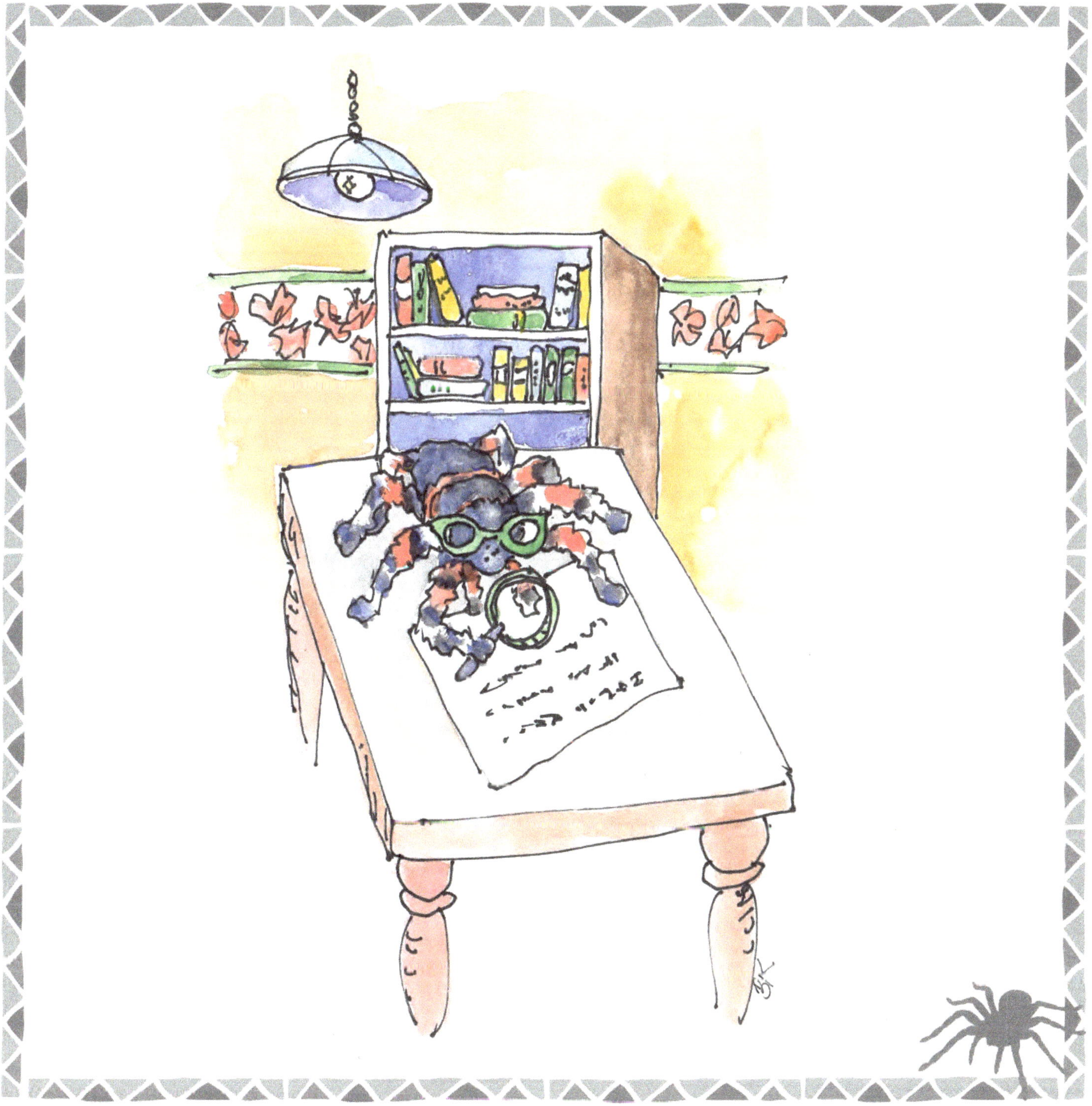

A red-kneed spider like MJ can feel lots of things,

Especially through her hairy legs vibrations drive her wild;

She may begin to kick the hairs off of her legs and body,

And anyone who watches her has laughed and even smiled.

MJ would not think of biting if she's handled gently,

And mostly she is calm and slow as round her cage she'll roam;

But thinks that chasing crickets is a very tasty sport,

Though several times a week she pounces if they're in her home.

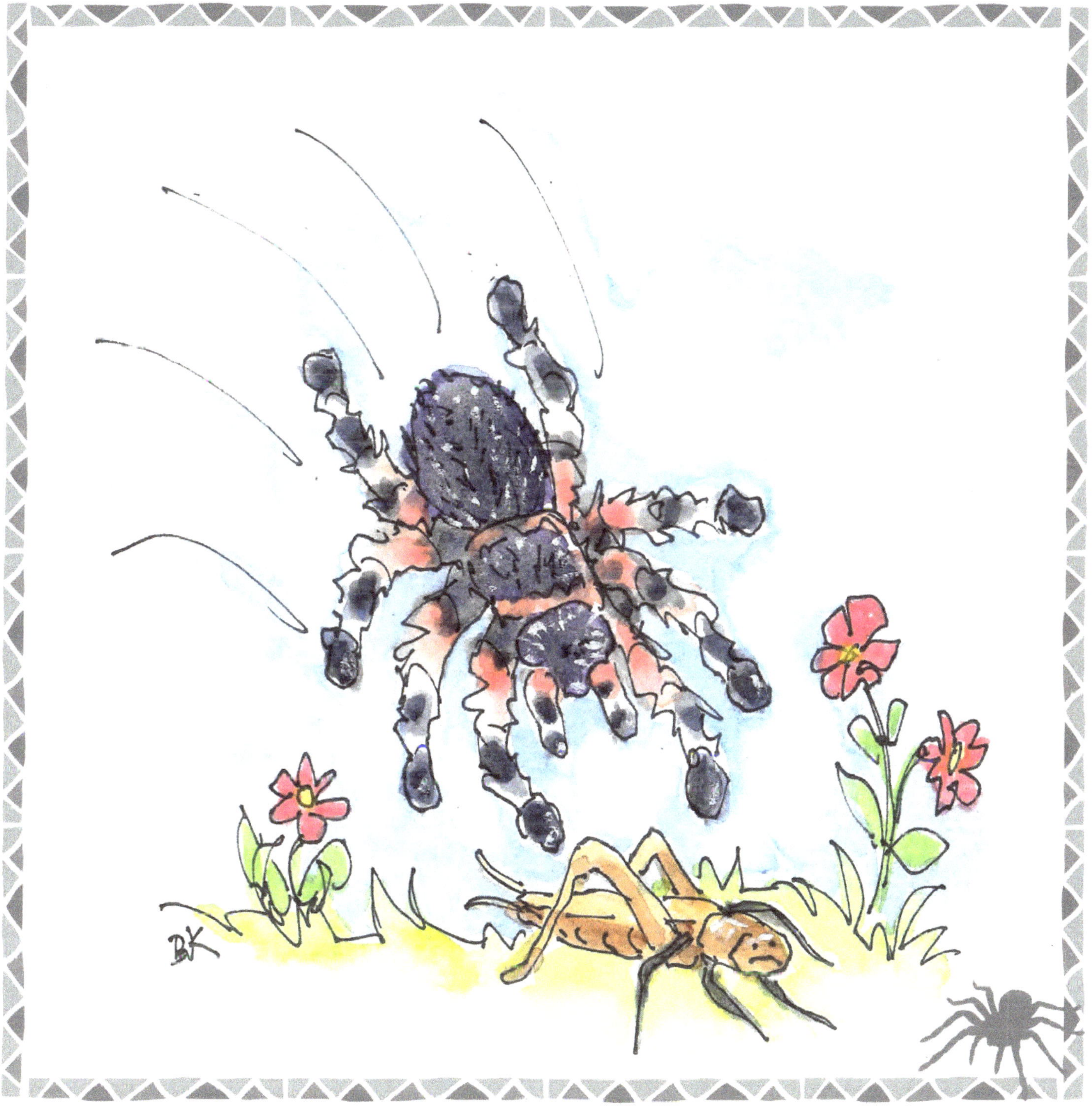

Something really strange will
happen when you've looked away,

Your pet and friend tarantula
onto her back will change;

You may think she is sleeping or
that she just cannot move,

But now your friend is trying to
molt and that is very strange.

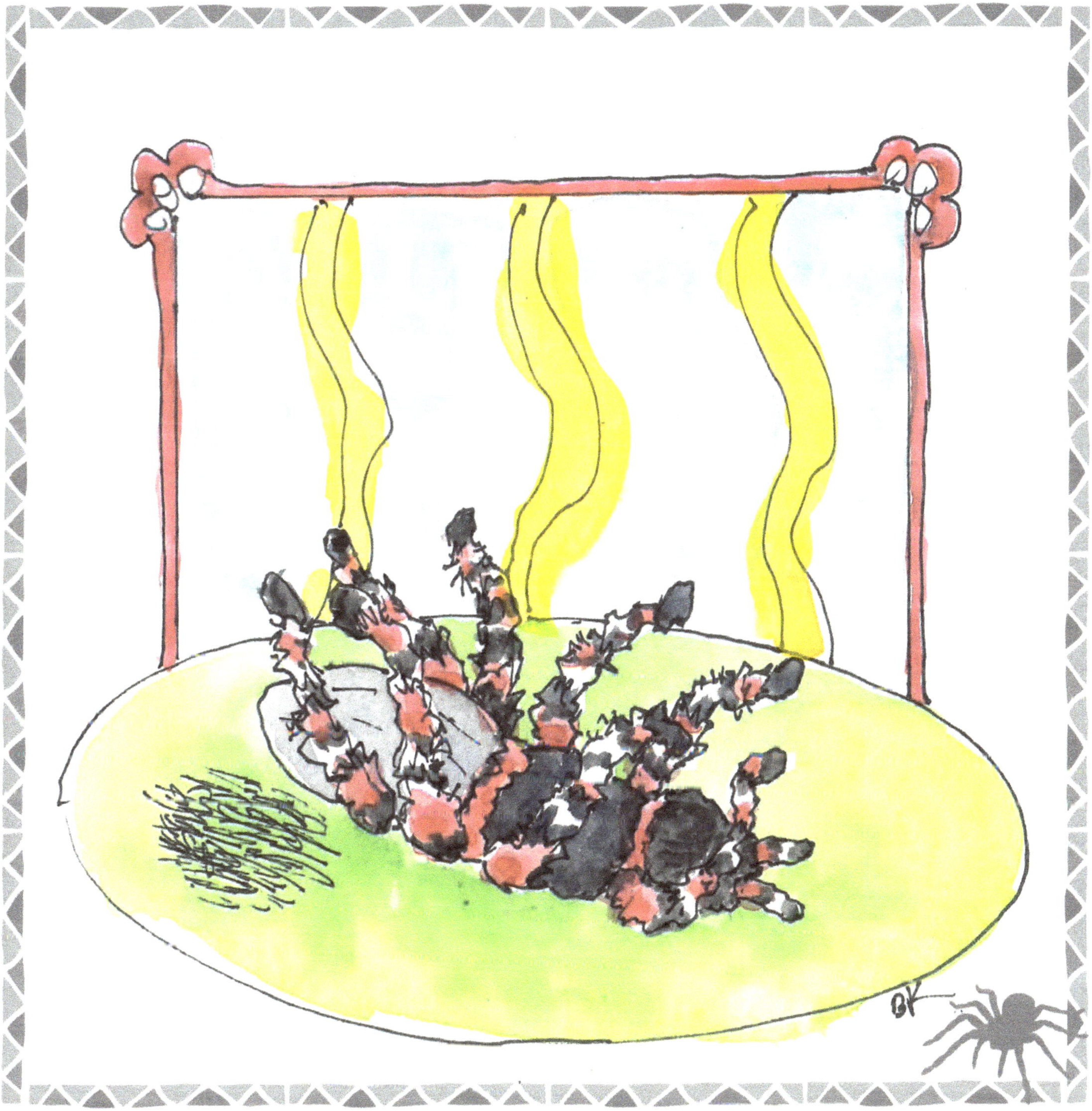

Twice a year and as she grows MJ will shed her skin,

My goodness there she was for sure but now not one, but two;

MJ molted in the night and what I saw was double,

An old skin that she shed I saw, and also MJ new.

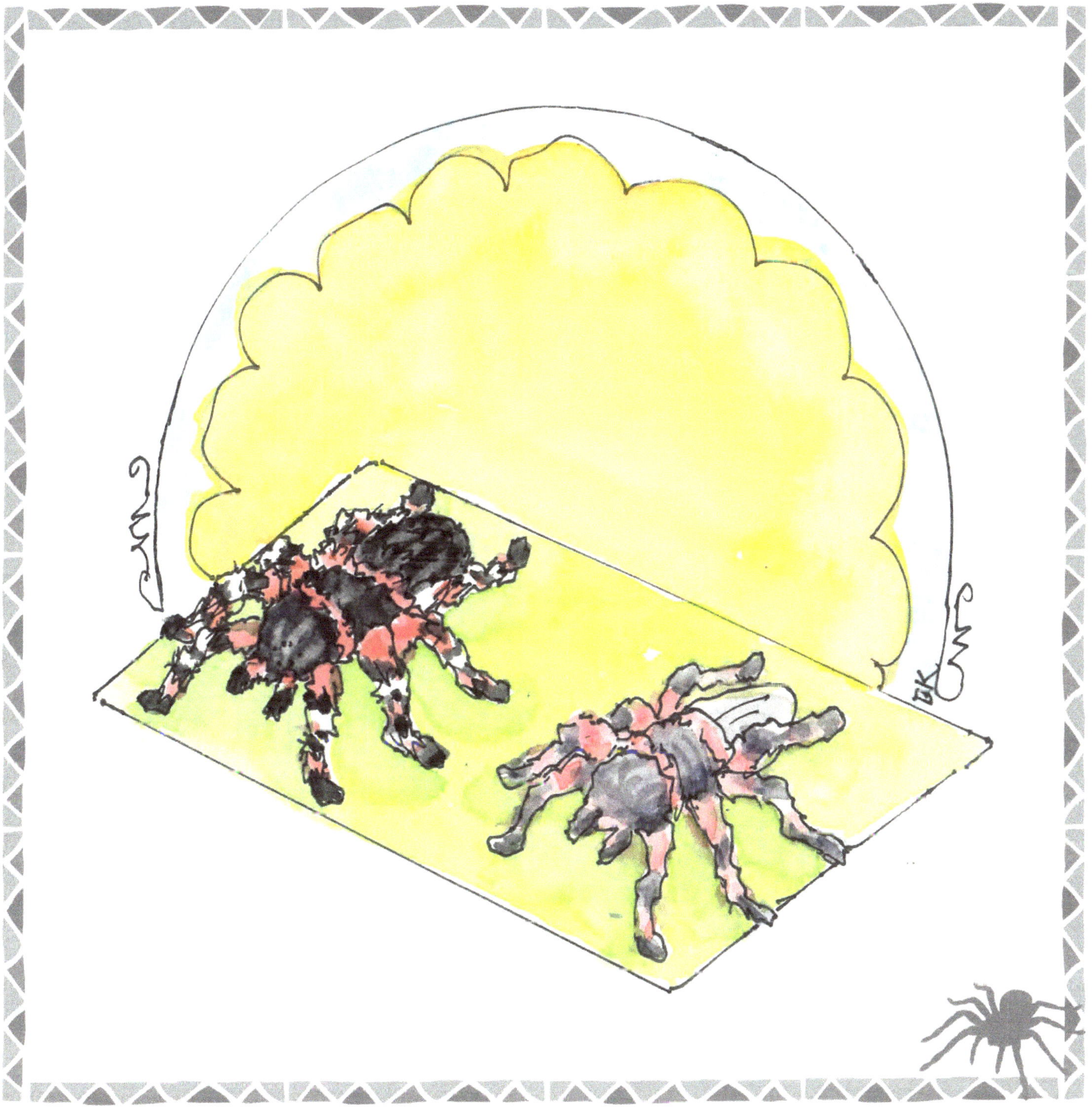

More stunning than the day before her colors how they glisten,

And now the molting made her thirsty, and so very sleepy;

On her sponge so big and damp I knew she'd get a drink,

So magical the molt, I saw, while others thought it creepy.

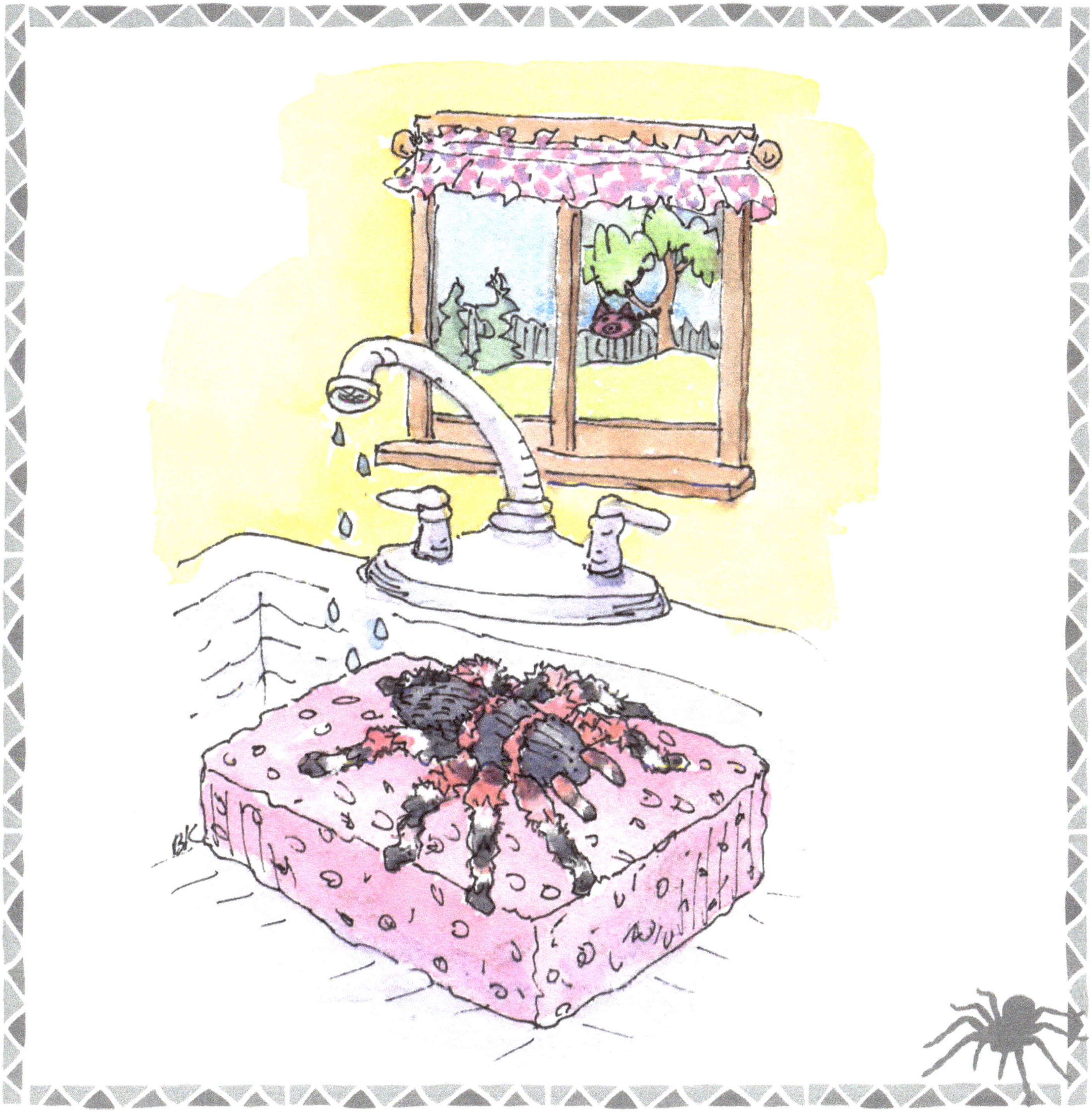

Boy tarantulas aren't as big and don't live long as girls,

But both of them need gentle care for they are very clever;

The exoskeleton needs to shed as they grow more each day,

Their curious lives we must protect from now until forever.

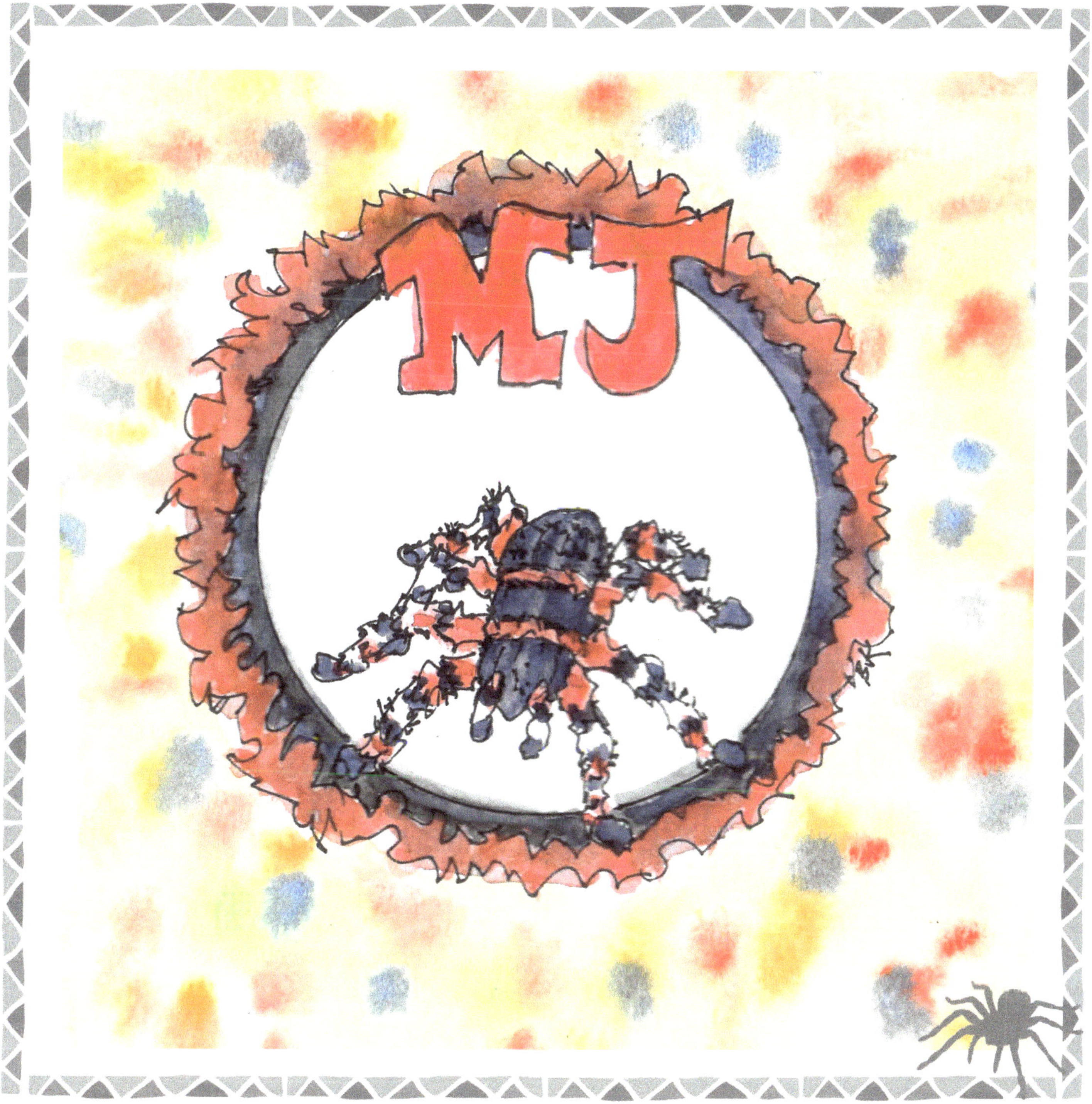
MJ

Tarantulas are a gift for sure from nature such a treat,

We must defend them where they live and from Earth's climate change;

And celebrate their birthdays as the girls can live to thirty,

And love the fact they are unique and beautiful and strange.

The End

Happy 30th Birthday!

Mexican Red Knee Tarantula Facts:

1. Red Knee Tarantulas can be identified by their dark brown body and eight legs with orange-red joints.

2. Red Knee Tarantula females have larger bodies and shorter legs than the males.

3. Red Knee Tarantulas are found on the Pacific coast of Mexico, living in dry areas, where they dig burrows for protection.

4. Red Knee Tarantulas live alone as they are solitary animals. They are considered near threatened due to climate change, local farming, and the pet trade. In the United States only captive grown spiders are allowed to be sold.

5. Red Knee Tarantulas are docile, slow moving, colorful, large, and live a longtime. As they require little space and care, they are a popular pet for all ages and the most common pet tarantula in the world.

6. Red Knee Tarantulas eat small insects, crickets, and mealworms in captivity several times a week. They ambush their prey from burrows. And with a venomous bite of their hollow fangs (paralyzing the prey), they suck up the juices (yikes!).

7. Red Knee Tarantulas may not have to eat for a month after a large meal, or when they molt.

8. Red Knee Tarantulas have eight eyes and can see backwards and forwards at the same time, even though their eyesight is

better at noticing movement, rather than shapes or colors.

9.   Red Knee Tarantulas have hairs on their legs that are very sensitive to vibrations. At the end of each leg is a small area that is also sensitive to touch, taste and smell.

10.   Red Knee Tarantulas are easy to handle and quite harmless to humans. They only bite if they feel threatened. While their bite is not fatal, it can feel like a bee sting. When feeling threatened they may actually kick out irritating hairs from their legs and abdomen as a defense.

11.   Red Knee Tarantulas go through a molting process, shedding their external skeletons (kind of like a hand pulling out of a glove), and necessary for them to be able to grow. Young tarantulas molt more frequently (about every 2-4 weeks as spiderlings, then gradually less as they reach adult size). An adult tarantula may even molt closer to every other year once they become larger. They may become lethargic as the molting process nears, and lose hairs on the back of their body. The actual molting takes several hours, and the tarantula looks dead as it usually lies on its back. When the molt is complete, the skin of the spider is renewed and the molt looks like another spider in the aquarium. Do not feed after a molt for several days. Do not hold your pet for several weeks after a molt as the new skin is fragile and sensitive. A tarantula can even regrow a lost leg. Injuries can stimulate molts to happen more frequently, helping to repair/regenerate the spider.

12.   Red Knee Tarantula females can live to be thirty years old, while males have a shorter life of about 10 years.

13.   Red Knee Tarantula adults may have leg spans of 6", and the

aquarium should be 2-3 times wider than the length of the spider's legs. The height of the aquarium needs to be only as tall as the span of the spider's legs when standing on end. A side opening to the aquarium is preferred, as tarantulas love to hang upside down on the screen of the top.

14. Red Knee Tarantulas will need a five to ten gallon tank, with a locking screen top, although smaller is better as they are growing up. A smaller area helps them to find their prey easier. The aquarium substrate can be four inches of eco earth, with a shallow dish of water for drinking, and a burrow (hollowed wood or piece of pottery) to hide. A small sponge can be placed in the water, as a tarantula likes to sit on the sponge to drink. The evaporation from the dish also helps to humidify the aquarium. Tarantulas can become dehydrated. Try to clean the water dish daily.

15. Red Knee Tarantulas do not need an aquarium light. However, a heat pad under part of the aquarium is beneficial. Maintaining 75 to 80 degrees Fahrenheit, plus some humidity, is important. They don't need vitamins or minerals added to their food.

16. Red Knee Tarantulas rarely become ill if taken care of properly. Holding them gently is important, as their fragile exoskeleton can be damaged if they fall, or they may even die.

17. Red Knee Tarantulas mate between July and October. The female actually makes a silk pad where she lays her 200-400 eggs, covering them with a sticky substance. She wraps the entire bundle with silk, making an egg sac, which she guards by carrying between her fangs. It takes 9 weeks for the eggs to hatch. After about 2 weeks the young spiders are

completely independent and leave their home.

~In the wild tarantulas are eaten by birds, lizards, and used by wasps to feed their young.

~Red knee tarantulas bite their enemies and brush the irritating and barbed hairs from their abdomens onto their enemies, causing irritation and even blindness. In humans these hairs might cause an allergic reaction that should only last a day or two.

~A female tarantula is an extremely serious commitment as her life span is very long.

~A tarantula is also venomous, though it has a mild venom, and is rarely a threat to humans.

~Purchasing a tarantula from a reputable breeder is wise, as they are practitioners of good animal husbandry, and eager to help new owners.

~And YES, a tarantula is a very scary looking creature. Many people do not like any kind of spider, especially one that is very large. These particular spiders are very popular in the movies because of their good looks and their gentle personalities.

The Williams Family and Sunshine the Yellow-bellied Marmot

Taking a risk to save something at-risk

Story and Artwork by

Jennifer Foreman de Grassi Williams

Dedicated to:

Anyone who dares to put their own life at risk to run into traffic to save a wounded or orphaned wild animal that is desperate for help.

The thousands of students I have had over four decades, many at-risk, who only needed one person to lend a helping hand, and blessed when that hand was mine.

My precious darlings Norah Alings, Sonja Hope, Harper Mae, and our newest little 'sunshine' baby, Reed William, who help me act way younger than my age.

The devoted work of Animals in Distress who understand that every life is invaluable.

Story number 3 is about an unusual animal that not many people get to see up close, a Yellow-bellied marmot called a Rock Chuck. When I used to commute 100 miles a day to my high school teaching job, the drive lent itself to all kinds of interesting experiences. The drive took me through some fairly barren desert between Boise and Mountain Home. It was across that desert that I was first introduced to colonies of rock chucks. At first glance a rather large rock chuck looked like some kind of brush you'd find on a front porch to scrape the mud off of your boots. With their short little legs they would stand like sergeants yelling something at the top of their lungs in a high pitched and shrill-like command. How cute these guys making territorial noises, and then scurrying fast with stubby/sturdy/kangaroo legs. One day I happened on one that had just been struck by a car. I HATE roadkill, especially when whoever did it doesn't stop to help, or at the very least remove the unfortunate critter from the roadway. I am one of those who cannot pass without at least looking for any sign of movement in an otherwise lifeless body. There have been times when just holding a little critter that is taking its last breath is a blessing in knowing that death was not experienced alone. In any event, this little guy had just enough strength to move his tail... flagging me down with all he had in that tail! I scooped him up and for two months fed his half paralyzed body, around the clock, with an eyedropper. As the healing began to take place he let me know that he was still a wild animal, not meant to have as anyone's pet, and he'd nip at every opportunity. After another month, and on a warm sunny day, I placed a cat collar around his neck with contact information and headed to Hill City. It was with a prayer

Sunshine

and a hug that I said my good-byes in the middle of the wilderness. And off he went into the nearest rock pile. About 6 months later, I received a call from someone who said they had found his collar. I wondered what the next chapter had been for my little marmot friend, and hoped he was in a burrow conducting his polygamous business, surrounded by the pitter patter of baby marmot feet. My next encounter with a rock chuck, besides the one I rescued from my neighbor's garage, was with one of the cutest creatures I have ever seen. Long story short, a student wanted to adopt one of my pet rats, but in exchange for a rock chuck she had inherited and didn't want. Upon entering her house, I almost couldn't see Sunshine amidst all the rescued, exotic birds that had completely taken over. Sunshine was sitting on a desk with birds surrounding her, though she didn't seem to mind at all. It was love at first sight for me. Sunshine stood up like that funky mud removing brush thing I described, front legs held like a wallaby, stubby back legs buried under her very Buddha-like belly. She looked at me and let out a few chirps, and then let me pick her up and cradle her like a baby. That was all it took. I brought her home, like she had been our pet that had run away for a few days, created a place in our wash room for her, and let her begin a life of terrorizing our cats, begging for avocados, squeezing down vents, escaping to the outdoors, and running after, and nipping, the ankles of anyone that entered her territory… her rock pile … inside of our house. She would let out a shrill whistle, and you couldn't tell if it was a fire alarm that needed a new battery, or a Fourth of July firework gone crazy. It was only Sunshine. Best of all, and when she was in the mood, I could cradle her like a newborn and she would 'purr' just like a kitten would do. She 'rocked' our world… as she displayed, surprisingly, many gentle characteristics.

But then, and in an instant, she would revert to her very basic wild animal red zone. I learned so many things from her that I could relate to my life as a teacher. Risk is inherent when you allow yourself to step out of your own comfort zone. The hope is that when you give yourself permission to do it, you are that lifeline to something (someone) that really needs you, human or animal.

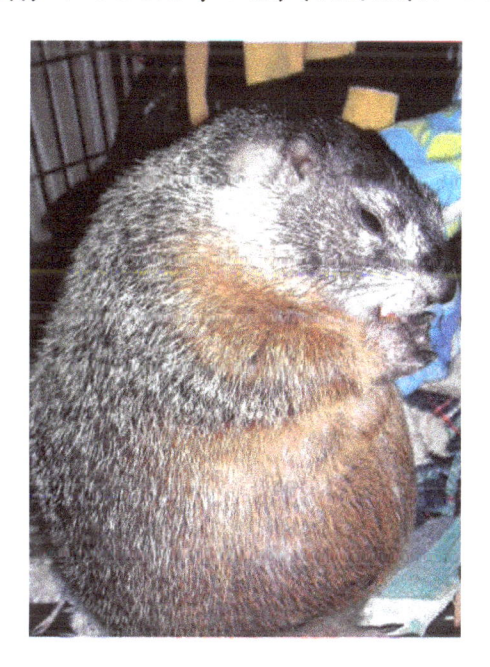

There we are atop the rocks when you go driving by,

Some people call us rock chucks when they play the game 'I Spy';

I am furry like my babies though we look like brushes,

And we stand and chirp and wave just hoping you'll say "hi".

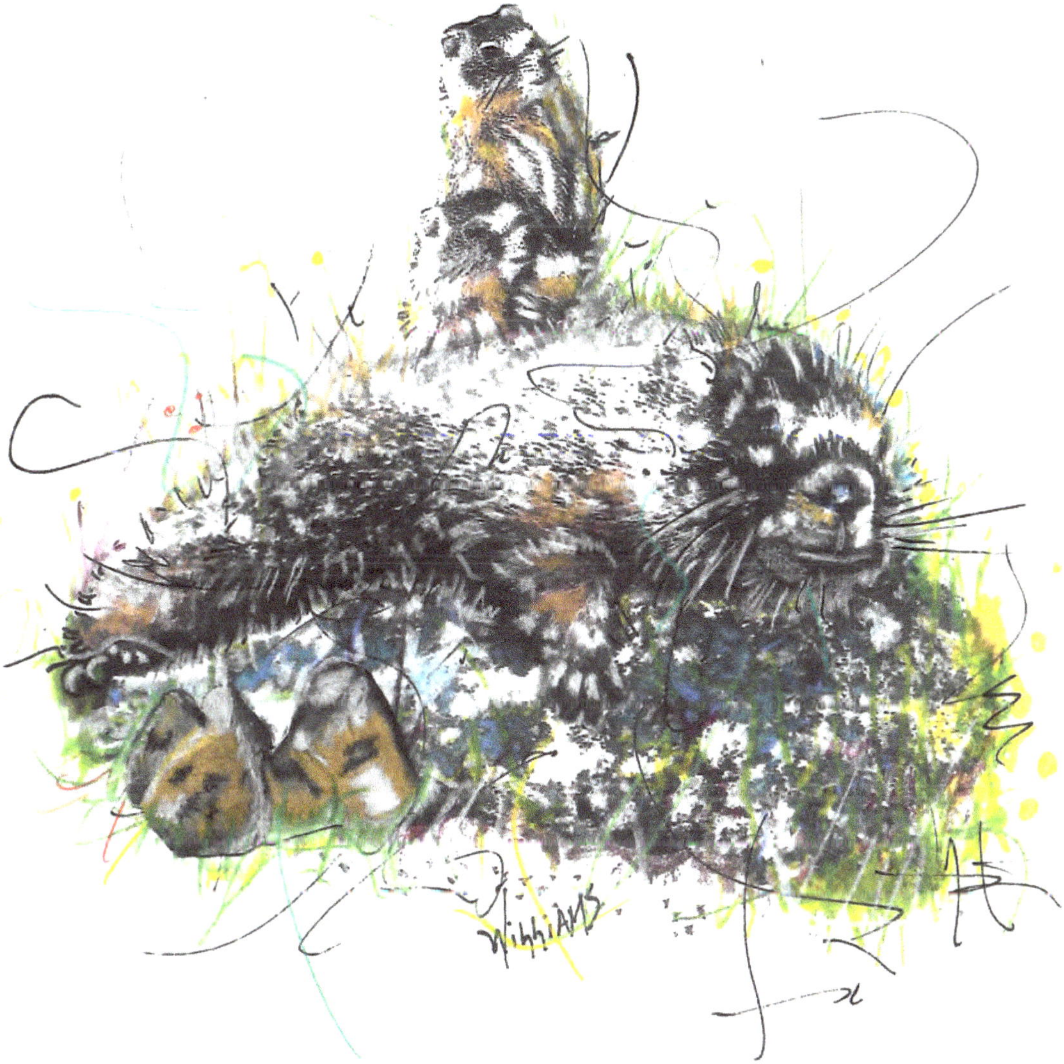

When I was a tiny girl no bigger than a rodent,

I lived with birds inside a house who really liked to tweet;

They fluttered and they chattered from the night until the morning,

Like a jungle with their chirps and singing oh so sweet.

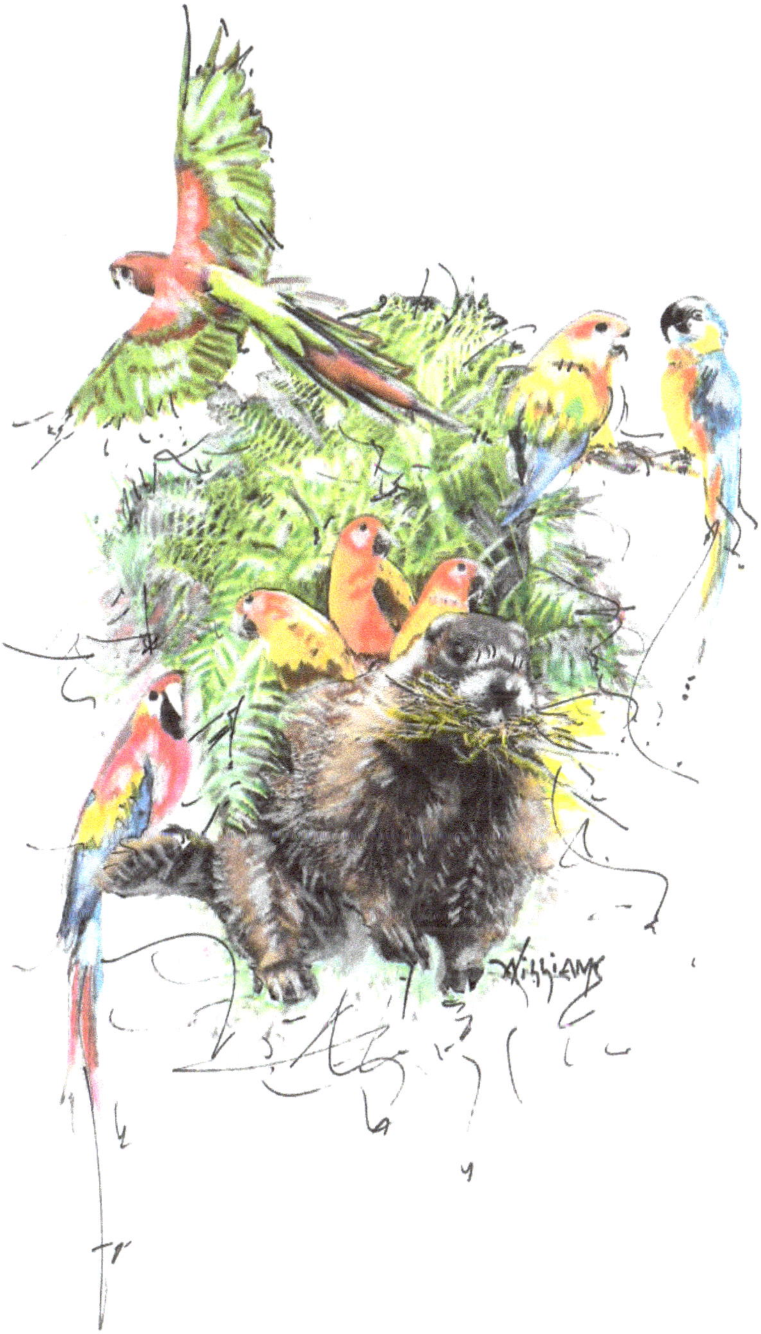
Williams

My family how they loved me and adored how I would play,

And they would let me roam around the plants and all the flowers;

They knew that I loved sitting in the warm of the big sun,

But also knew my short legs could run fast if I felt showers.

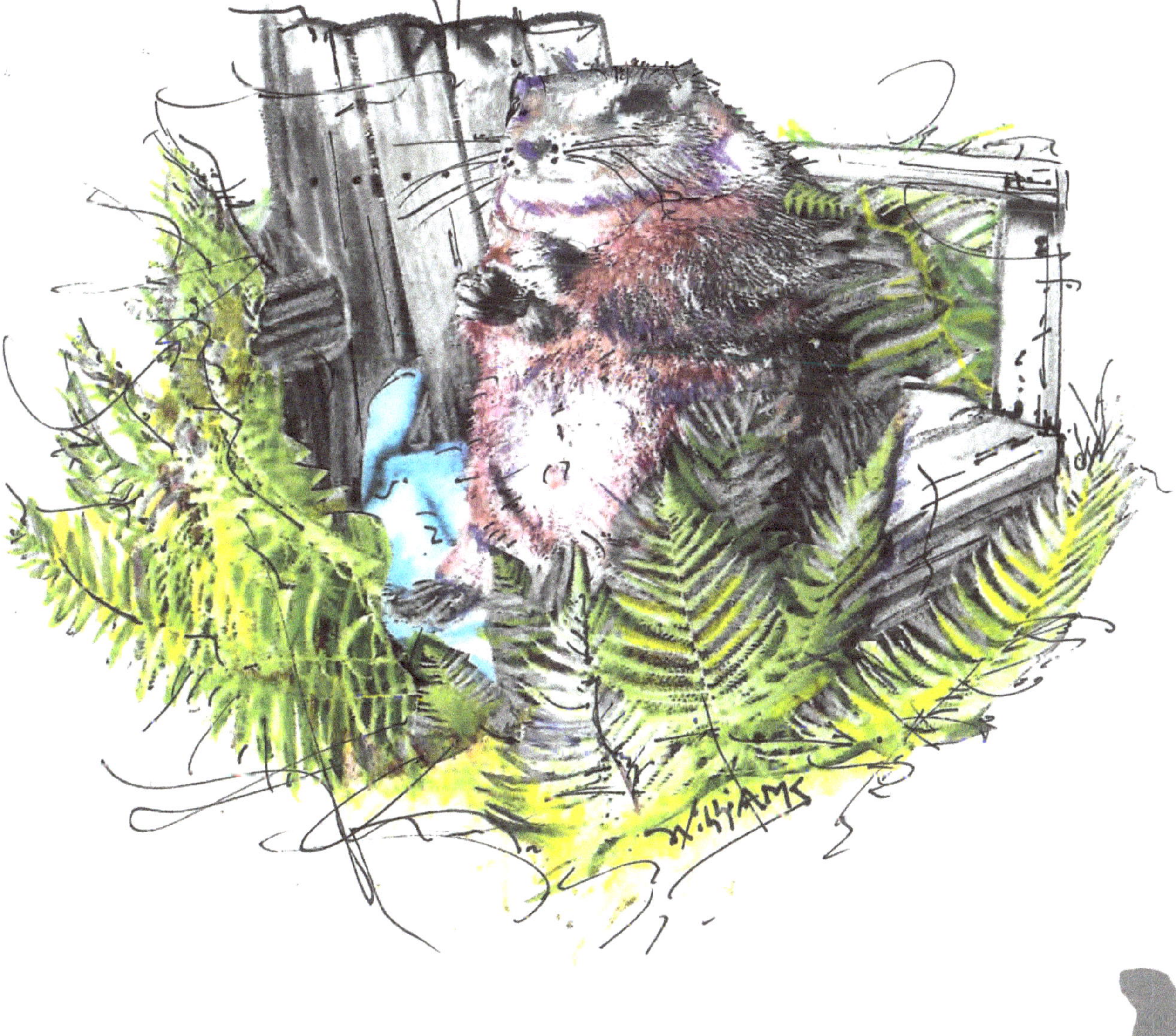
WilliAMS

I could sit in a big patch of fruits and pretty blossoms,

And dream of mountains, and rock piles, and my daily naps;

I spend a lot of time just eating plants, and seeds, and grasses,

But how I love my AVOCADOS, and my table scraps.

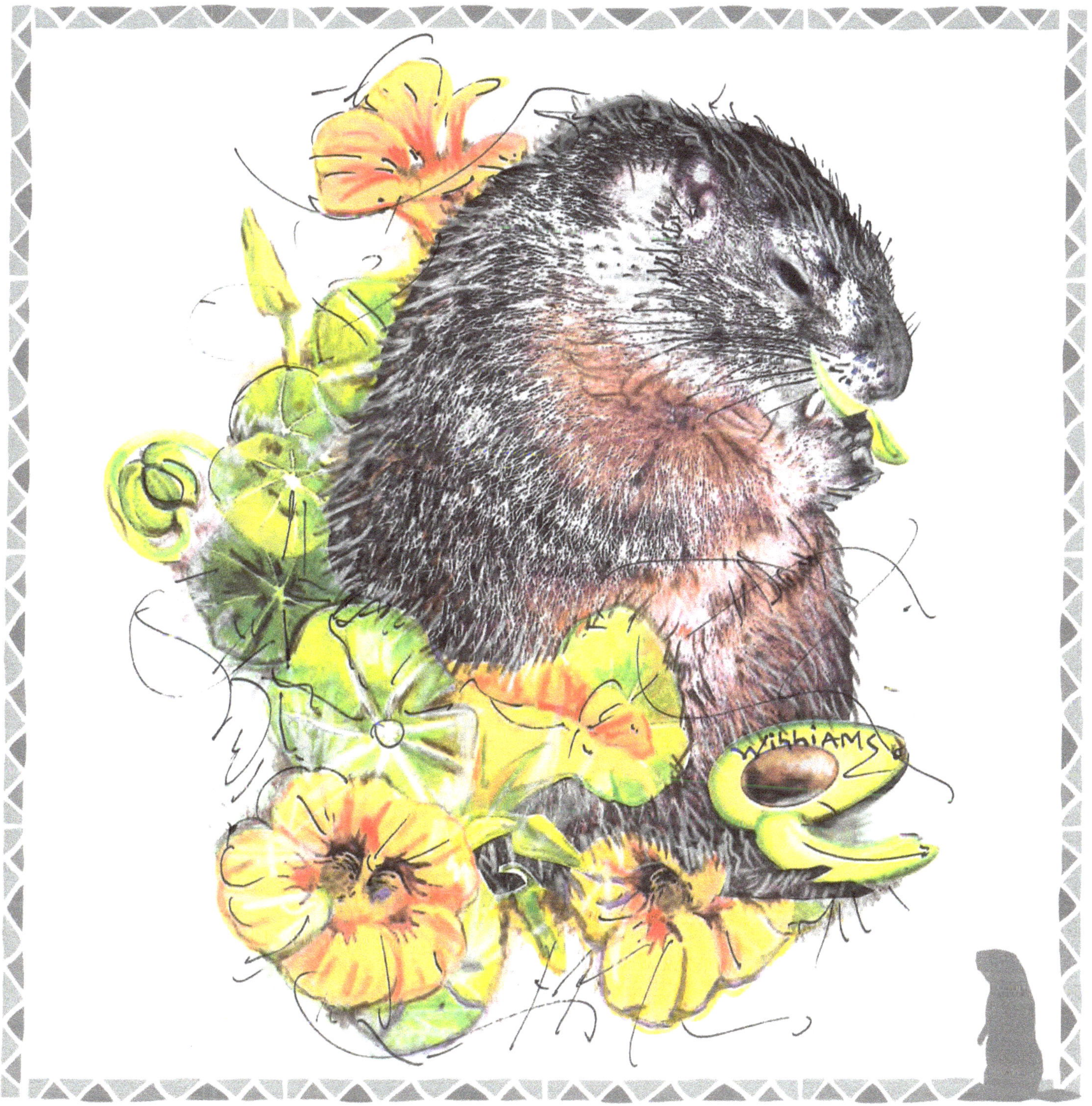
WILLIAMS

Being held and rocked to sleep inside of my blue blanket,

I look just like a baby in a crib with a blue binkie;

And if you listen closely I will purr just like a kitty,

And love the little kisses I get, though my fur can be quite stinky.

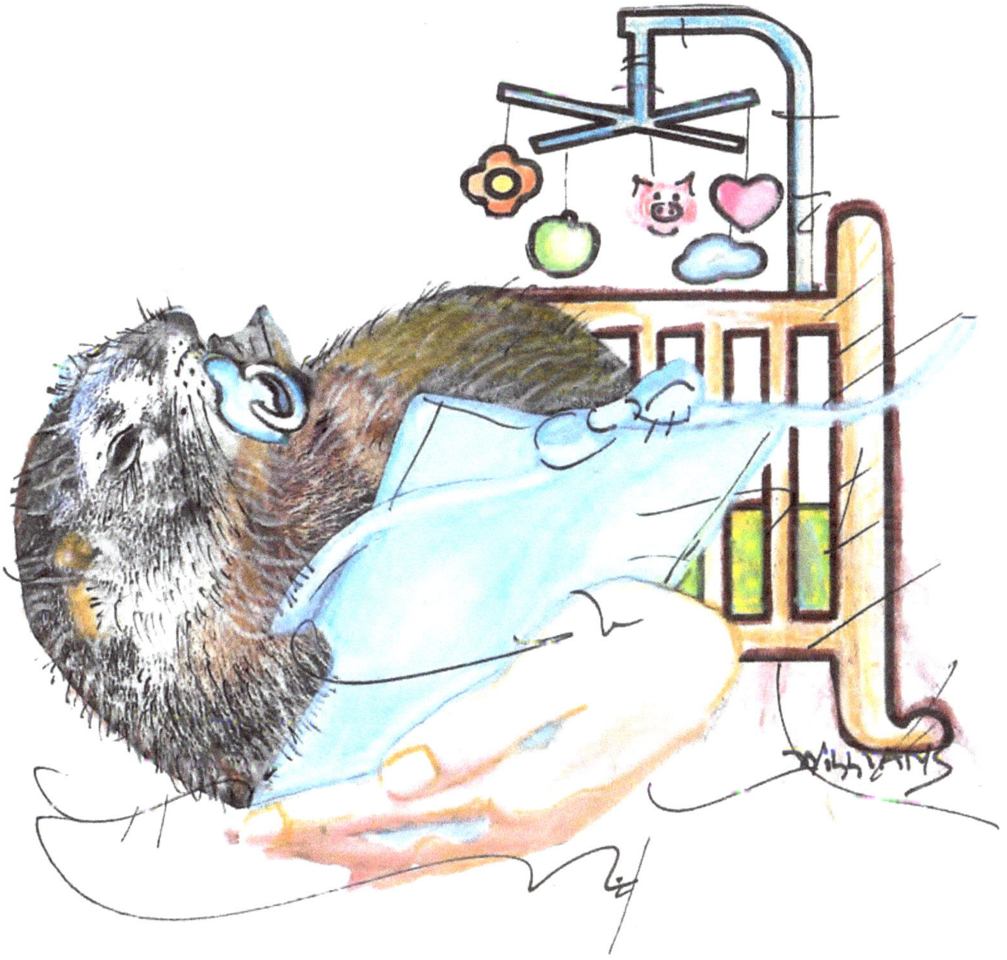

In the yard I have a place
just by the garden gate,

And there a big ol' pile of rocks
is where I hide and seek;

It makes me think of the warm
desert where I had been born,

Close to badgers and coyotes and
things with a sharp beak.

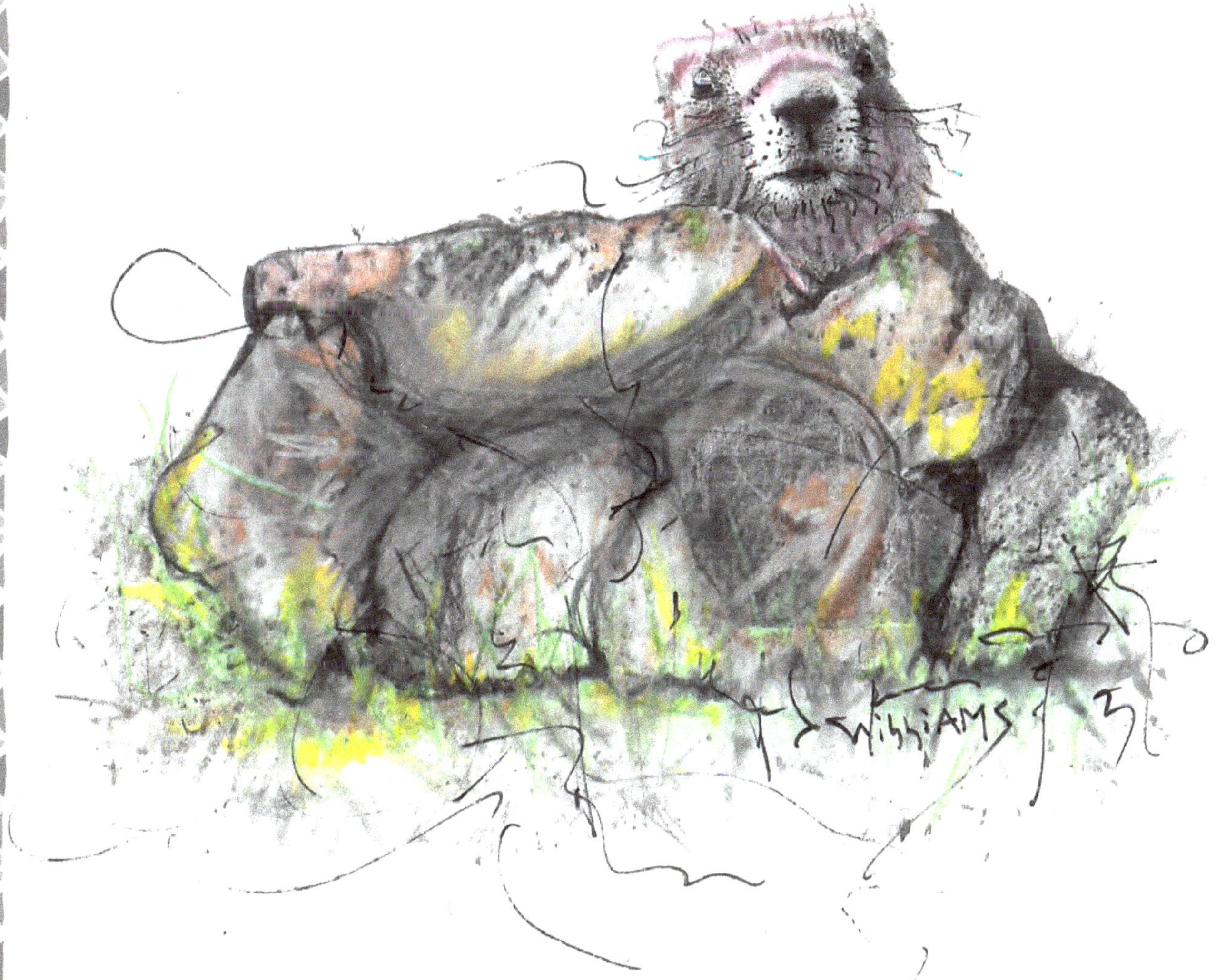
WILLIAMS

People cannot buy me in a pet shop like a dog,

The desert is my home where I am free and very wild;

My human family is afraid that I'll get lost forever,

So gave me a red collar, with a bell and then just smiled.

ROCK CHUCK CROSSING

I am a little trickster and down vents I love to go,

And wait there for 2 hours, or more, before I leave my space;

I like to bite the bare toes or the ankles that pass by,

But I don't do it to be bad, just to protect my place.

Williams

There is a secret garden where I sit and meet my pals,

Andy cat, the squirrels, and Diego how we play;

We talk about the Earth and how to keep her very healthy,

And then we tell some jokes and giggle, and stay there for the day.

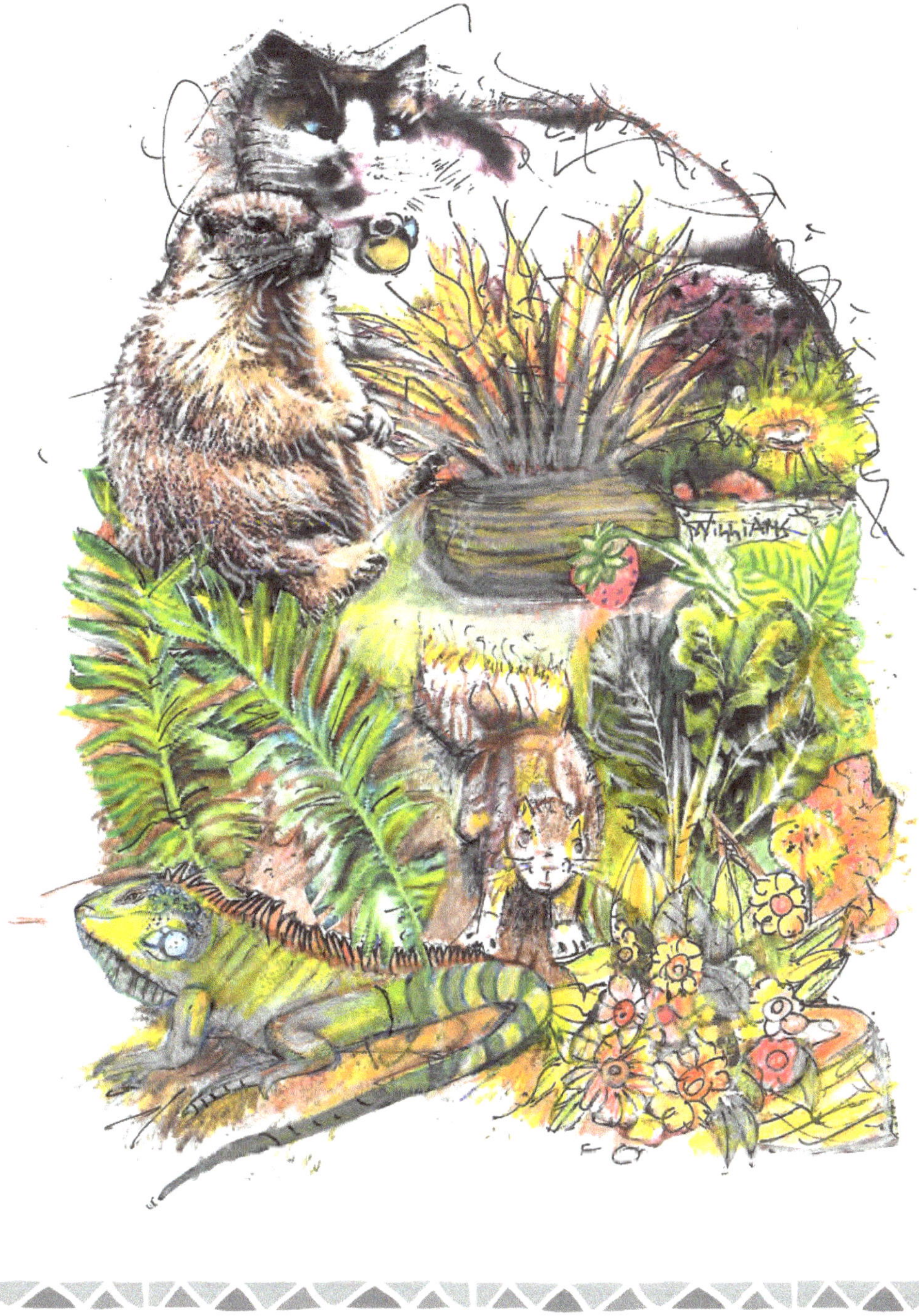

Rock chucks aren't quite woodchucks like Punxsutawney Phil,

We both are marmots, large ground squirrels, but Phil is called a groundhog;

It's his job to tell us whether spring will come quite early,

But when he does I hop inside his hole just like a frog.

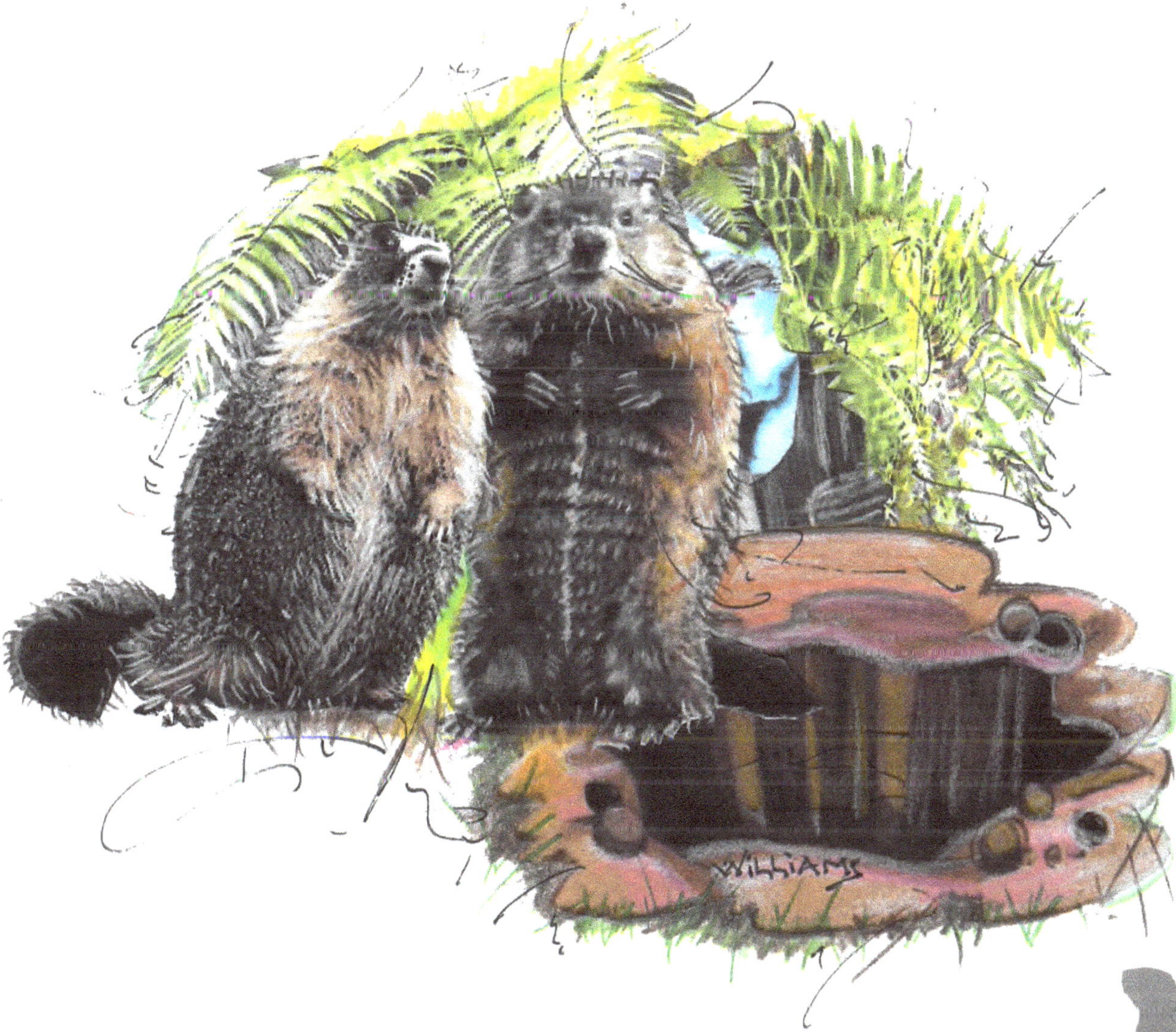
WILLIAMS

It isn't very often that a rock chuck can be seen,

As something that has feelings, can be loved, and understood;

For I am still a wild animal and not so easily tamed,

But with my human family I can show them that I'm good.

The End

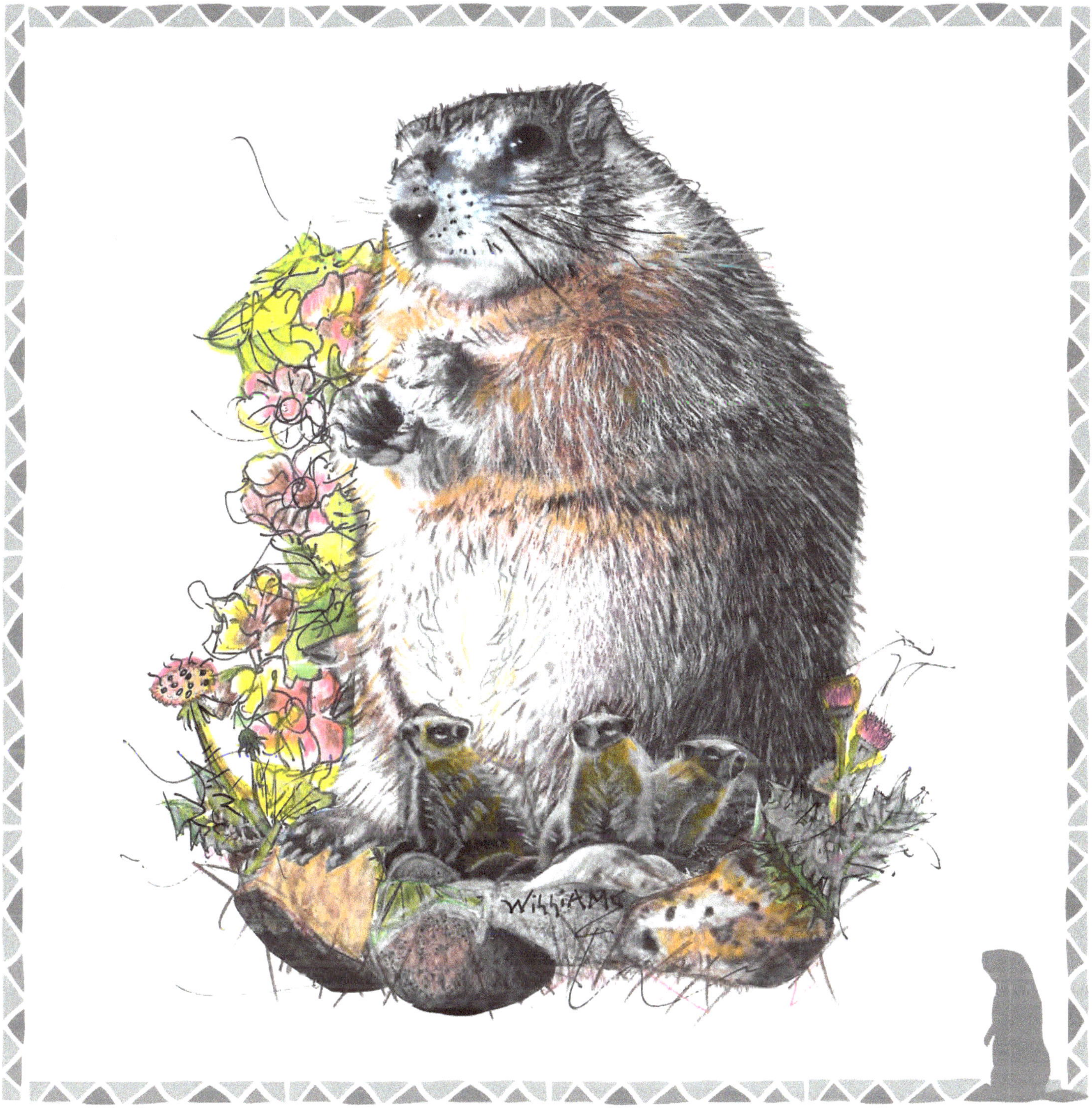
WilliAMS

Yellow-bellied Marmot Facts:

1. Yellow-bellied Marmots enjoy warm and dry places, like deserts, hills, and rock piles. They live in protected burrows where they raise their families, are safe from predators, and hibernate.

2. Yellow-bellied Marmots love the sunshine. Their belly is yellow (or orange-brown), which is why they are called yellow-bellied marmots.

3. Yellow-bellied Marmots can live alone, in colonies (and as pairs), and males may have babies with more than one female, usually mating once a year after hibernation.

4. Yellow-bellied Marmots have a gestation of 30 days, with mom having 5-9 pups.

5. Yellow-bellied Marmot moms keep their babies in the burrow for about 3 weeks while nursing them.

6.   Yellow-bellied Marmots can live 13-15 years in the wild, but predators and hibernation can cause premature deaths.

7.   Yellow-bellied Marmots spend their day lying in the sun, grooming themselves, looking for food, and stay in an alert position for predators.

8.   Yellow-bellied Marmots make very loud trilling, whistling, and chucking noises when alarmed.

9.   Yellow-bellied Marmots don't hibernate together.

10. Yellow-bellied Marmots can show friendly behaviors, mostly to others they know, by the way they greet, play, or groom each other. They can be aggressive with marmots from other burrows, or males might try to protect their territory by marking the area with their scent, or waving their tails back and forth. Sometimes males and females act aggressively toward their own young to encourage them to leave home.

11.   Yellow-bellied Marmots communicate with each other through a series of 6 different whistles. They also scream and have a distinctive teeth chatter (trill, whistle, chuck) to alert others, when they feel threatened, or if they are feeling anxious or excited.

12.   Yellow-bellied Marmots are herbivores (99% vegetarian) and eat plants, seeds, flowers and grasses.

13.   Yellow-bellied Marmots have to be on the outlook for predators like golden eagles, coyotes, badgers, (and black bears sometimes). Many times they have to stay in their burrows for a very longtime to stay safe.

14.   Yellow-bellied Marmots can affect the ecosystem by the seeds they eat and distribute. They create places for other animals to live when they abandon their burrows.

15.   Yellow-bellied Marmots can (quite rarely) carry the plague, which is caused by a kind of bacteria.

16.   Yellow-bellied Marmots are often hunted for no reason, for food, and for their fur, because they are listed as unprotected. A hunting license is required.

17.   Yellow-bellied Marmots have sweet faces and are considered to be small or medium in size to other rodents. They have sturdy bodies, and wide heads. The fur on their bodies is course, like a squirrel, and looks brown all over, except for lighter patches on their necks, yellowish bellies and white spots between their eyes.

18.   Yellow-bellied Marmots lose their fur during the summer, but eventually it grows back.

19.   Yellow-bellied Marmots are one kind of marmot. Woodchucks and groundhogs ('whistle pig') are also marmots.

20.   Marmots are the only animal that have a US holiday named after them: Groundhog Day.

The Williams Family Saves Moose the Kangaroo Mouse

When tiny is mighty

Story by

Jennifer Foreman de Grassi Williams

Watercolors by Bobbi Kelly

Dedicated to:

Everyone who understands that it isn't the size of the life that matters, but life itself that matters.

Our newest little blessing: Reed William
When Tiny is Mighty

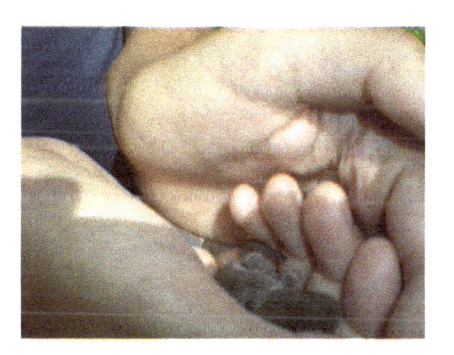

Story number 4 is about a finger-sized baby wild kangaroo mouse that amazed us with his instincts to accomplish many things. I have to say that I was in awe of the miniscule piece of flesh my friend pulled out of her pocket at my front door. "I knew you would take this," she said. A friend of hers had found it, whatever 'it' was, on a rock by a dam. It was squeaking very loudly in an effort to find its mom. If I hadn't seen it breathing, I really don't think I would have recognized it as being a life form. At first I didn't really know what it could be, except that it was totally dependent on us for life. I thought of how kangaroos are brought into this world and their miraculous and instinctive will to live~ amazing to me how wild animals survive against many odds.

When I stared at this little life, I could tell from its noises and movements that it was trying to communicate so many things: fear, hunger, pain, desperation. I knew I had been given a responsibility, and I was in love with this little being already. As with all babies, the priority was to get it warm, make it feel safe, and then figure out what it needed to eat. I always keep puppy or kitten formula in my refrigerator, as it works on any warm blooded animal baby I have ever had. This little one was way too tiny for an eye dropper, but a small syringe without the needle was perfect. Quite truthfully, I was not sure what it was until a couple of days later, and after doing some research. It was a wild kangaroo mouse. The usual rule of thumb, or in this case something that looks like a finger, is to always release an adult mouse back into the wild as they can carry Hantavirus (which can be deadly). They can also harbor ticks, worms, fleas. Plus an adult does much better in the wild and is happier, as such a wild animal never loses its fear of humans... even if held a lot. The story is a bit different for a helpless baby who cannot take care of itself, and who has not learned how to be a wild mouse. "Hand-raised baby wild mice tend to be affectionate and loyal to their human caregivers, and are smarter than domesticated mice." I knew we would keep this little guy and be fascinated to see how his instincts would dictate his life. We created quite a habitat for him in his glass aquarium, which afforded us total access/view to his life and habits. To name him was a challenge...

such a little guy, but such a big spirit, like a Moose. The life expectancy of a wild mouse is about 5 years. Moose lived a good 7. He never knew another mouse, but certainly grew used to us picking him up. We got to watch him go through all stages of baby to senior, and he earned his long and gray hair by the end of his life. It was amazing that he had no parents, siblings, or role model, yet he was capable of so much on his own. He was as endearing and adorable as a baby and the same as a little old man.

Steps after getting baby warm in my hand were to:

1. Rehydrate (Pedialyte is good) by giving several drops before an attempt at formula, like puppy/kitten milk.

2. Determine age by looking at a chart, or know that baby mice grow hair at about 3-4 days, open eyes after 10 days, and start a jumping stage after that (called the "popcorn" stage).

3. Care needs to be taken so that baby does not aspirate when given fluids. Baby should be held upright when being given fluids, and turned upside down if bubbles are coming out of its nose.

4. Feed every 2-3 hours initially. When eyes begin to open after a couple of weeks, then feed every 4 hours. Water down the formula, and check with a vet or online as to how much baby needs.

5.   As mouse gets older, it can eat hard food and drink out of a rodent water bottle hung on the side of the cage. Never give a bowl of water as the mouse can drown. Hard foods include commercial rodent food, baby food, white rice, and kitten food.

You may not quite believe it when you see this furry guy,

That as a baby, baby mouse he had no hair at all;

His front legs are so very short, with back ones really long,

And he can hop up awfully high though he is very small.

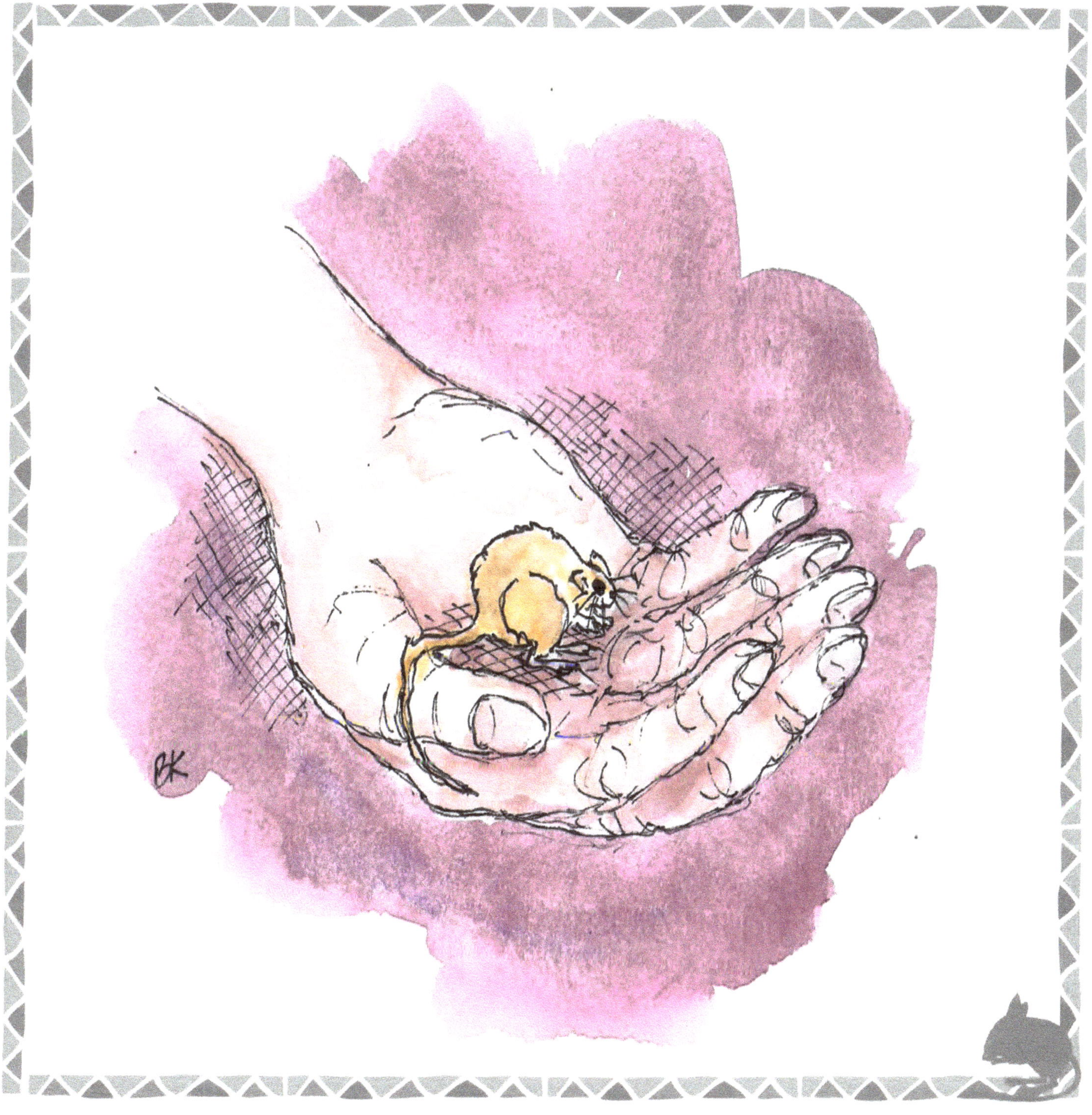
BK

A kangaroo is really big and not at all a mouse,

But like the kangaroo that's big this mouse can be quite wild;

Moose is what we call him even though he's very little,

And in the world of grown up mice, Moose is just a child.

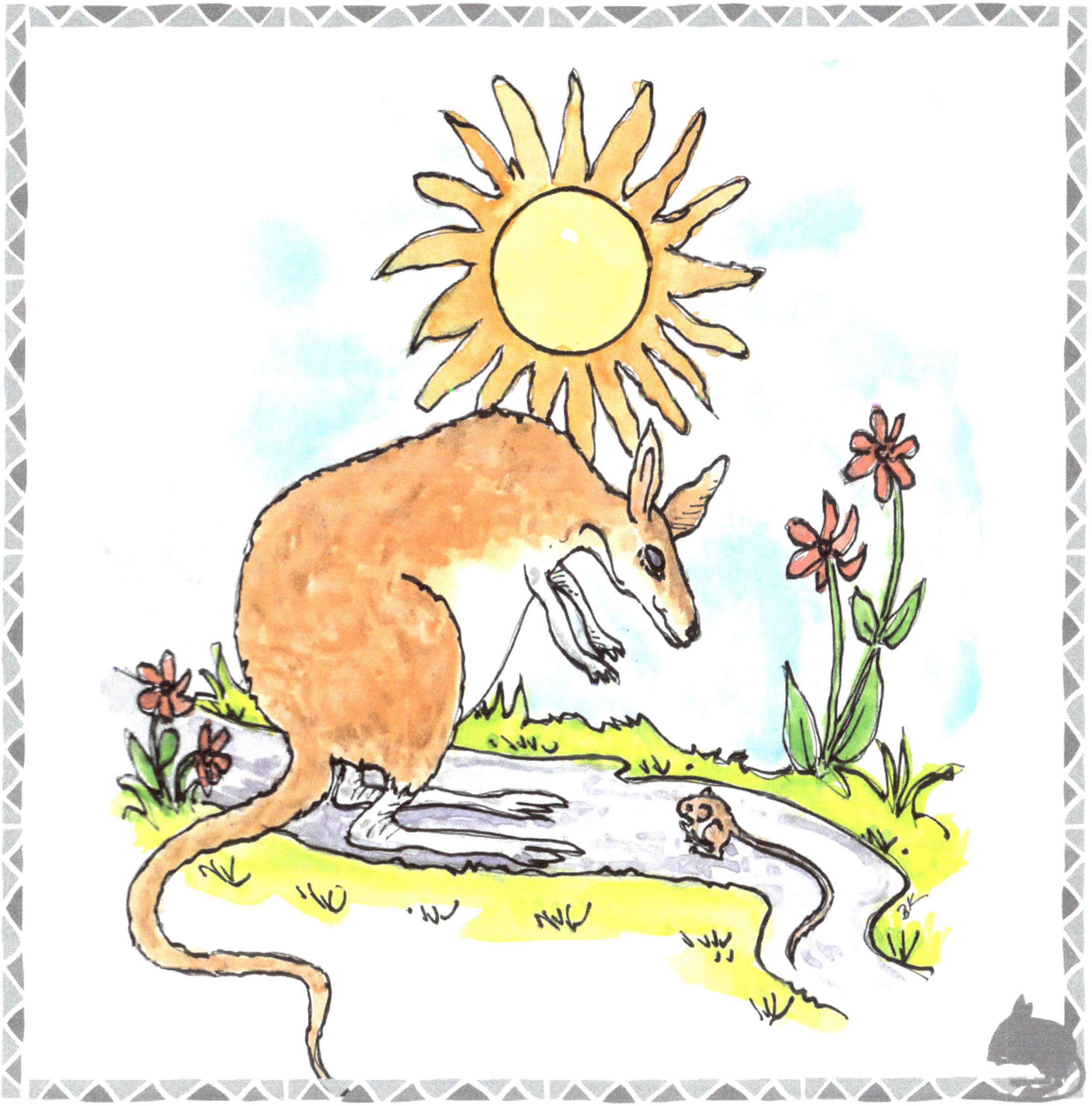
BK

Moose the mouse is very cute and likes to live alone,

His big, big whiskers feel the air to sense if cold or hot;

He also likes to wash his hands, his face and tiny paws,

And loves to stay up late at night, at least that's what I thought.

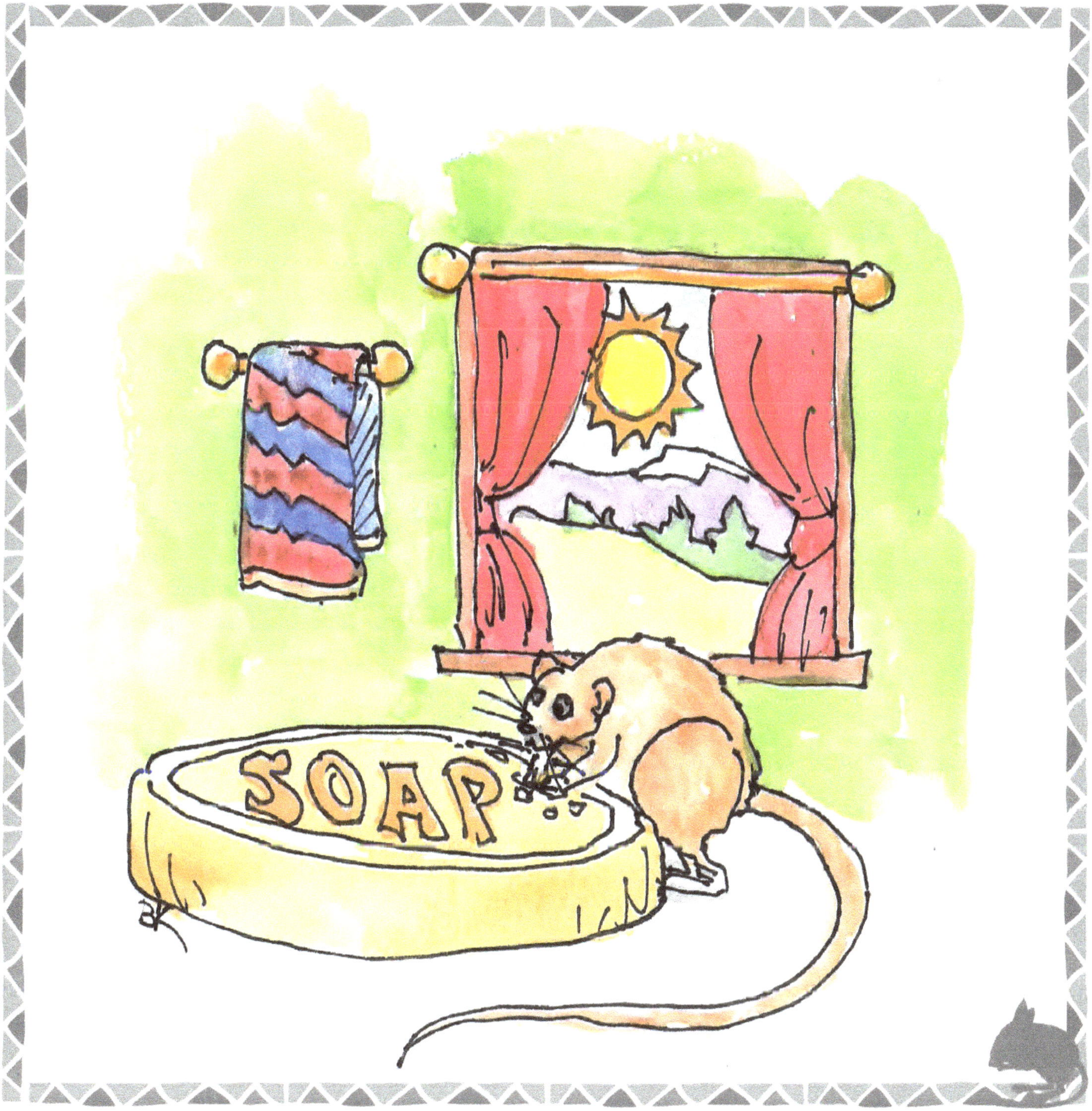
SOAP

Moose the mouse tucks food away
inside of his cheek pouches,

And holy cow if you could see the
grains and seeds and insects;

His cheeks fill up like red balloons
that might just float or pop,

He stores it there like pet mice
do, and nobody objects.

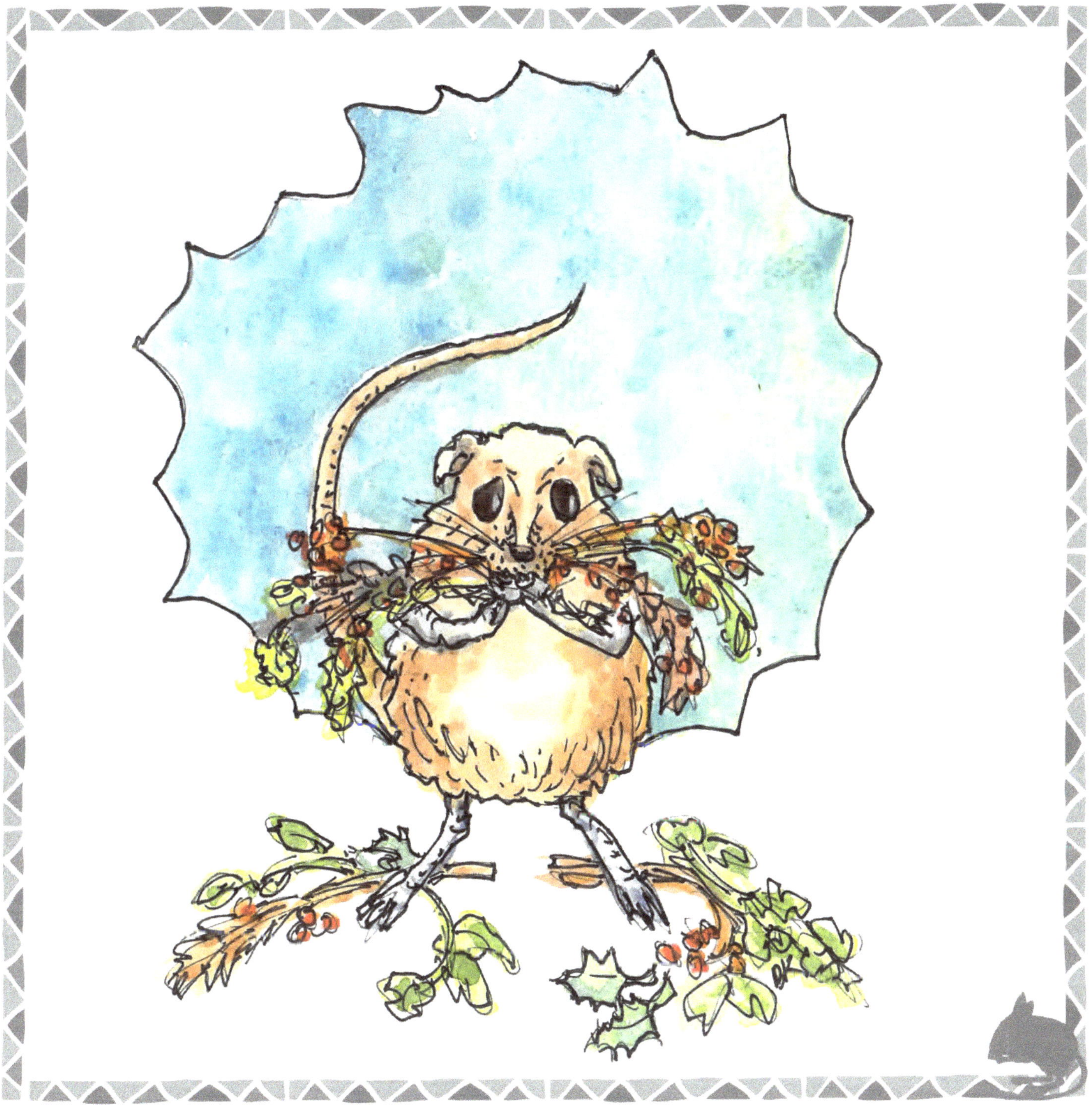

A mouse that seems just like a little baby kangaroo,

Can live inside a burrow, where he isn't very bold;

He drinks a little water, though he doesn't need too much,

The cold and moon just make him hide, and that is what I'm told.

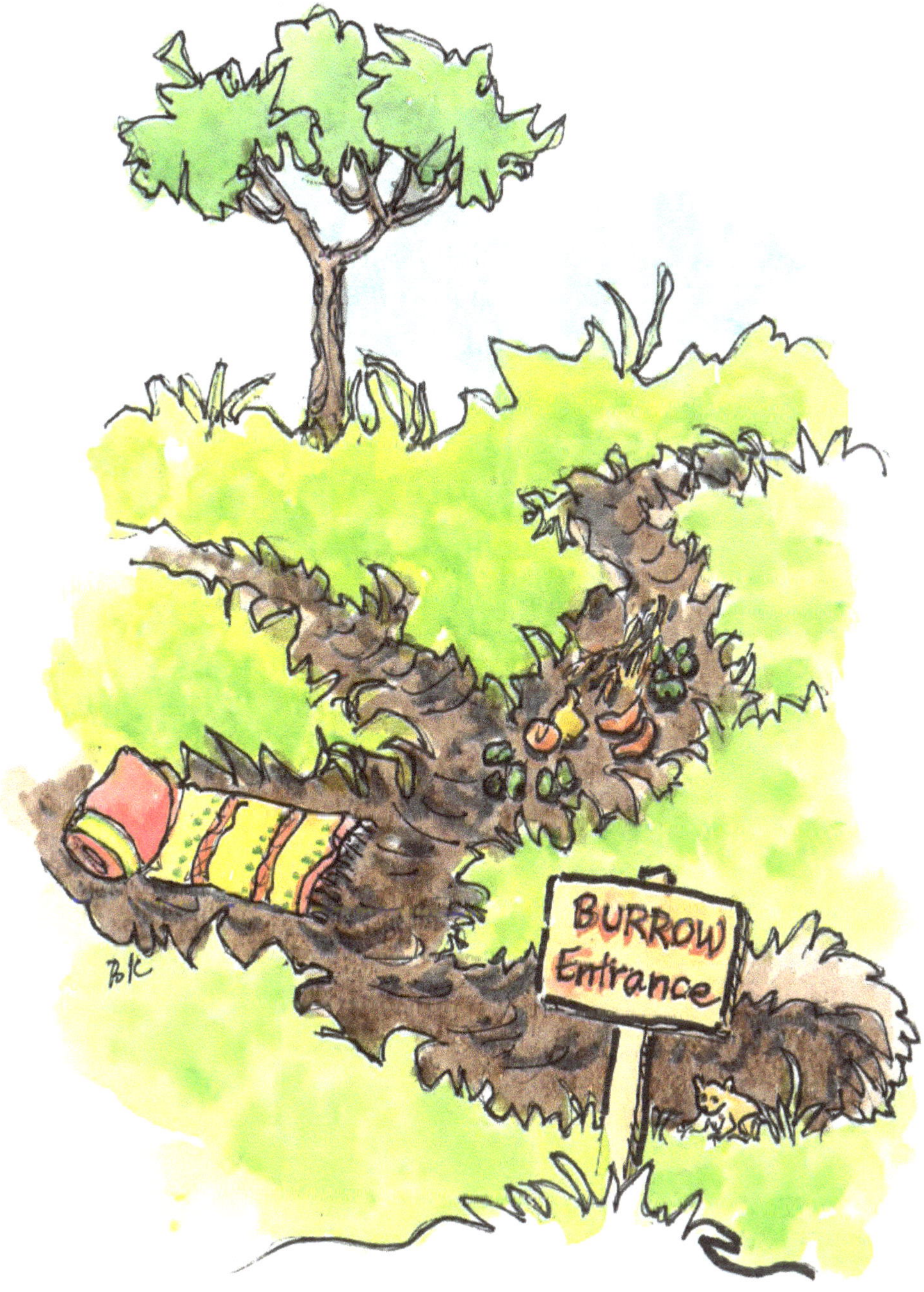
BURROW
Entrance

While dry and warm inside his burrow Moose can get some sleep,

But only if his habitat is safe upon this earth;

For he can live five years or more and sleep upon his nest,

And dream of all the kids he'll have when mama mouse gives birth.

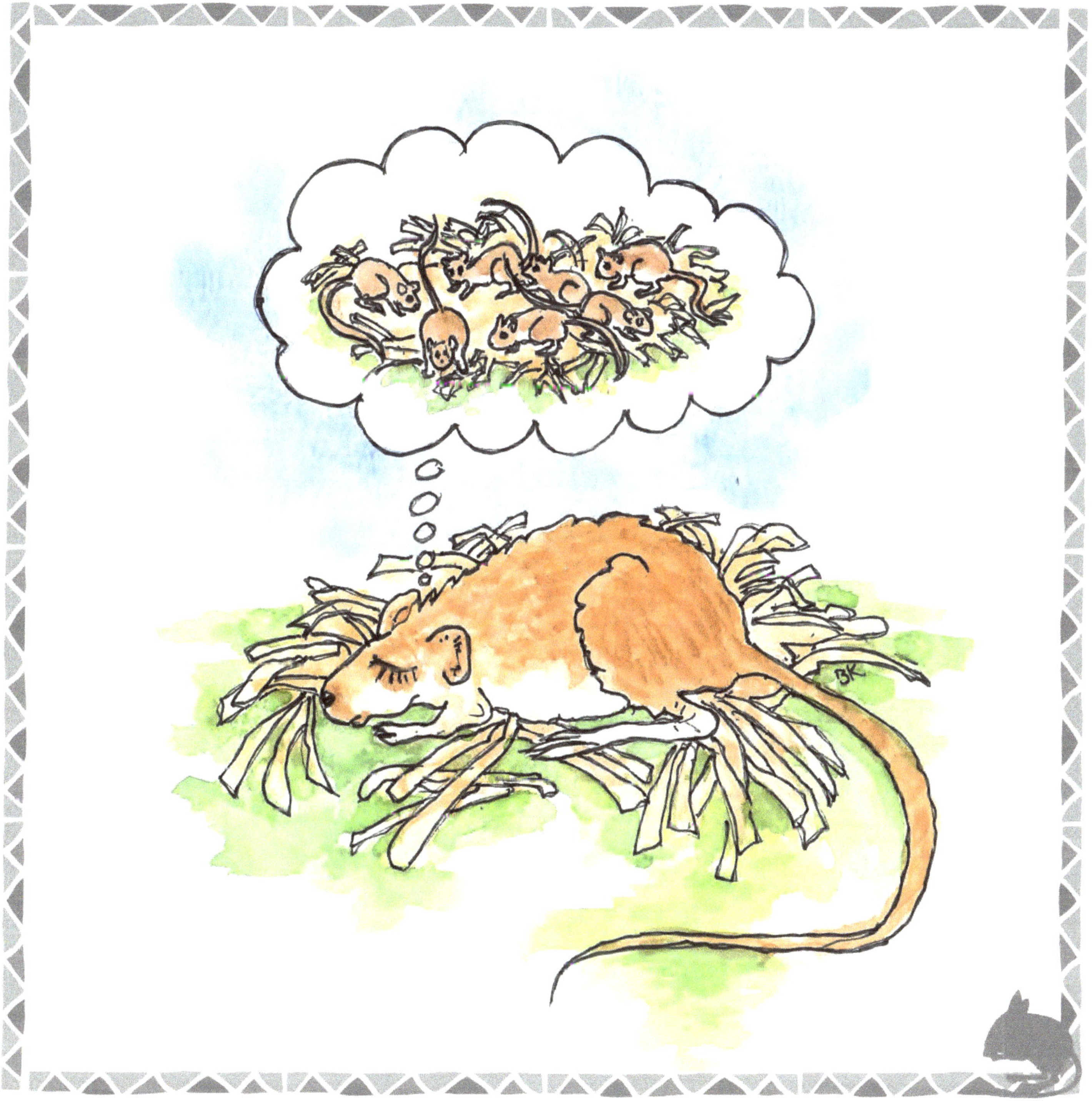

Moose the mouse just loves to live all by himself for sure,

And will protect his home and burrow from things that wander near;

Like snakes and owls, and badgers too, and foxes that come close,

He'll run and hide until he knows the coast is very clear.

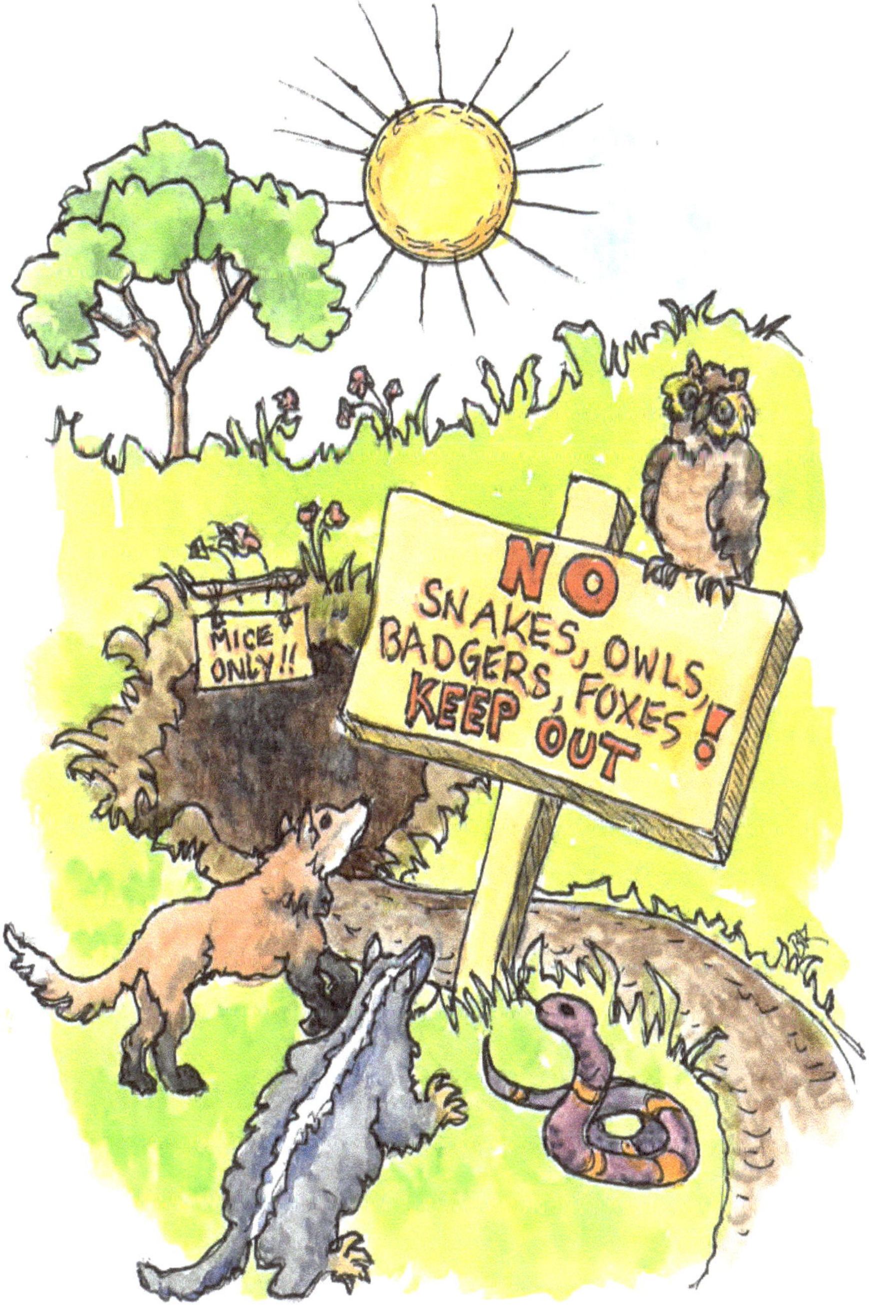
MICE ONLY!!
NO
SNAKES, OWLS,
BADGERS, FOXES!
KEEP OUT

This sweet fluff ball in the night will gaze into the sky,

He knows that night allows him to be safer than the day;

And even though the stars and moon can make him move quite slow.

He sniffs the nighttime air and then he jumps and wants to play.

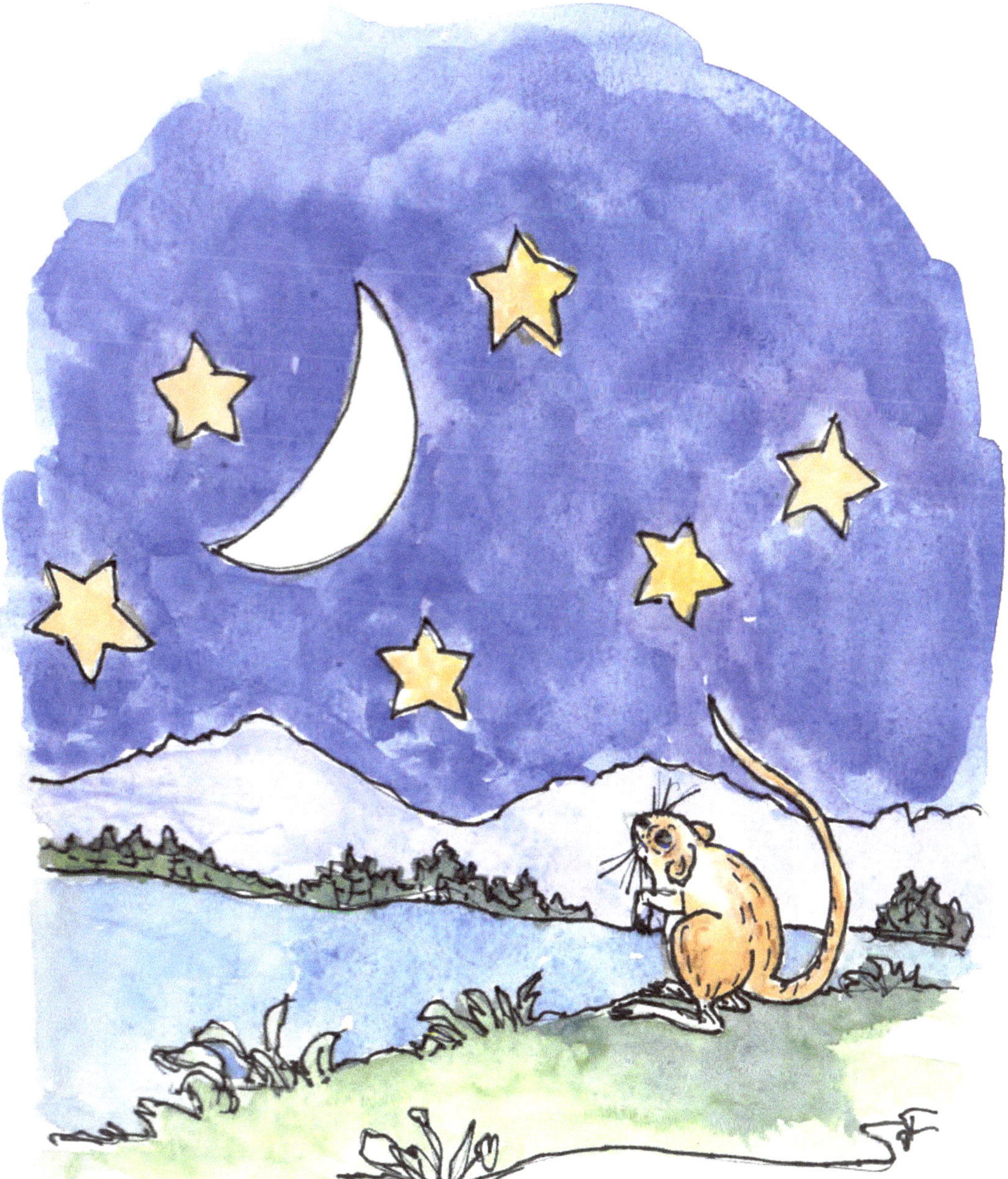

Moose really likes the sunshine and when the temperatures get hot,

But fears that global warming won't be good for him or you;

So many other animals are starting to move North,

Because the kind of food they need is disappearing too.

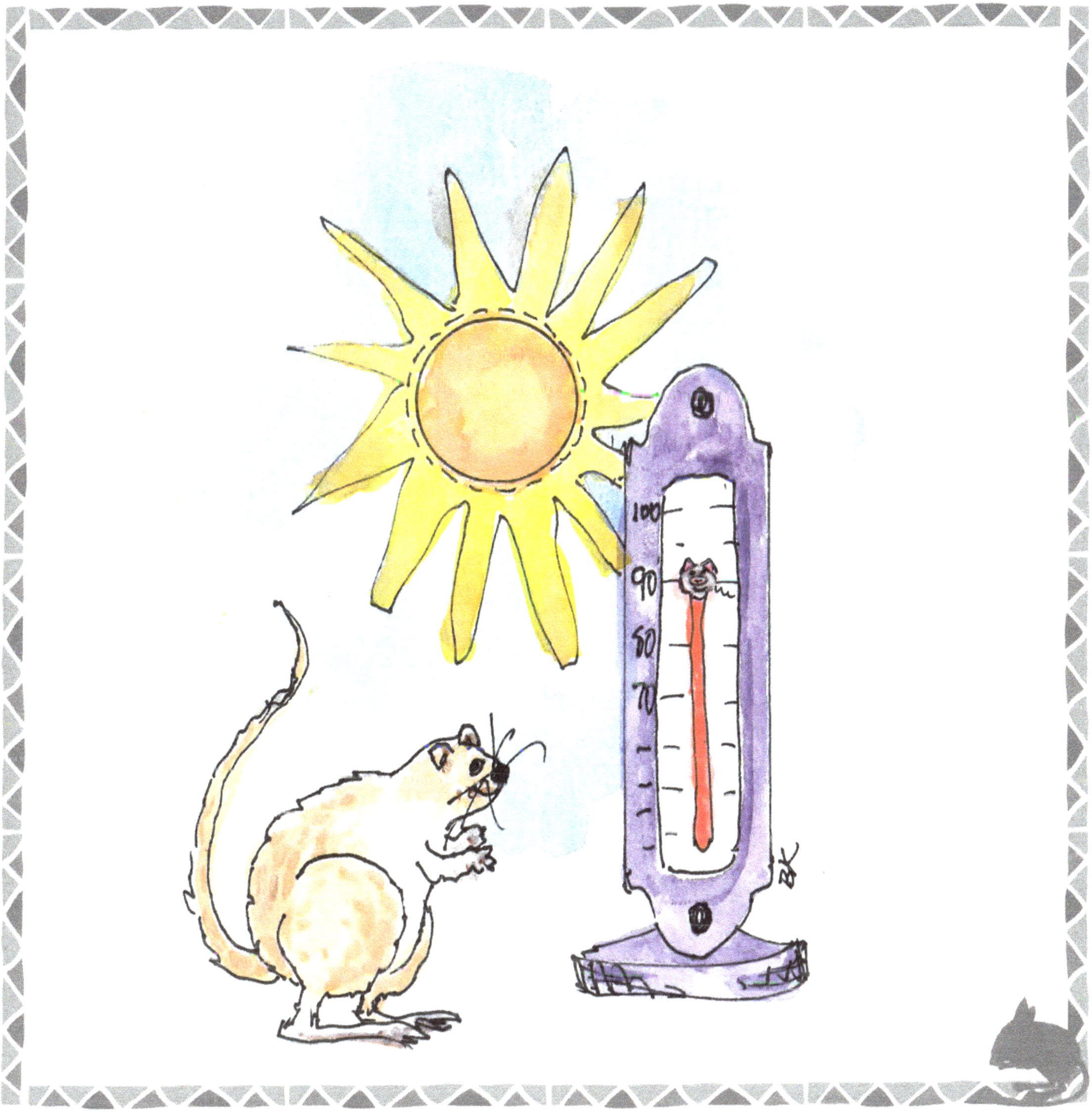
100
90
80
70

Moose always has such full days as he gathers all he needs,

And never spends much thought on how his fur is turning gray;

He thinks he'd look quite silly using glasses or a cane,

Hopping like a kangaroo or playing all the day.

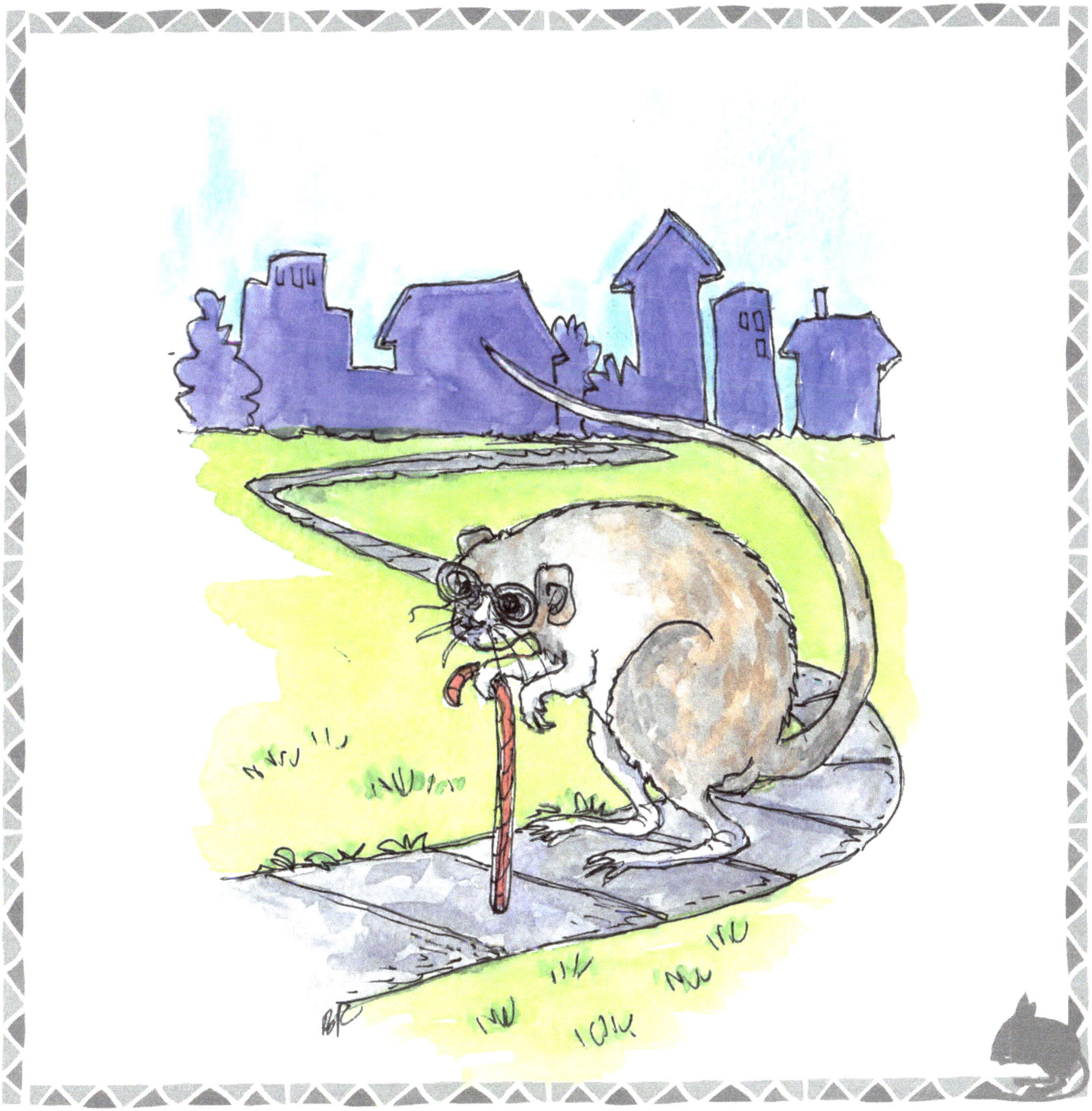

You wouldn't really think that such a tiny little guy,

Could build so many tunnels with a purpose that he knows;

He likes his tiny trumpet and his red ball where he sits,

And plays and runs to have some fun, then rests his tiny toes.

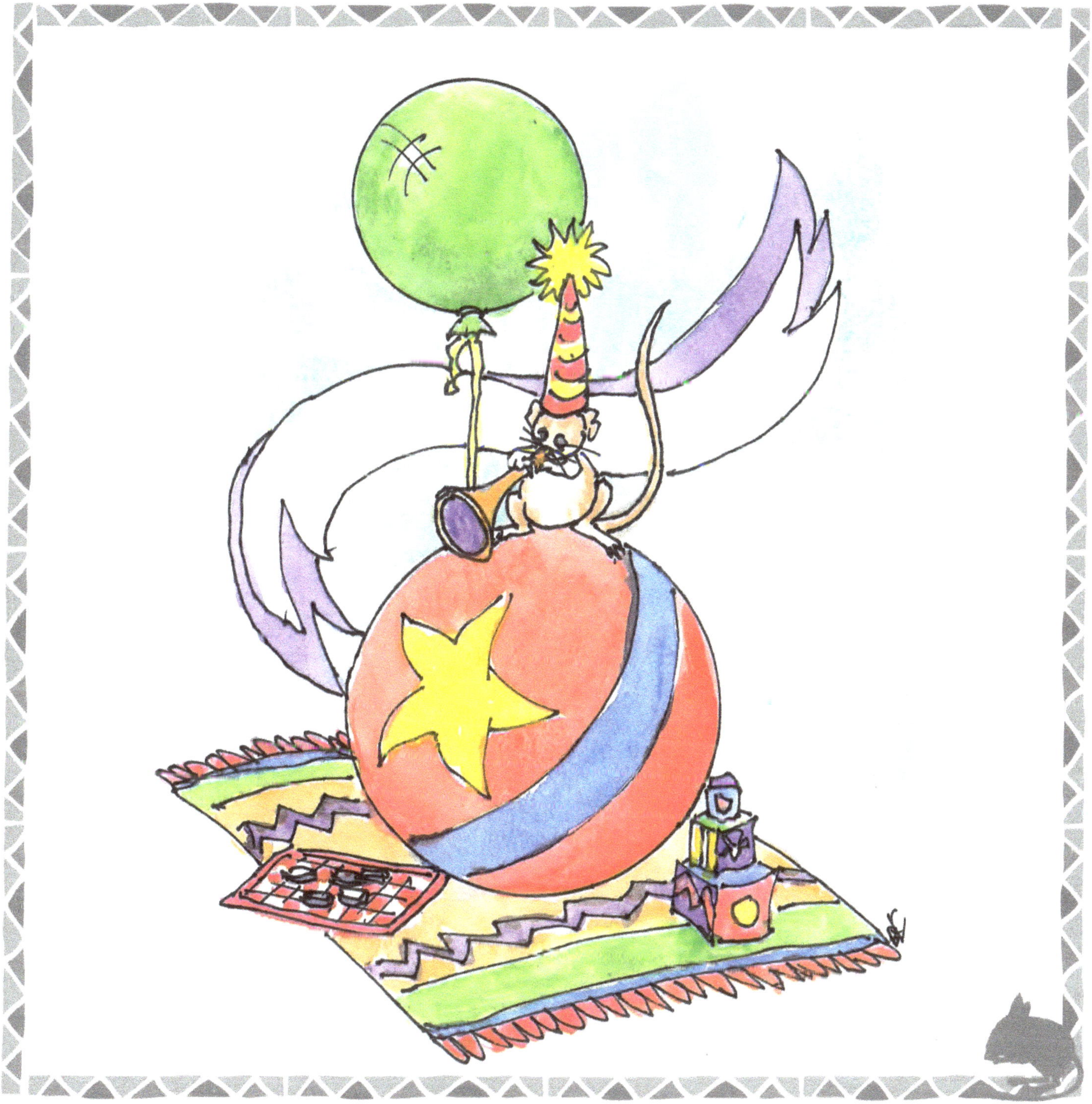

It is said somewhere I read that
Cat is to a mouse,

Just like a dog is to a rat, though
Moose can hibernate;

And when he came to live with
us his size was like a sausage,

For though he was a big surprise,
his life with us was GREAT.

THE END

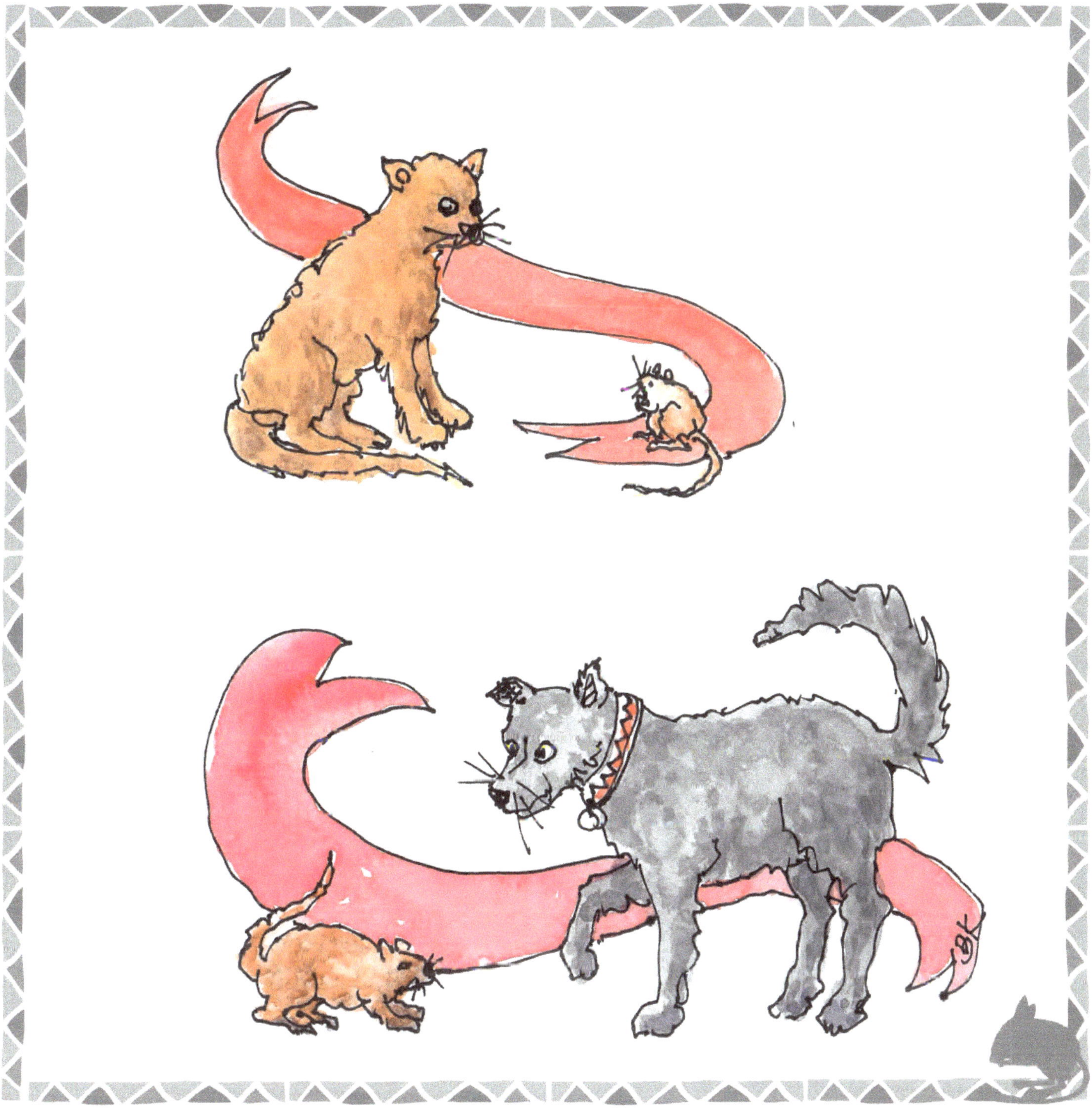

Kangaroo Mice Facts:

1. Kangaroo Mice have large heads and long whiskers, though their bodies are very small.

2. Kangaroo Mice have thick tails, which they use for fat storage, helping them during hibernation.

3. Kangaroo Mice can be dark or light in color.

4. Kangaroo Mice have short front legs, and long back ones. Dark Kangaroo mice mostly hop on their two hind legs (bipedal) as they forage, but can also move on all four legs if living in an aquarium.

5. Kangaroo Mice metabolize water from the seeds they eat. Their kidneys can concentrate the urine, and this helps to prevent any water loss.

6. Kangaroo Mice are not endangered, but considered threatened as their numbers are declining due to human activity (creating a decline in their habitat).

7. Kangaroo Mice live about 5 years.

8. Kangaroo Mice are very clean.

9. Kangaroo Mice have more than one breeding season a year, and have elaborate nests in their burrows.

10. Kangaroo Mice have 2-7 babies.

11. Kangaroo Mice live solitary lives, but can be very territorial and aggressive when they encounter others.

12. Kangaroo Mice are nocturnal, and most active after the sun sets.

13. Kangaroo Mice forage for grains, seeds, and insects, and carry food back to their burrows in their cheek pouches.

14. Kangaroo Mice don't seem to be moving

northward, like other animals, due to global warming.

15. Kangaroo Mice have predators such as snakes, badgers, and owls.

16. Kangaroo Mice hibernate. The fat deposits in their tails act as a source of energy during hibernation, which are fatter going into hibernation and skinnier close to spring.

17. Kangaroo Mice don't typically make good pets. They may seem docile at first, but bottom line is they are wild animals.

18. Kangaroo Mice can carry diseases.

19. Kangaroo Mice are very sensitive to temperature, having decreased energy levels when it gets colder and when there is moonlight.

Pet Mice Facts:

1. Pet Mice have pointed snouts and ears that are rounded, plus an almost hairless tail. They have long whiskers that also help them to feel along the surface of things.

2. Pet Mice include a number of mice species, but the house mouse is the most popular.

3. Pet Mice are mostly nocturnal with poor eyesight, but can smell and hear very well.

4. Pet Mice have predators like wild dogs, foxes, coyotes, birds of prey, cats, and even snakes.

5. Pet Mice live for approximately 3 years.

6. Pet Mice have tails that can grow as long as their bodies.

7. Pet Mice can suffer from respiratory issues.

Bedding material made of aspen is good, or hay.

8. Pet Mice do well with a commercial mouse food. They also like a variety of fresh fruit, vegetables, scrambled or boiled egg, lean meat, peas, chickpeas, and mealworms.

9. Pet Mice do well in a glass aquarium or wire cage with a water bottle, mouse toys and exercise wheel, plus a variety of places to hide like tubes, cans, boxes, etc.

10. Pet Mice build very complex burrows that have routes to escape, and long entrances.

11. Pet Mice are very clean rodents and keep their burrows clean too. They often have separate burrows for sleeping, storing their food, and going potty.

12. Pet Mice thrive in temperatures that are between 86-90 degrees, and use their whiskers to sense the change in temperature.

13. Pet Mice are covered by the Animal Welfare Act, which means you are required to care for them properly. However, the "US is the only country in the world that does not include within its animal welfare laws and regulations the mice who are subjected to research and testing. The federal Animal Welfare Act (AWA) was amended in 1970 to include all warm-blooded animals who are commonly experimented upon. However, the term "animals", for purposes of the protections delineated in the statute, is defined so as to expressly exclude mice, rats and birds—the very animals who constitute roughly 95% of animals in research!"

~Like rats, there is no doubt we have completely discounted that mice, too, experience pain and fear, shown by the fact that we still count on them as specimens in a lab. You've only to have a pet rat, or mouse, to know that finding another non-living option to use in all kinds of experiments would be the kind and ethical thing to do.

The Williams Family Fosters Rabbits, Parakeets, and Snails

Lives that cross by accident

Story by

Jennifer Foreman de Grassi Williams

Watercolors by Bobbi Kelly

Dedicated to:

My Family, My Friends, and Anyone who has ever rescued a hurt, abused, abandoned little creature, because we know that animals are not objects we can treat like trash, but are nature's gifts, and we are responsible for the plight of all living beings.

With love to infinity for:

Norah

Harper

Sonja

Reed

Story number 5 is divided into three mini anecdotes, mostly factual, about a unique assortment of miniature beings that came to live with us, though purely unintentional on their parts and ours. Their presence in our lives taught us new things, or at the very least that a trail of slime is quite important. I am reminded, sadly, that these, like other beings we could all name, are in many cases 'throw away' animals. I find infinite joy, and have since I was barely able to walk, in the many creatures we are lucky enough to share our lives. Too often, however, there are animals that people just don't like, don't want anymore, have no use for, get tired of, or find frustration in the care they need, can't afford to feed, are the products of a broken home or somebody dying, are considered pests, or worse yet are not even looked to as being capable of feeling fear, loyalty, maternal instincts, hunger, pain, sadness, or love. Many 'overlooked' beings that aren't particularly warm and fuzzy, don't bark or purr their satisfaction, can't even be appreciated for their own place and value in the natural world. They too have the challenges of having babies, a routine, instincts, community, transferring information, creativity and ingenuity. This book embraces several of those little lives that crossed my path quite by accident.

 The first poem is about parakeets. Parakeets can be as friendly or aloof as you'd like depending on the time you invest in them. We acquired three when our children were very young: Pepsi, Cola, and Sprite. When we were on vacation a neighbor girl was caring for them and forgot to fill their water bowl. They passed away by the time we returned. I was stricken with sadness and panic simultaneously as to how I would explain these deaths to our youngest daughter. I asked our local pet store if they had any parakeets, but all that remained were three they could not sell. One had a bent beak. One had a goiter. The last had many of its feathers missing. Ah, these were my kind of birds! I replaced our deceased pets with these and upon seeing them my daughter said, "Mom our birds look so different". I explained that sometimes going on vacation for a while made your pets look a little different upon your return. That was a true statement, but I could not bring myself to tell her the whole truth, or burden her sweet mind with how it feels when a pet dies. Many years later I accepted a parakeet from a student who was going off to college and begged me to take her bird. Of course I had to get a friend for it. This is where you get into a 'bird spiral'. Parakeets can live a very long time, and can mourn when their cage mate passes. I decided to hang a mirror in the cage and found that the single bird was quite content talking to itself, 'thinking' (I believe) that there was another friend who never talked back in that mirror, but talked at the same time.

The next poem involves two rabbits (bunnies) that

were 'dumped' at the creek below our house. This was not the first (or last) incident of random people throwing animals away like garbage at our creek, which can also be a lovely place where newborn ducks, lizards, snakes, and birds find life quite good. I watched as a man got out of his truck and I wondered what he was putting behind some bushes, so decided to see for myself after he drove away. Under a clump of grass, and very confused and afraid, were two dwarf rabbits. I was picturing this man, who probably got tired of his child's pets and decided this would be (or not) a humane place to leave them~ RIGHT!!!! I imagined what excuse he would make to his son or daughter about the disappearance of the rabbits. There are coyotes, foxes, and cars nearby. The rabbits would not have stood a chance in the wild, let alone with the fall and winter months. So Blackie and Marshmallow came to live with us. They shared a very big dog run in our yard where they could dig, and 'binkie' and laugh (if rabbits could laugh out loud they would have) at the antics of a large gray pigeon we rescued and he too lived in the dog run. His name was 'Curry Bird' and he would continually do his mating dance for the two rabbits. It was a sight. They, of course, paid no mind to the stomping and cooing CB.

The last little poem is about one of the most interesting, and destructive, bits of life I've known: garden snails. When I was a young girl my brother would squash them in his hands. I was mortified. As a teenager I watched in horror as my father would kill them with salt, and I'd cry. As an adult I bought my father a cement snail the size of a loveable Olde English Bulldogge with a metal sign that read "try to kill this one". I have such fondness for their interesting ways that I collect them (sometimes upwards of 50) after we have watered our yard, or after a rain, and relocate their homes to a delightful area of our back hill that contains shelter and plenty of compost and dead leaves for food. So there you have it. This book reminds me of the animals people give away, throw away, or kill. ALL life has value. It is our job to be kind, and in the words of my dear Mother, "Do no harm".

Sonja

Three little parakeets loved chatting with each other,

They chirped and sang from morn 'til night and that you couldn't miss;

And certainly you'd hear them play with all the toys they loved,

Smart little birds said so many words: "cutie-patootie" and "kiss".

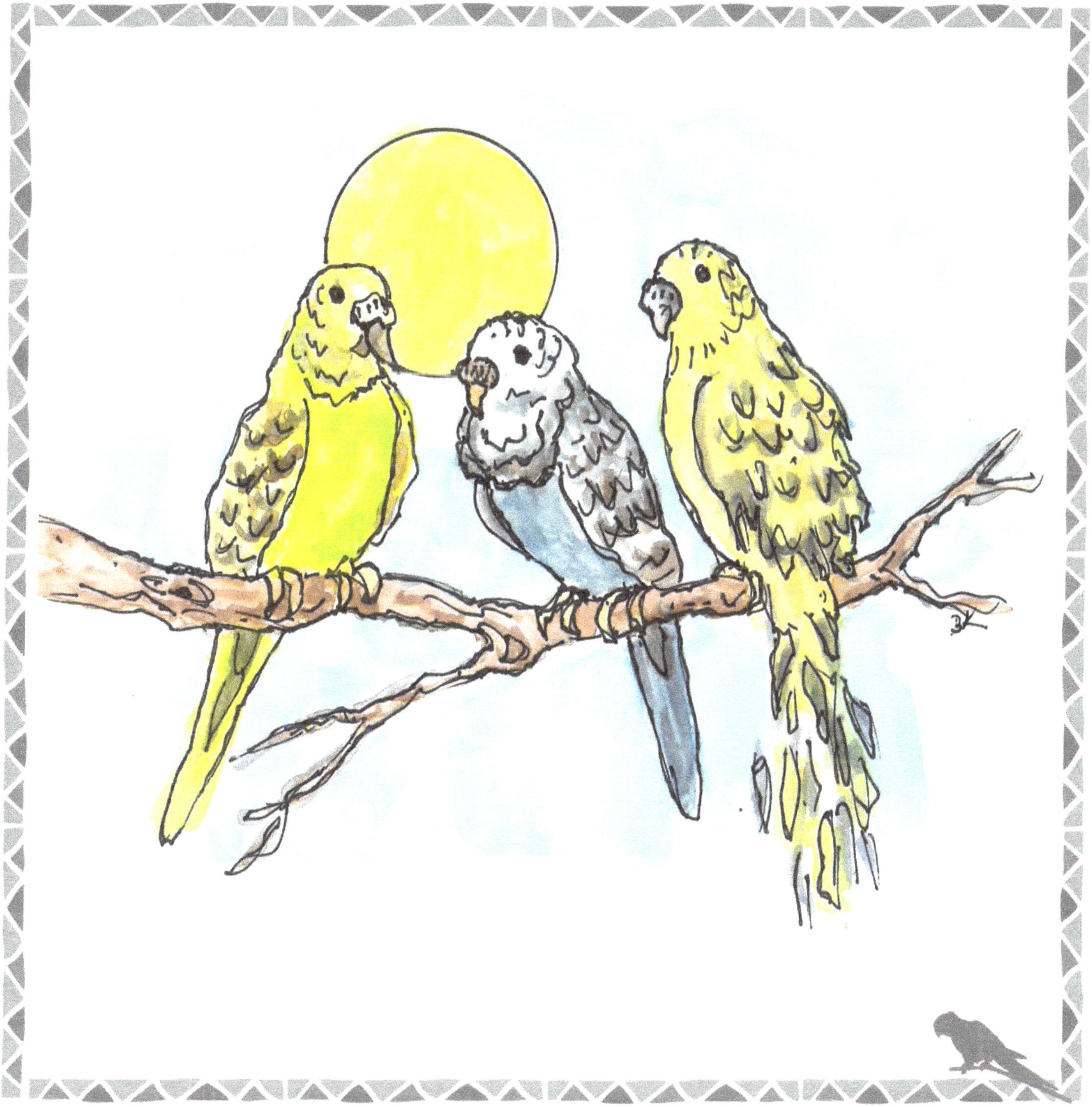

Pepsi, Sprite and Cola were so colorful and bright,

And sometimes you could hear them splashing in their water bowl;

These little feathered balls are clever to their bones,

So huggable and friendly from their heart into their soul.

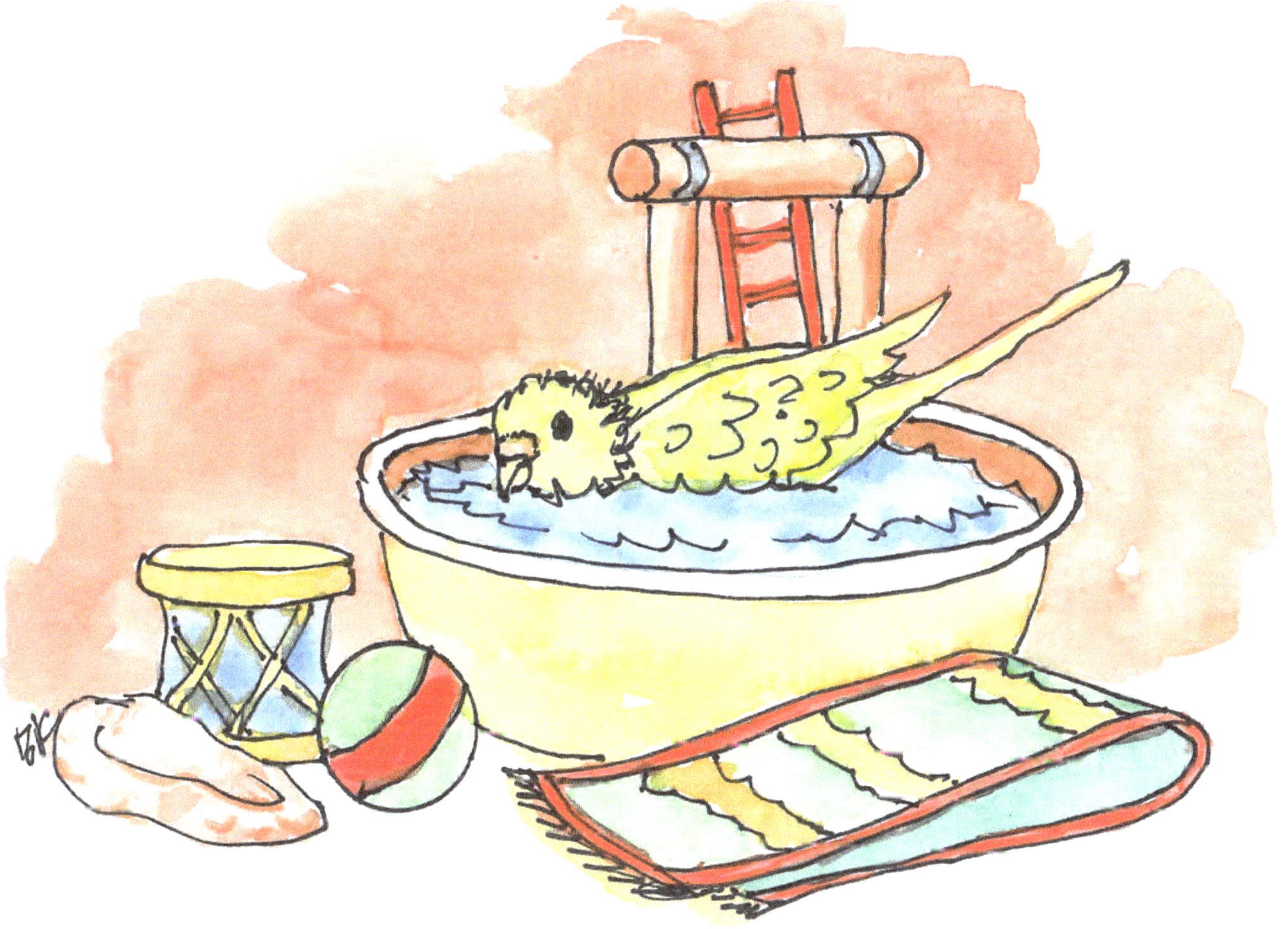

A person really could not tell by listening to their sounds,

That parakeets can learn the things they hear at home all day;

For they can speak more words than most of us can understand,

And even learn from our dear pets like dogs and what they say. (bark)

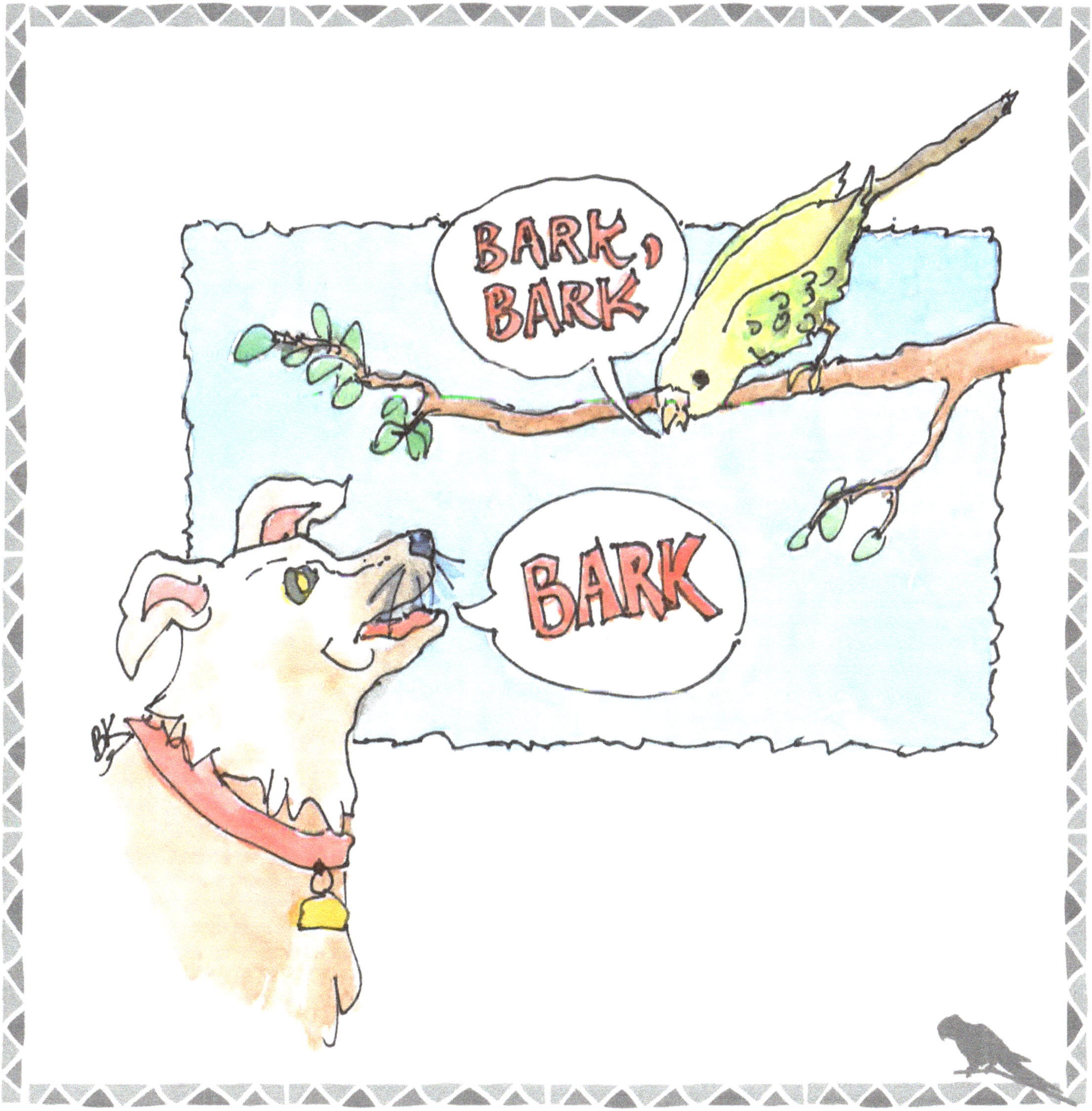
BARK, BARK
BARK

Quite early in the morning, or so very late at night,

You may not really know it but your little Budgie may~

Be looking in the mirror and think that he's alone,

So listen very closely to what your Budgie has to say.

The End

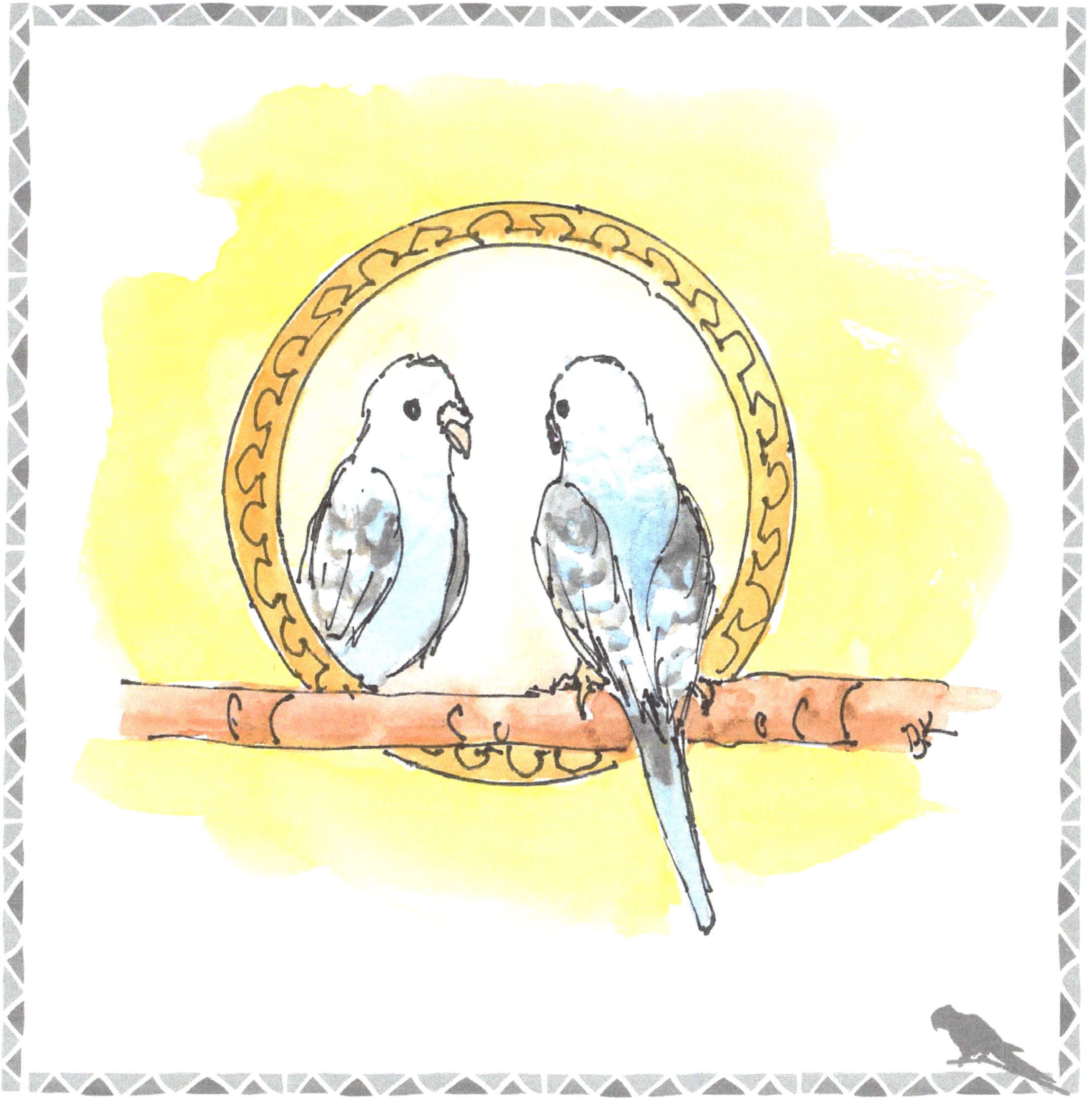

"Hiss," said the little snake just sitting by the creek,

For he had never seen a rabbit 'til this very day;

But nibbling on the grass and weeds sat two young rabbit friends,

Planning what they'd find to eat and what they'd like to play.

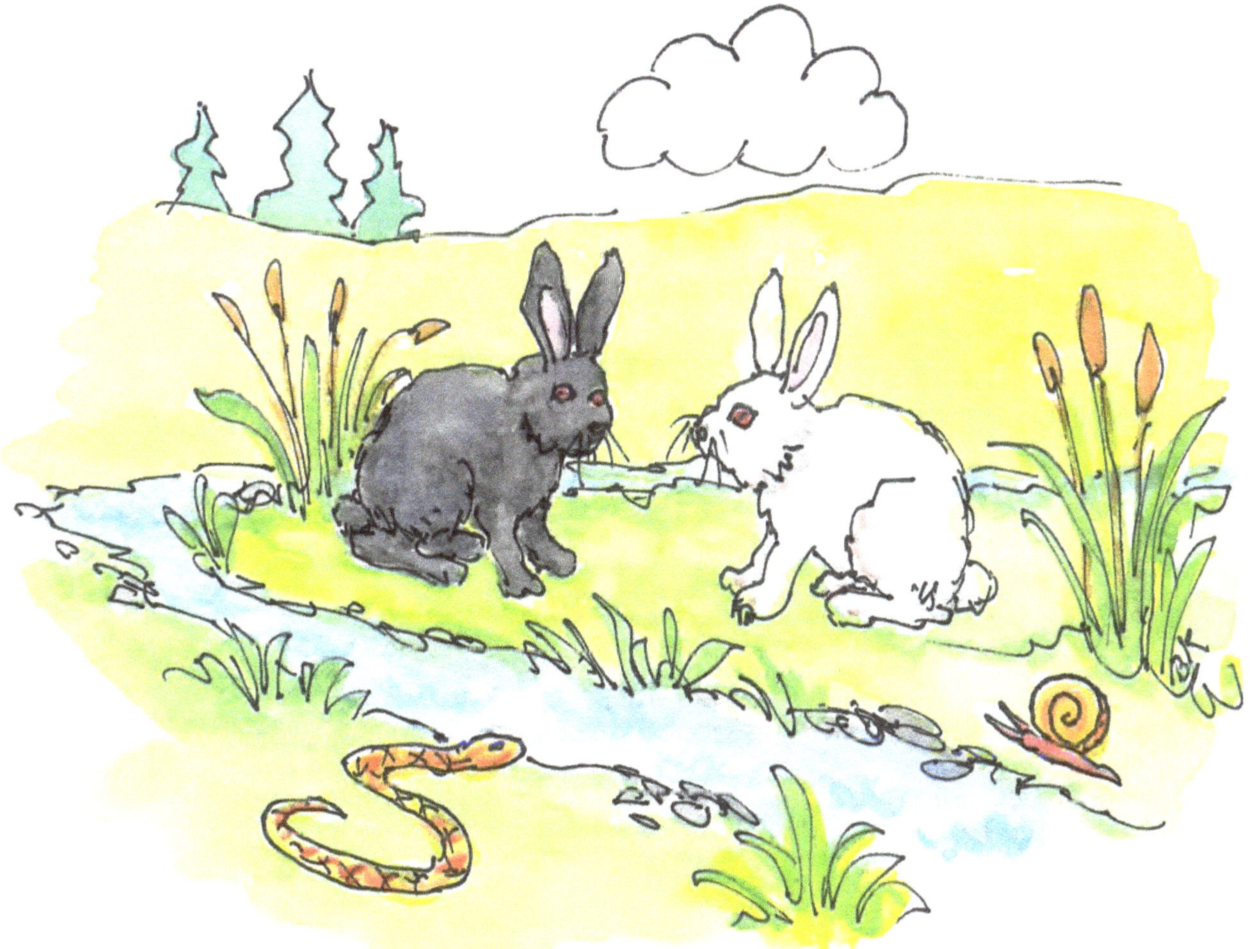

Marshmallow's white fur made Blackie's fur a little darker,

Looking for each other as they played among their toys;

They liked to hide inside their cardboard castle just to see,

Their pigeon friend named Curry bird, who danced and made such noise.

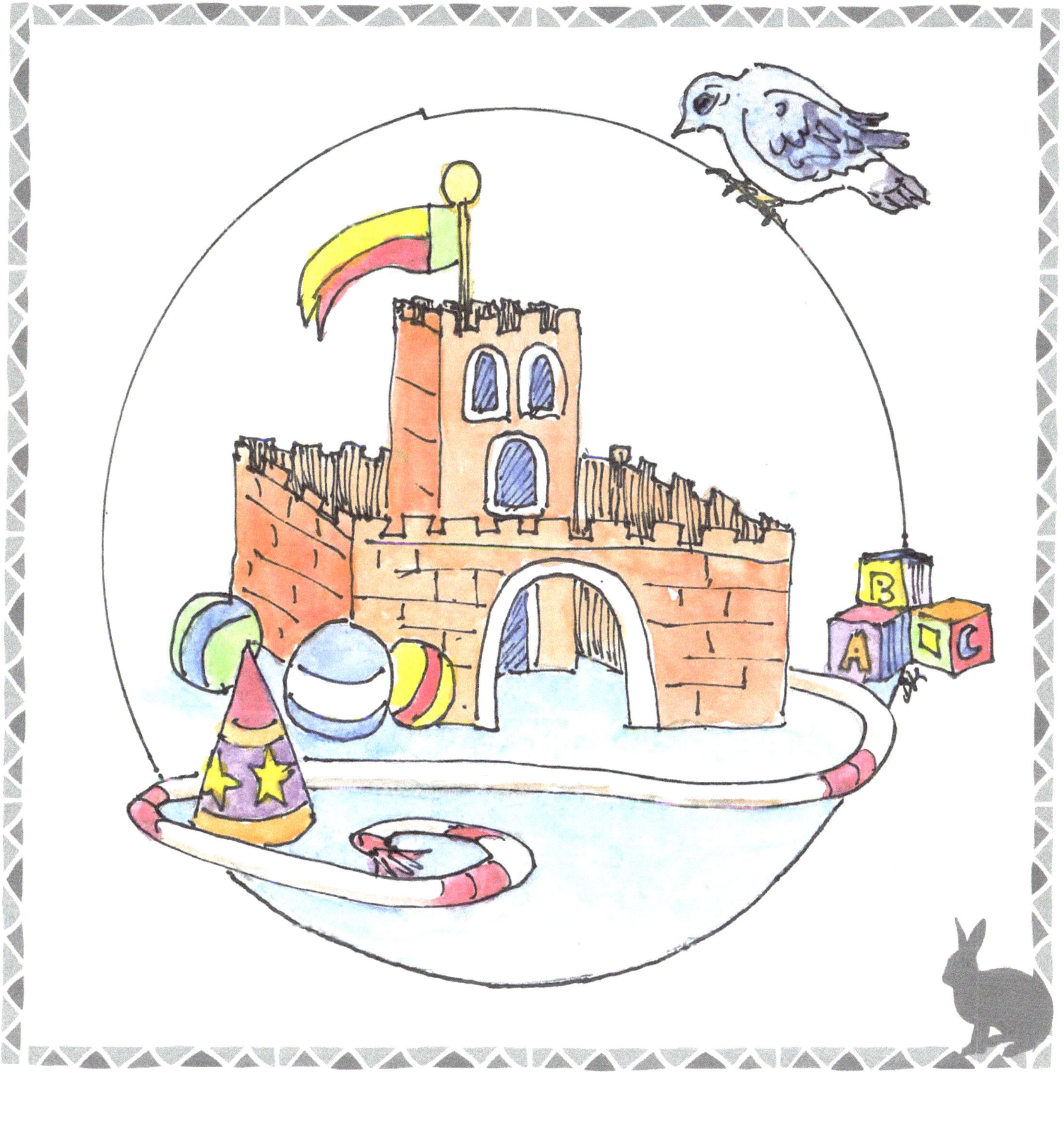
B
A
C

A boy rabbit is called a 'buck', while girls are pretty 'does',

And babies are their little 'kits' though can't meow like kittens;

Mama's can have many 'kits' that look like colored eggs,

And when you see them hopping round they look like ears in mittens.

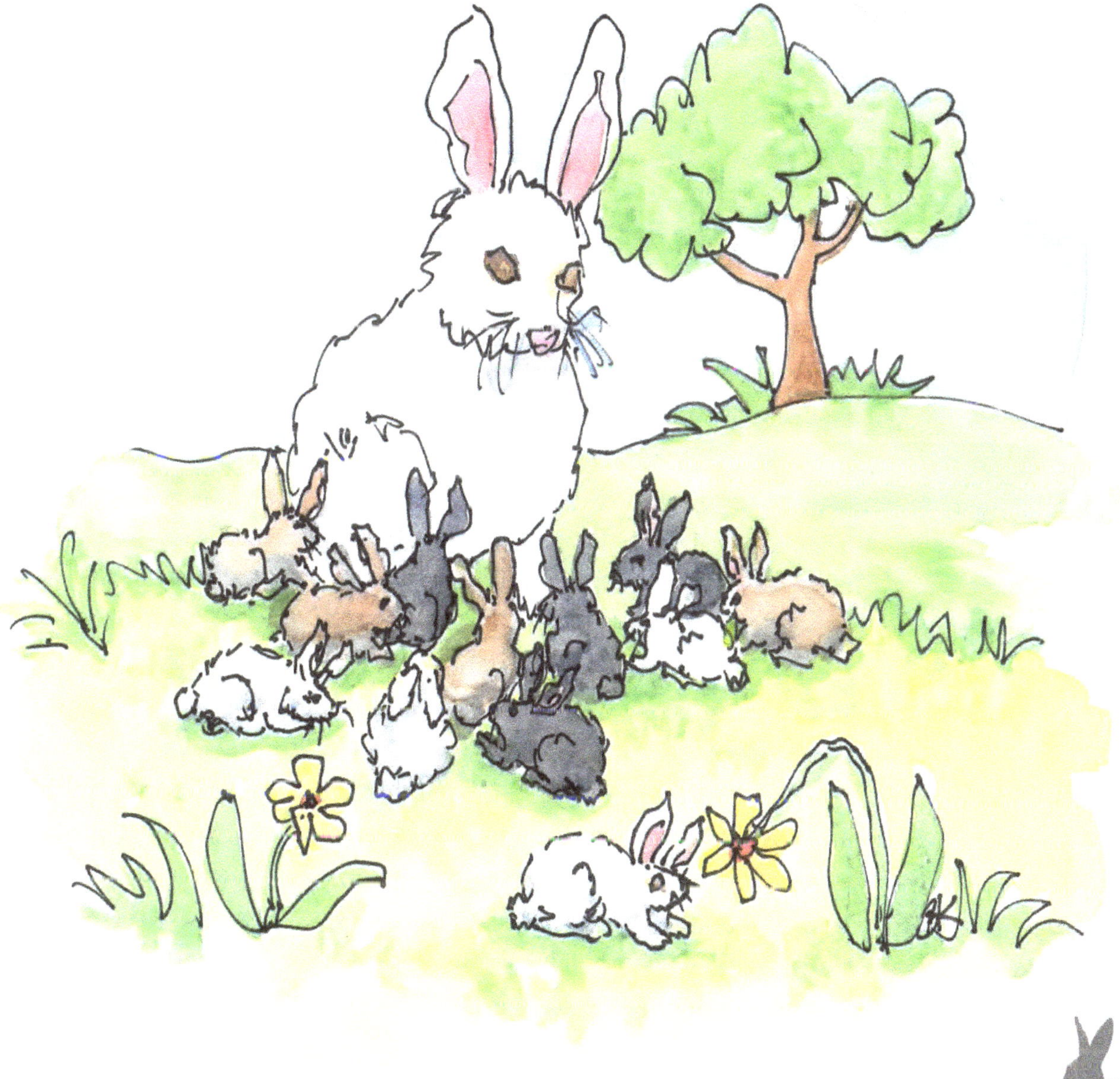

Rabbits are the same as bunnies and are cute and fun,

They look like great big balls of fluff and take a lot of care;

And if you wonder why they twist and twirl as they spin,

They do it cuz they're happy, it's a 'binky' in the air.

The End

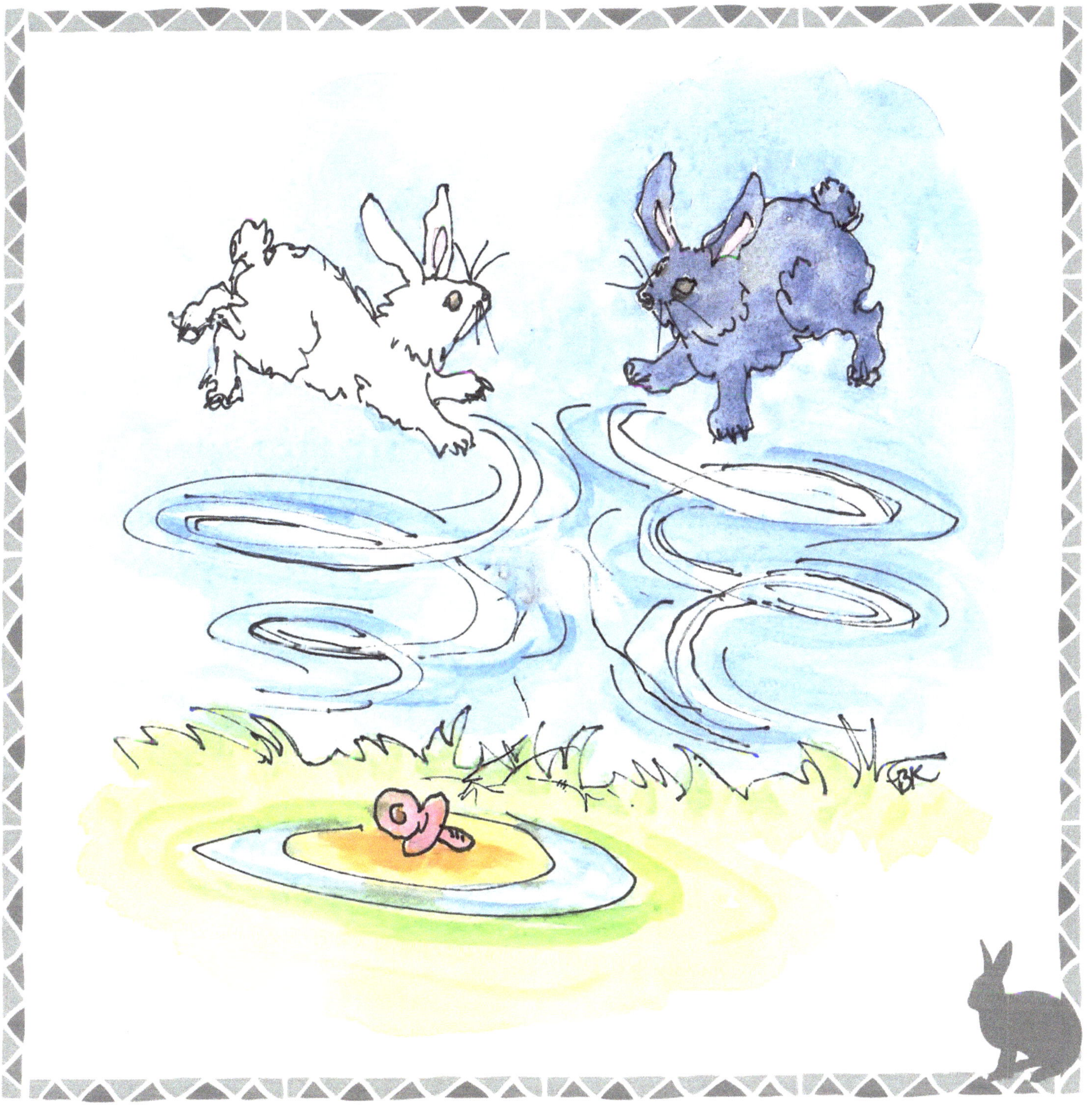

"Icky," said her mommy as she
came into the house,

Crawling on her arm was her
new friend that she had found;

The little snail poked his head
from way inside his shell,

And in the garden more were there
just crawling on the ground.

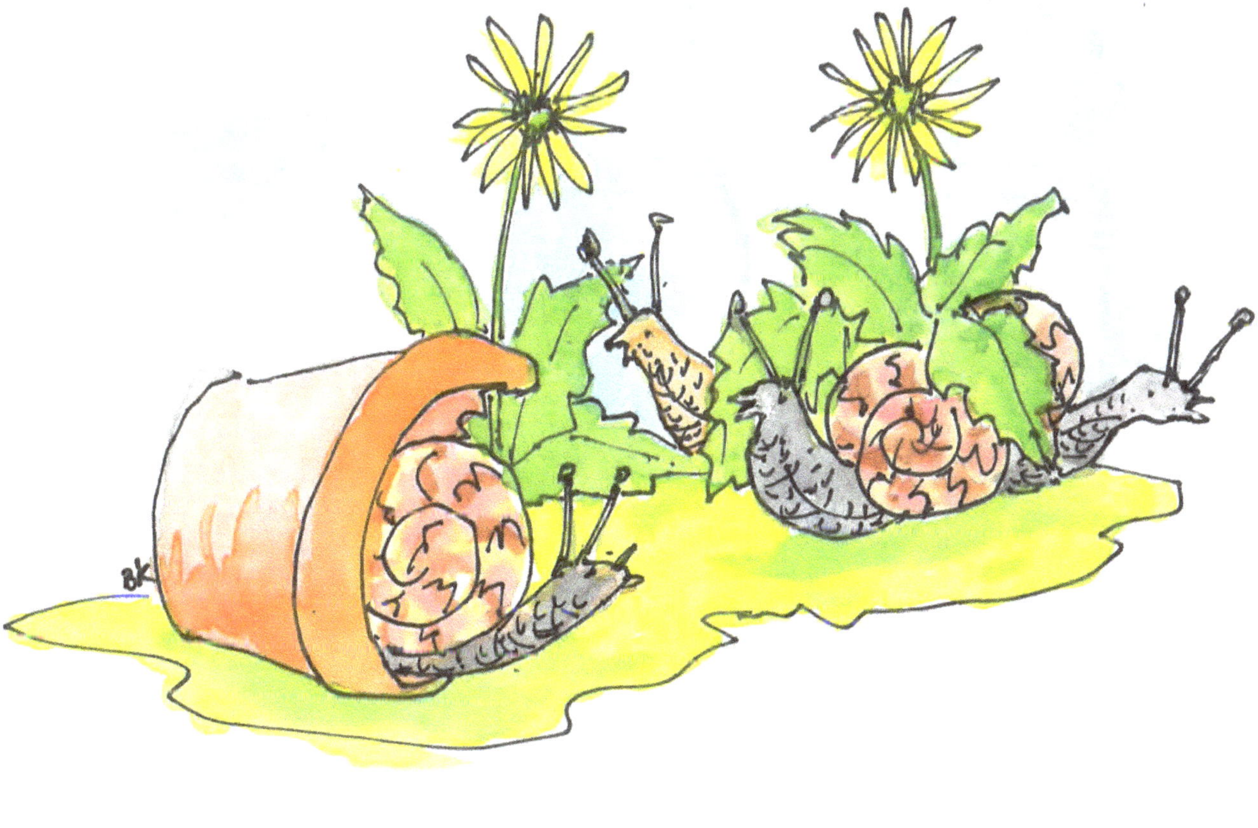
BK

Snails are so beautiful with shells they call their home,

And even on their back you'll see their babies if you're lucky;

Snails are so friendly and they never bite or scratch,

And eat the dead leaves and the weeds and anything that's yucky.

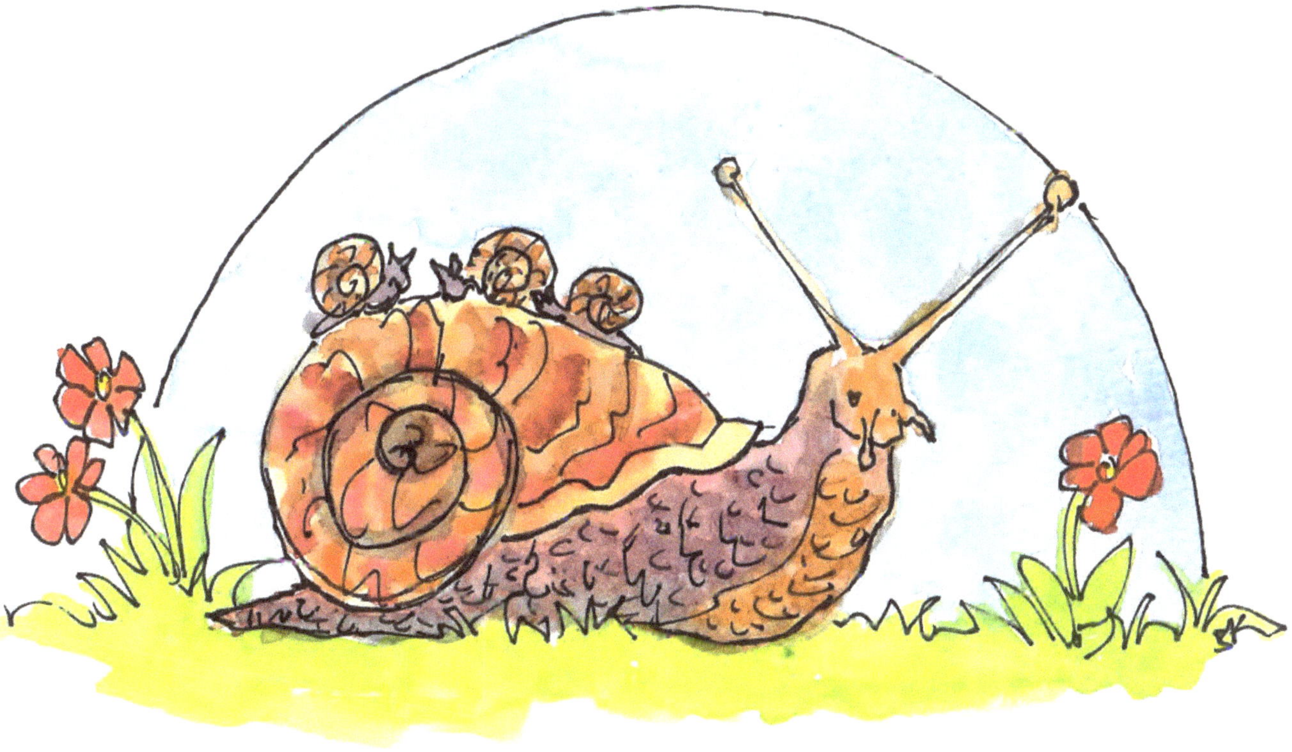

Snails are like ocean clams for
they are mollusks too,

But in your yard they like to hide
and also like to climb;

Cucumbers and apples are some things
they like to eat,

And inside of a chicken shell they'll
find and eat the lime.

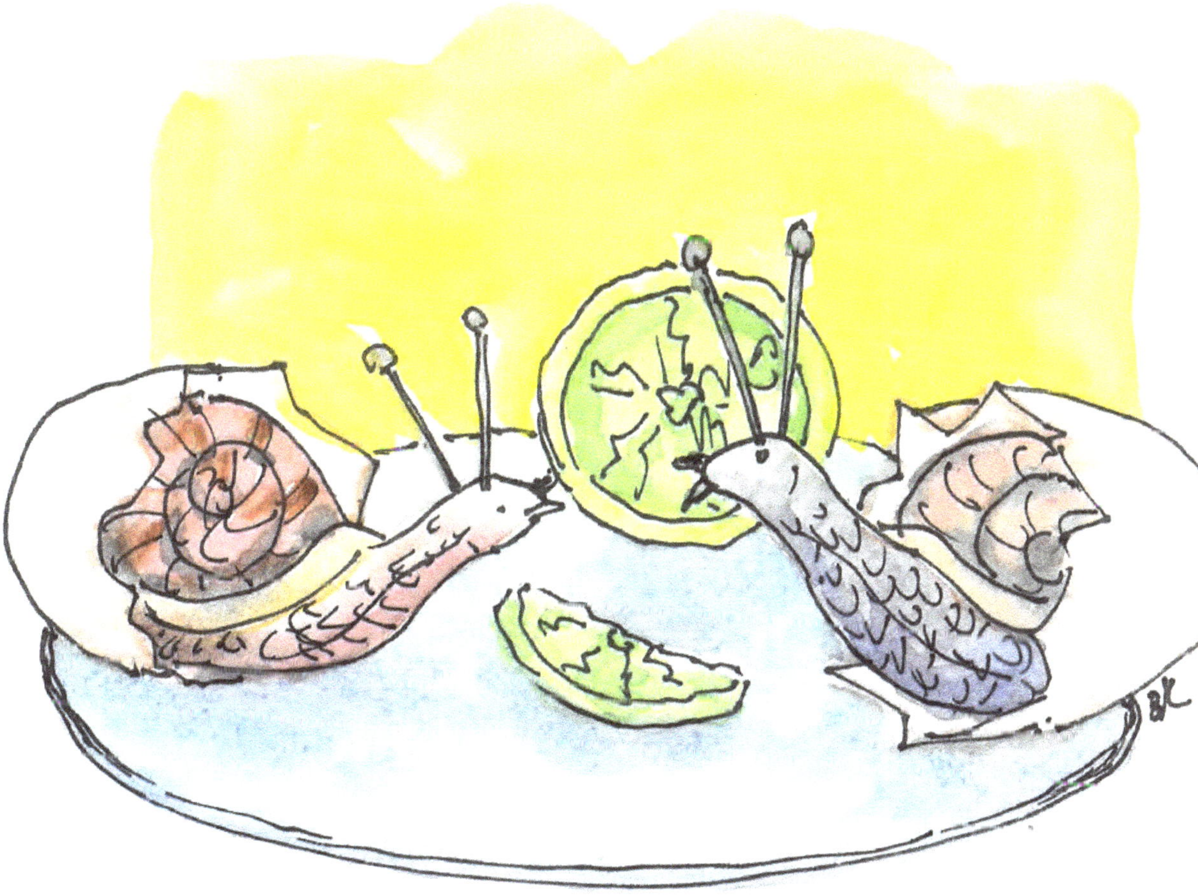

Snails can be very large or tiny
as a pinhead,

Garden snails have smooth, smooth
shells, but some are even hairy;

And slimy slugs look just like snails but
they don't have a shell,

And I suppose a giant snail
might look a little scary.

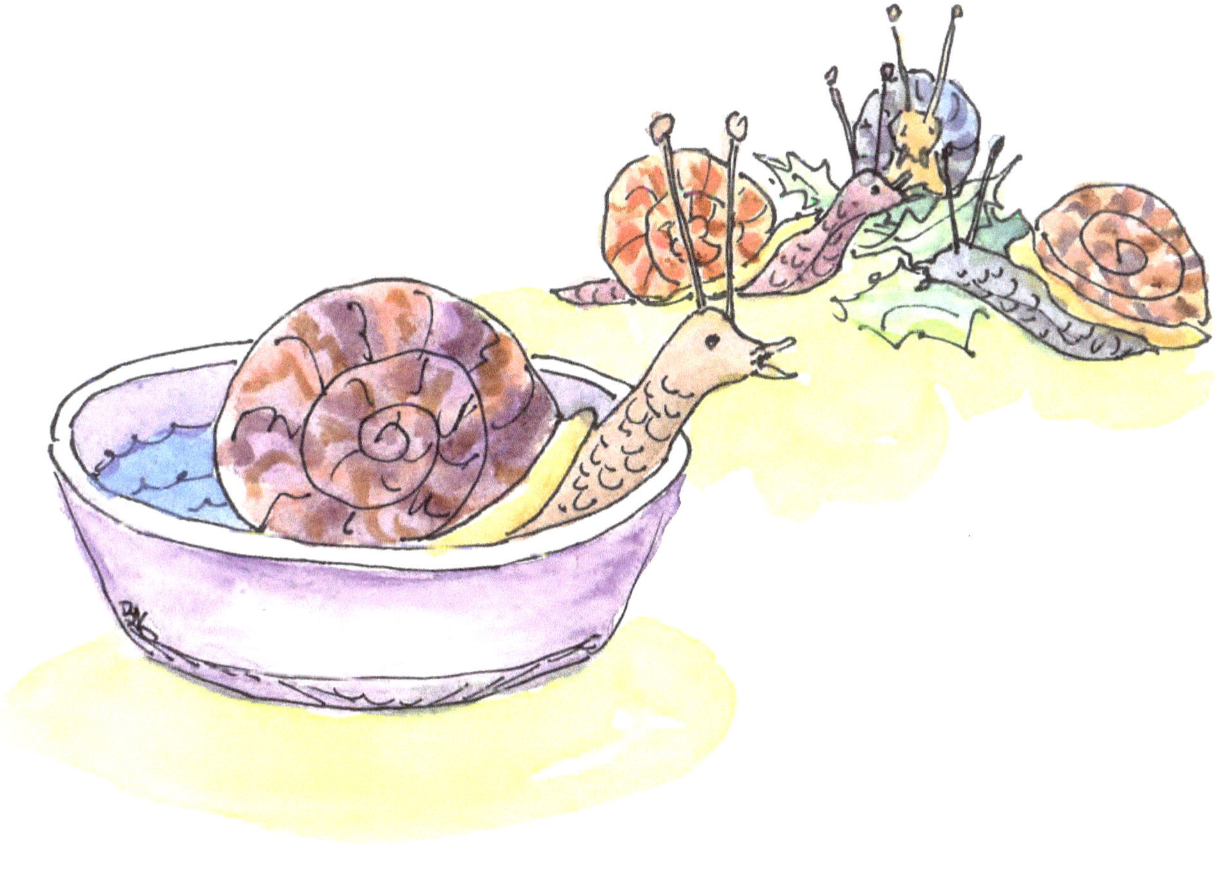

Snails are such gentle things
and even help to heal,

Their slime can help to mend a
cut by scissors or a knife;

Garden snails are so cute
and their antennae too,

And their shells might just symbolize
the circle of all life.

The End

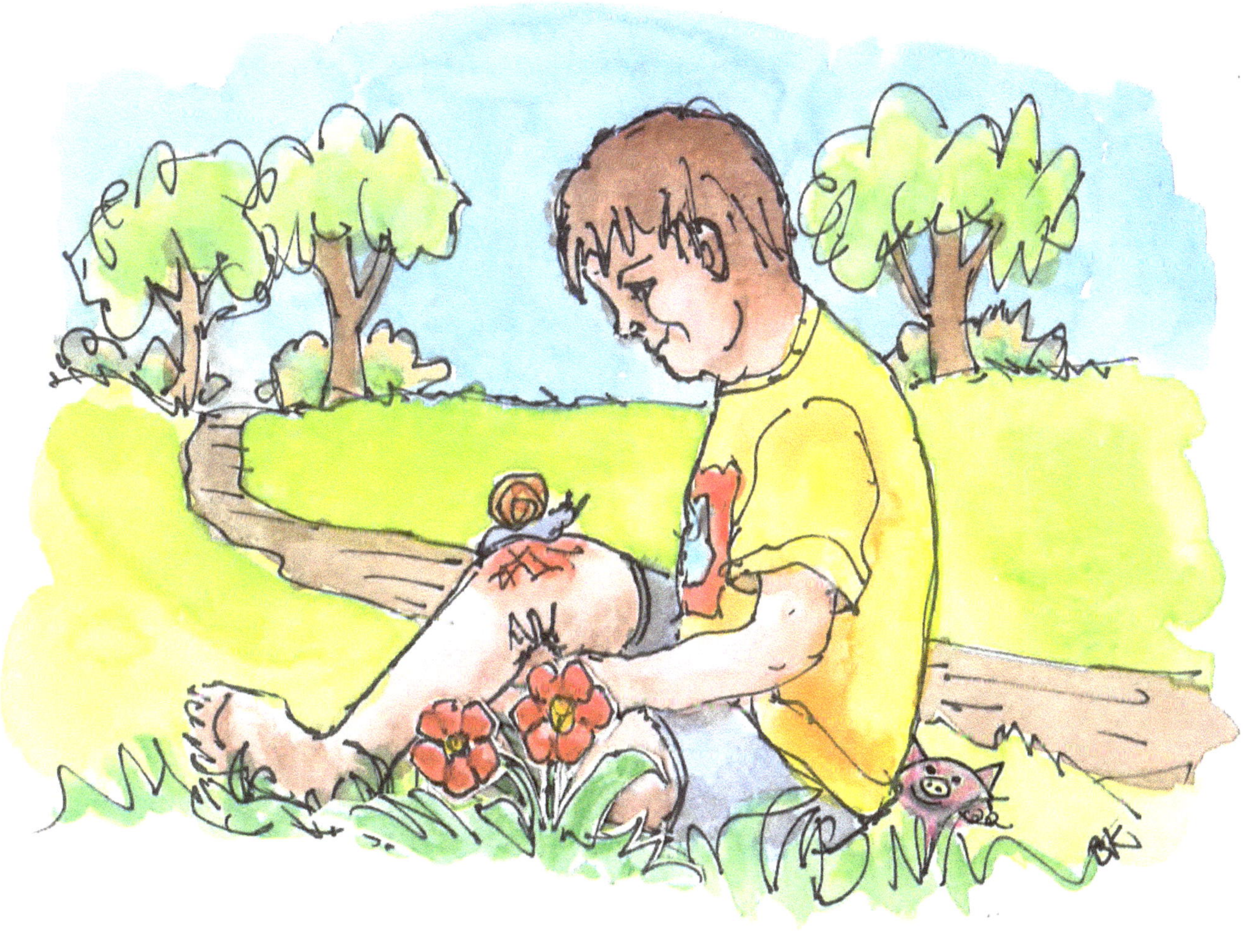

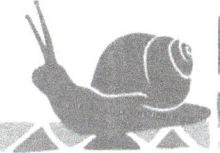

Pet Parakeet Facts:

1. Pet Parakeets live approximately 7 to 15 years.

2. Pet Parakeets have very loving and friendly personalities, which makes them a popular bird to have.

3. Pet Parakeets are smart and very easy to train. They can be taught very basic commands.

4. Pet Parakeets can learn to speak. Simple words like kiss or cutie are easier to learn than long phrases. Repeating a word over and over will help. It may take several months for a parakeet to be able to 'talk'. Parakeets have been known to speak 1000 words.

5. Pet Parakeets learn to be handled and actually like it. At least a half hour a day is good and allows your bird to get used to the idea.

6. Pet Parakeets like a big cage. Creating as natural an environment as possible is best. Placing a hut at the top of the cage with a soft

interior for sleeping is something it may like. There are a variety of materials that can be put on the bottom of the cage, including recycled paper.

7. Pet Parakeets should have their cage cleaned weekly.

8. Pet Parakeets need to have their cage placed away from drafty areas. Placing a cage at or below eye level is great, unless other pets (cats/dogs) can reach it.

9. Pet Parakeets can be sensitive to odors, so a kitchen is probably not a great place to hang a cage.

10. Pet Parakeets originally came from the Australian outback, which is a mixture of desert, grasslands, woodlands, and open scrub areas.

11. Pet Parakeets eat a variety of foods in the wild. Pet stores carry seed and pellets for them. They also like a little fruit (apples, bananas, melons), vegetables, sprouted seeds, plus millet sprays and honey sticks. Clean water is a must and should be

changed daily.

12. Pet Parakeets nest in hollow cavities of trees (like the eucalyptus). They do not build nests.

13. Pet Parakeets love interacting with their owners, and also love toys in their cage.

14. Pet Parakeets love to groom themselves, and might even like a mist of water from a spray bottle every now and then.

15. Pet Parakeets may need veterinarian care if they become lethargic, stop eating, groom less often, sneeze, have any discharge or indication of mites (especially on the face), sit on the bottom of the cage for long periods of time, or have feathers that stay fluffed.

16. Pet Parakeets have two toes facing forward and two facing back.

*Parakeets are also called Budgie birds.

*Parakeets, like other animals, can carry diseases that may be contagious to humans. Washing hands after contact is recommended.

*Parakeet means "long tail".

*Parakeet plumage is naturally green and yellow. However, captive breeding has created a variety of colors.

*A parakeet's beak grows about 3" a year. Above their beak is a colored area called a "cere". In general the male has a blue or lavender one and a female has a brown or white "cere".

*Funny that if a parakeet regurgitates for you, it might be that they look at you like family, actually trying to feed you like they feed their young.

*The Guinness World Records for "the most talking bird" has a Budgerigar named Puck having a vocabulary of over 1700 words.

Pet Rabbit Facts:

1. Pet Rabbits are very unique and have specific needs in order to live long and healthy lives. They require toys and companionship to be happy.

2. Pet Rabbits like to live in groups, or at least pairs, because they are very sociable. They do not make good pets for people who have never had pets.

3. Pet Rabbits come in a variety of sizes, colors, and personalities. They can have ears as long as four inches, and can grow to four feet. They are born with their eyes closed and no fur.

4. Pet Rabbits can live 8 to 12 years depending upon the breed. Miniature or dwarf breeds usually live longer than larger breeds.

5. Pet Rabbits are herbivores and mostly like plants. Rabbit food can be purchased from a pet shop.

6. Pet Rabbits that live inside the house ('house

rabbits') can live free in rooms that have been rabbit proofed, or they can have a safe space like a cage or pen. If they live in a pen, their space should be large enough for them to hop around in, or they should be let out daily to get exercise. When rabbit proofing, care should be taken to cover wires and baseboards, and block anything they might chew (under beds, houseplants, etc.)

7. Pet Rabbits are very sociable, so don't isolate them.

8. Pet Rabbits should have access to fresh hay all the time. Baby rabbits like alfalfa and adults eat timothy, grass, or oat hay.

9. Pet Rabbits like fresh vegetables, rabbit pellets, and fresh water. Ceramic water bowls work well as rabbits won't tip them when drinking.

10. Pet Rabbits are inclined to potty in the same area. Set cat litter near to where their food and water bowls are used. Recycled newspaper pellet litter is good (regular cat litter and wood shavings are

not healthy choices), and hay can go on top of that. Funny that rabbits like to eat and poop at the same time.

11. Pet Rabbits need to be stimulated as they can get bored easily. Cardboard rabbit houses are great as they can gnaw and chew windows and doors, while seeking refuge when needed. Adding a few toys will stimulate interest and natural chew toys are a good distraction to chewing on things they shouldn't.

12. Pet Rabbits are very clean and like to groom themselves a lot. As rabbits shed a couple of times a year, they need to be brushed. Clipping their nails is important too. Their teeth and nails never stop growing.

13. Pet Rabbits should have health checkups too, just like any other pet. Spaying/neutering can be good for overall health, reduce aggressive behavior, and it is no secret they can reproduce a lot.

14. Pet Rabbits have some very quirky

behaviors. It is a good idea to understand them so you have a happy life together. They 'binky' when they are expressing total joy by jumping and twisting in the air, or running while doing it. They can also 'purr'. They flop and do 'nose bonks'.

15. Pet Rabbits are pretty clean animals and don't like baths, because they hate water.

*Rabbits and bunnies are the same.

*Baby rabbits are called 'kittens' or 'kits'. Females are called 'does' and males are called 'bucks'.

*Rabbits may eat their own poop, called 'cecotropes', which contain nutrients that are good for them.

* Rabbits are natural prey animals. They never will try not to act like they are hurt, even if they are.

* Rabbits are 'crepuscular', which means they are most active at dawn and dusk. In the wild they live in a burrow, or a group of burrows called a

warren.

* Rabbits, sad but true, are the next most common pet at animal shelters behind dogs and cats.

Snail Facts:

1. Snails make great pets.

2. Snails can be kept in glass aquariums for safety and easy viewing.

3. Snails should have a substrate of safe dirt and be free of chemicals. Terrarium earth from a pet store is best, covered with a variety of moist leaves and dandelions they love to eat. It should be thick enough to lay their eggs and to hide in.

4. Snails eat cucumbers, carrots, and apples, along with leaves and dandelions.

5. Snails will love a piece of pottery or bark to hide in.

6. Snails should have a lime source (egg shells), which seems to help them mate and lay eggs.

7. Snails should have their aquariums cleaned every few days of feces, mucous, and any dead leaves, dandelions, or other food materials.

8. Snails can appear sleepy if they are not getting enough oxygen. A screened lid on the aquarium should work well, but care has to be taken that tiny newborns don't escape through the cracks. Snails, like us, exhale carbon dioxide which puts them to sleep. The screened lid should allow the carbon dioxide to escape. A separate 'baby unit' should be made to house the babies.

*There is a species of snail that can grow to one and a half feet, while the smallest land snail has a shell .03 inches tall.

*The only big difference between a snail and slug is the shell. Actually, some slug families have internal shell plates.

*Snails and slugs are called Gastropods, and are actually mollusks (same as clams, mussels, and oysters).

*Snails are hermaphrodites, which means that both snails receive sperm during the mating process.

*Snails live in nearly all habitats on earth, from the deepest ocean to the highest deserts.

*Snail mucus may help in the healing of wounds due to its triggering of an immune response that helps the regeneration of skin cells.

*Snails that cling to rocks in the ocean surf have the same gel that has been studied in slug slime, and has been used as an adhesive for helping to repair heart defects where sutures are not completely reliable (only tested on pig's hearts).

*Sea snails were a symbol of rebirth and joy for Mesoamericans. They thought of the shape of the shell as a representation of the circle of life.

*Snails were pets for the novelist Patricia Highsmith who kept about 300 of them.

*Sea snails that are very large are called Conches and have been used as musical instruments.

*Some terrestrial snails have shells that are hairy.

*And, we won't even mention Escargot!

The Williams Family Nurtures Squirrels

Teaching us how to discover the forests in our lives

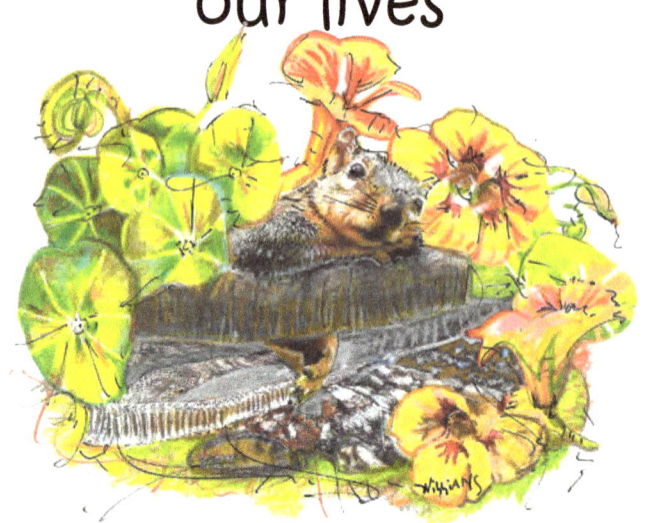

Story and Artwork by
Jennifer Foreman de Grassi Williams

May we always be nuts and pranksters~
Love, Wa

Story number 6 is my attempt to communicate a more intimate picture of squirrels that share their backyards and forests with us. So not everyone likes squirrels, but hard to find anyone who doesn't think they aren't fun to watch as they play, aren't amazed at how quick and adept they are, and can't at least admit that they are pretty darn cute! We've coexisted and nurtured generations of them living in our yard, and I am certain they have taught their babies that we are safe, and a very reliable food source. If you think that friendships can be forged with these little tricksters, I am here to say yes you can. We've had dozens of squirrels in the past thirty years who have really captured our hearts. They come to the window and look in like a young child waiting for mom to open the door, and guilt you into getting off of the couch to handfeed a walnut that you've already shelled and had waiting. The females are particularly friendly as they stand on two back legs begging, showing off their pregnant bellies and squirrel nipples...yep...can't resist a nursing mama. One of my very favorite mamas was Chippy. Chippy lived in our trees for years. I could stand in any part of my yard and call her name and here she'd come, crooked tail and all. One year I found a day old baby lying in my forest area. I knew that Chippy had a nest so called her name and down she came from a large pine tree. I held out the baby, hoping she'd accept it. Like a mother cat with her kittens she gently took the babe in her mouth, and up the tree she went. All you could see was a tiny tail wrapped around her neck with some exotic fur garment. I always check my yard after a big wind or storm, as there have been times when babies have blown out of their nests. As babes are totally helpless, blind and deaf at birth, there is no chance of survival without intervention. Some are taken to our local Animals in Distress organization where loving hands feed the young until they are strong enough to be returned to the wild. Many times I've raised them myself. Baby Stewy came to me as a newborn, and each day I would take him to my art classroom as he needed to be fed, around the clock, with a small eyedropper. What a great lesson for my students about compassion and respect for all creatures, and for many this was as close to anything wild that they would ever get. Countless kids wanted the opportunity to feed such a tiny and cute baby. Stewy was tame to a point. We'd let him out of his cage as he'd jump 6 feet from one person to another and entertained us with his antics. He also had an upstairs cage and one on the upper deck out of my bedroom door. One night I woke him as he needed to come inside to the warmth of his indoor cage. He turned into a hormonal teenage boy who had been woken too early in the morning. He lunged at me, his perceived mom, when I turned my back (twice), and I had scratches on my arms and a leg injury that needed stitches. It was 2 in the morning, so I left him outside to 'rethink' his temper. Long story short, I went to the doctor the next day for a tetanus shot and couldn't quite tell the doctor what happened so blamed it on a barbed wire fence. As I had tried to acclimate Stewy with the other squirrels in the yard, it just wasn't going to happen. Squirrels are very territorial and Stewy didn't stand a chance. A couple of times a pack of marauding squirrels came from another neighborhood to encroach on the territory of our yard, and it was like two rival gangs in a scene out of West Side Story. Stewy didn't fair very well, and I wondered if he could ever live among wild squirrels. In any event it was difficult, but the right thing to do, to find a safe place for Stewy along a river with water and a forest to be himself, and away from civilization. A wild animal is always a wild animal, and sometimes they revert to their animal 'red zone', their inherent primal place of territory and self-protection. These sentient animals should always be taken to experts if rescued. So yes, I am that lady that swerves for squirrels in the road ('I brake for squirrels'), and I am the one you see stopping to remove the ones that aren't lucky enough to win in the battle between squirrel and car! We've had squirrels manage to come down the chimney and run soot-covered through the house. Our yard has more peanut plants growing than a plantation, and a few of my flower heads have been chewed to their bases. Those are but small tradeoffs for the entertainment they continually provide. There are a plethora of squirrel stories that our cats could share. We've rescued many, perhaps more than any other animal we've had, and the stories are astonishing, but I have a mama at my door who demands a walnut and it isn't worth the guilt if I don't do it right now!

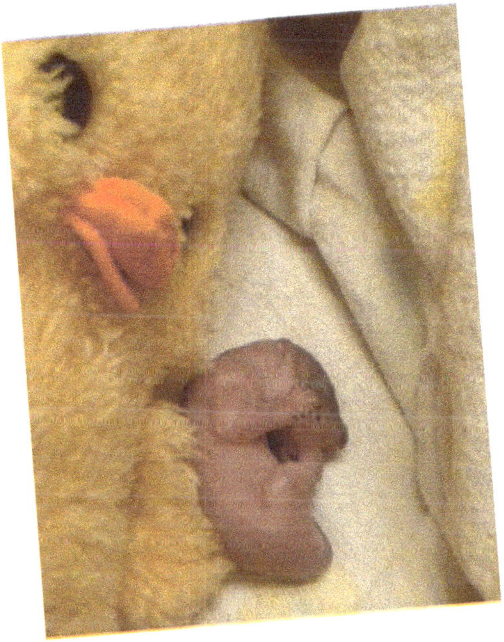

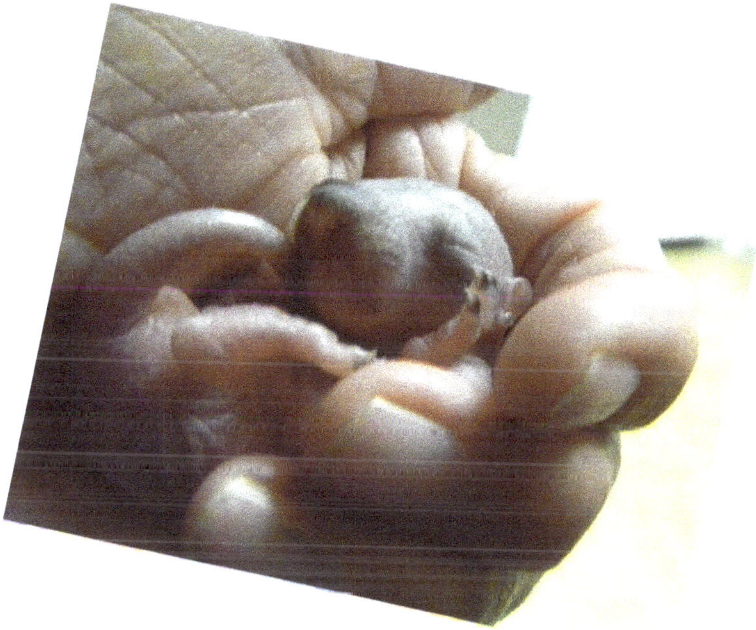

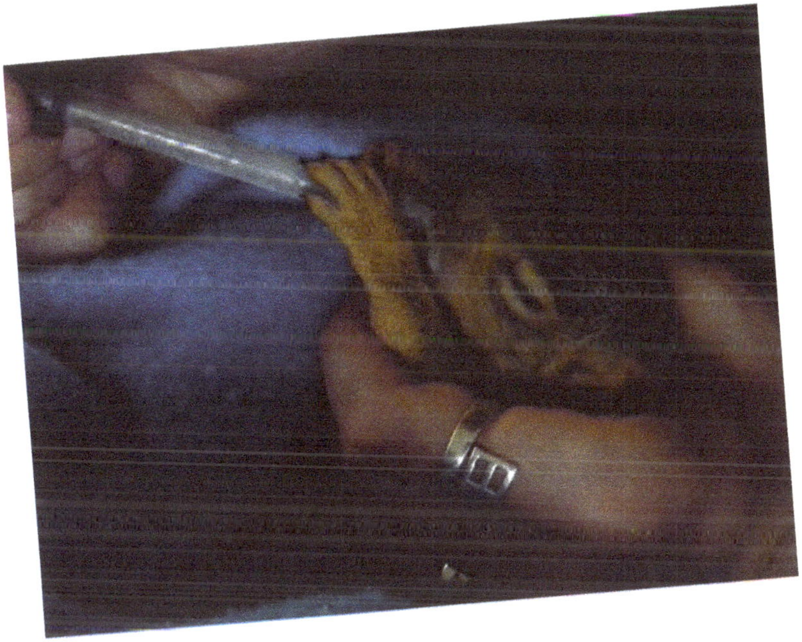

Goodness what a big surprise when
I felt something drop,

And then I saw a fur ball and
some tiny little eyes;

I felt a wiggle and a tail, and
heard a little squeak,

From his nest a squirrel fell and
I was so surprised!

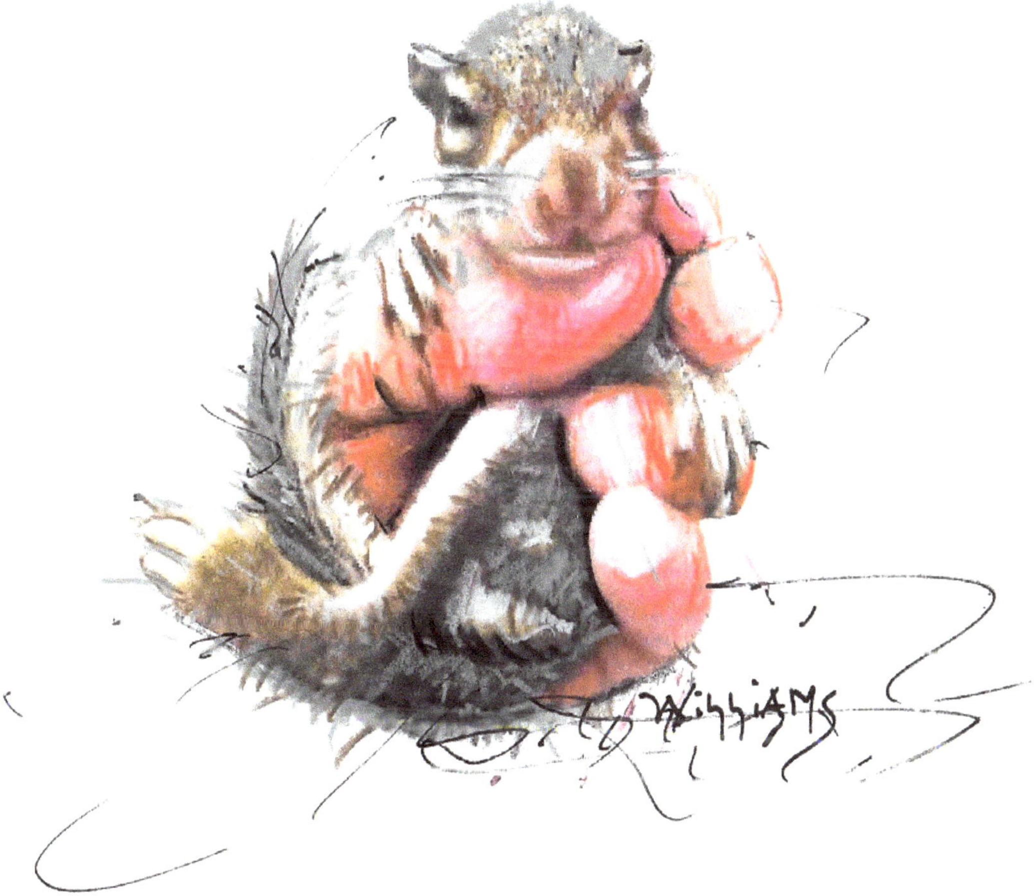
Williams

I looked up in the tree to try and find his mommy there,

And all the while sweet baby cuddled in my hand to hide;

I put him in a blanket on a heating pad to sleep,

And promised him some baby milk when we were safe inside.

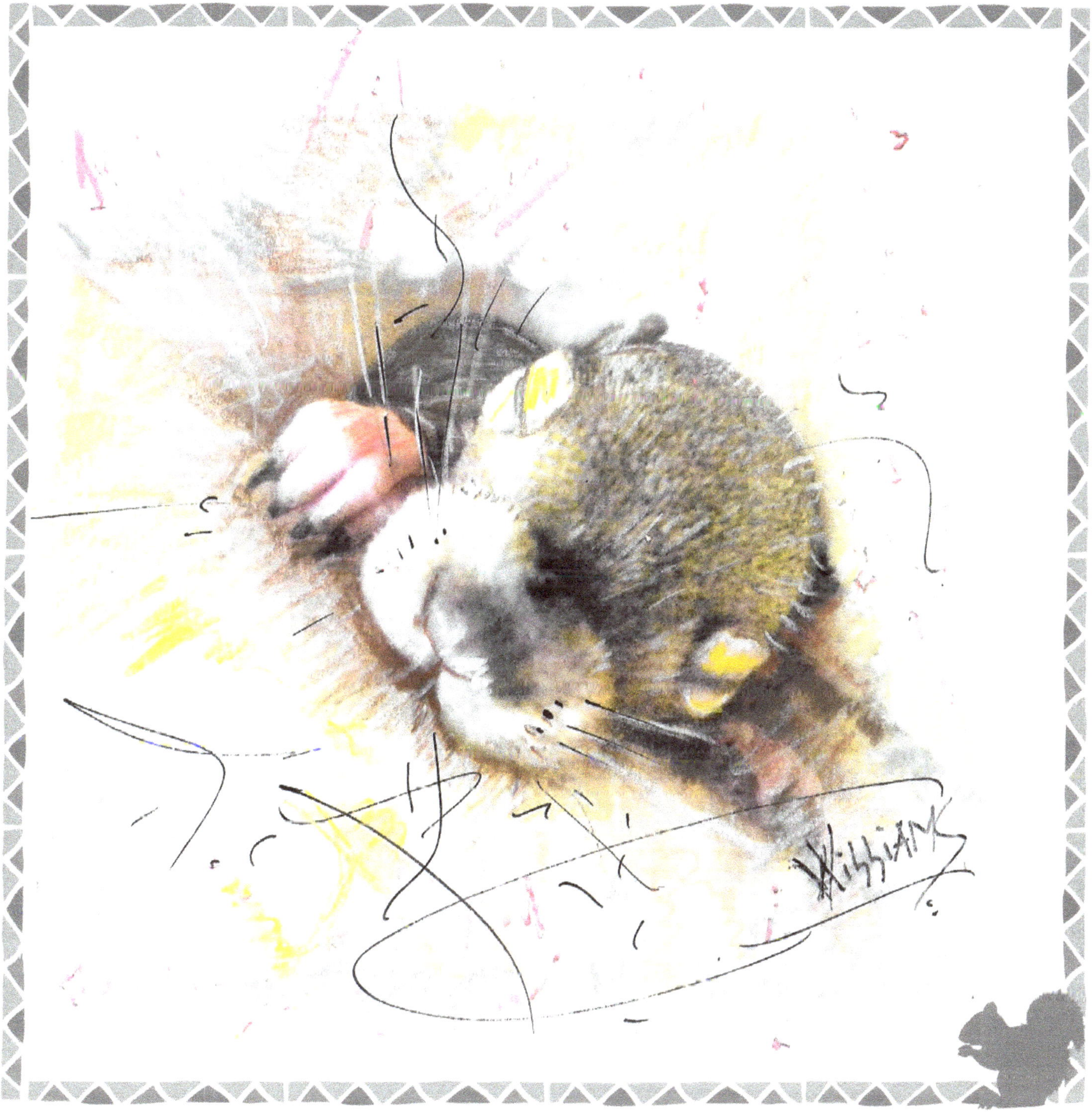

Because the night before was very windy in the yard,

On the ground were squirrel babes not knowing what to do;

The trees shook many pinecones down and glad that I came by,

I rescued one already and now another two.

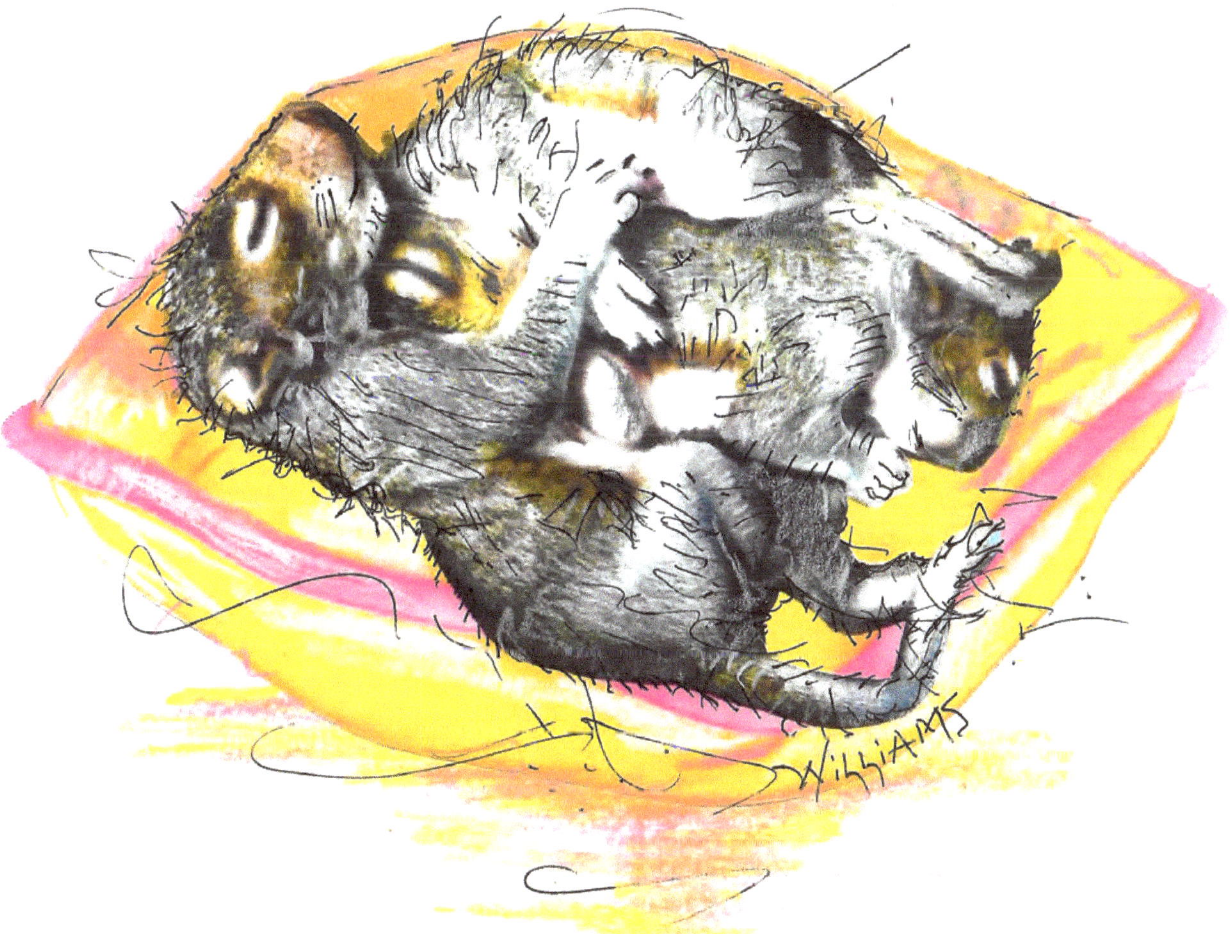
WILLIAMS

On their paws and tiny feet were nails sharp and pokey,

Oh how cute the little tails and their whiskers too;

Mama squirrel never came so help they really needed,

They drank from tiny baby bottles just like humans do.

Williams

How quickly did these little ones grow up and want to play,

And in the yard where flowers grow they'd climb the highest trees;

And butterflies would land on them and tickle their cute noses,

But soon they got so big and fast they could outrun the bees.

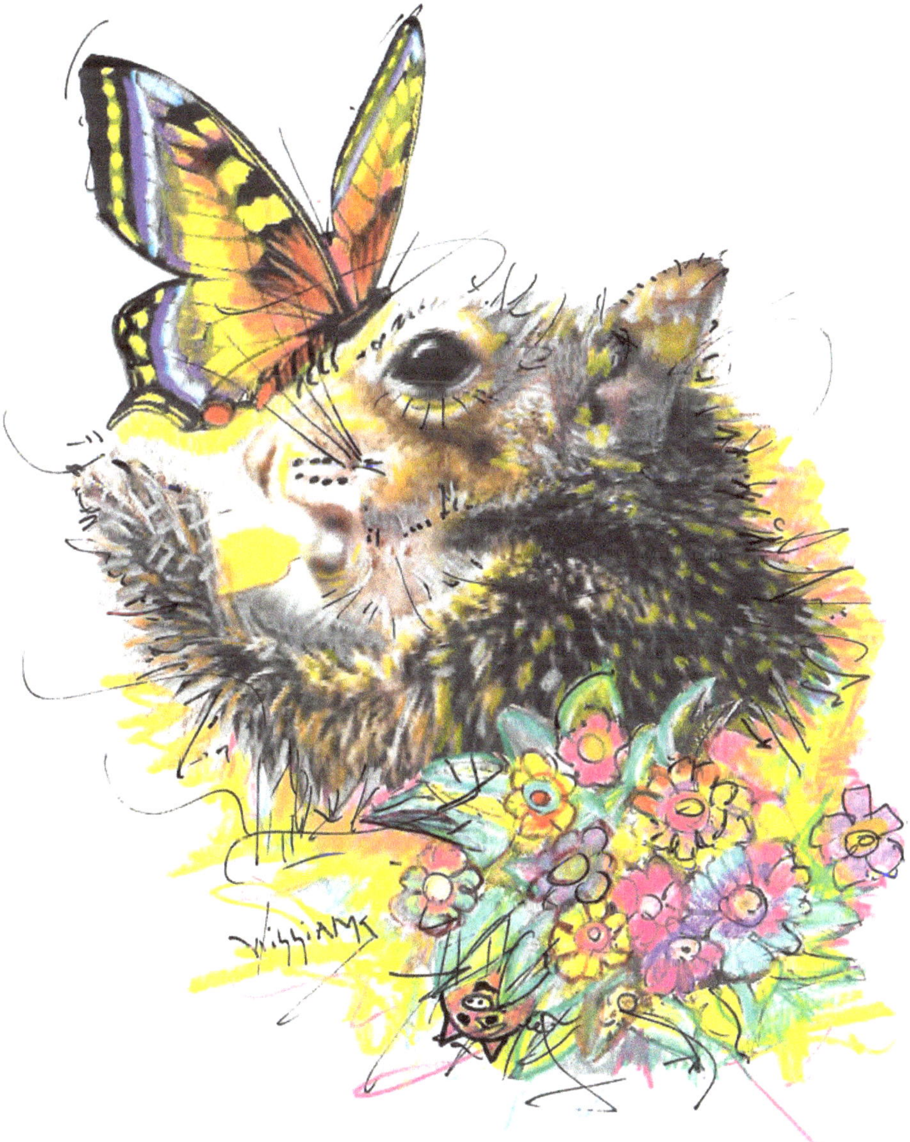
WILLIAMS

Stewy, Angel, Bee Bee Boo, and
Lucas with dear Peanut,

Watched as Chippy held her baby
like a cat would do;

And up the big old tree that was a home
to other critters,

Past a big raccoon that lived
inside of their tree too.

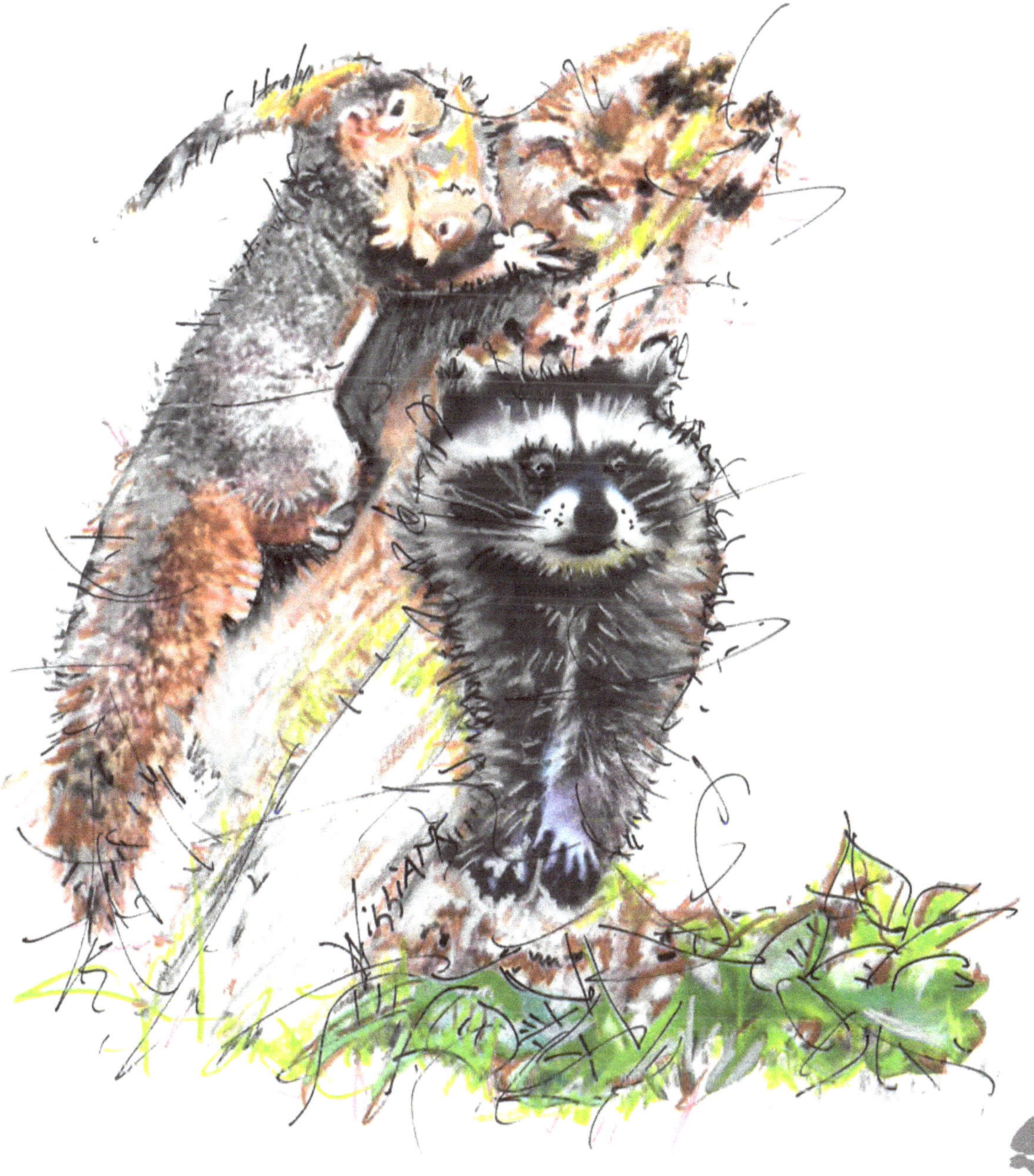

The tree was such a fun place with a "Catface" hole inside,

And from it hung a bucket with a monkey toy tied on;

Stewy and his friends would swing on monkey like a rope,

Spilling peanuts from the bucket to the bright green lawn.

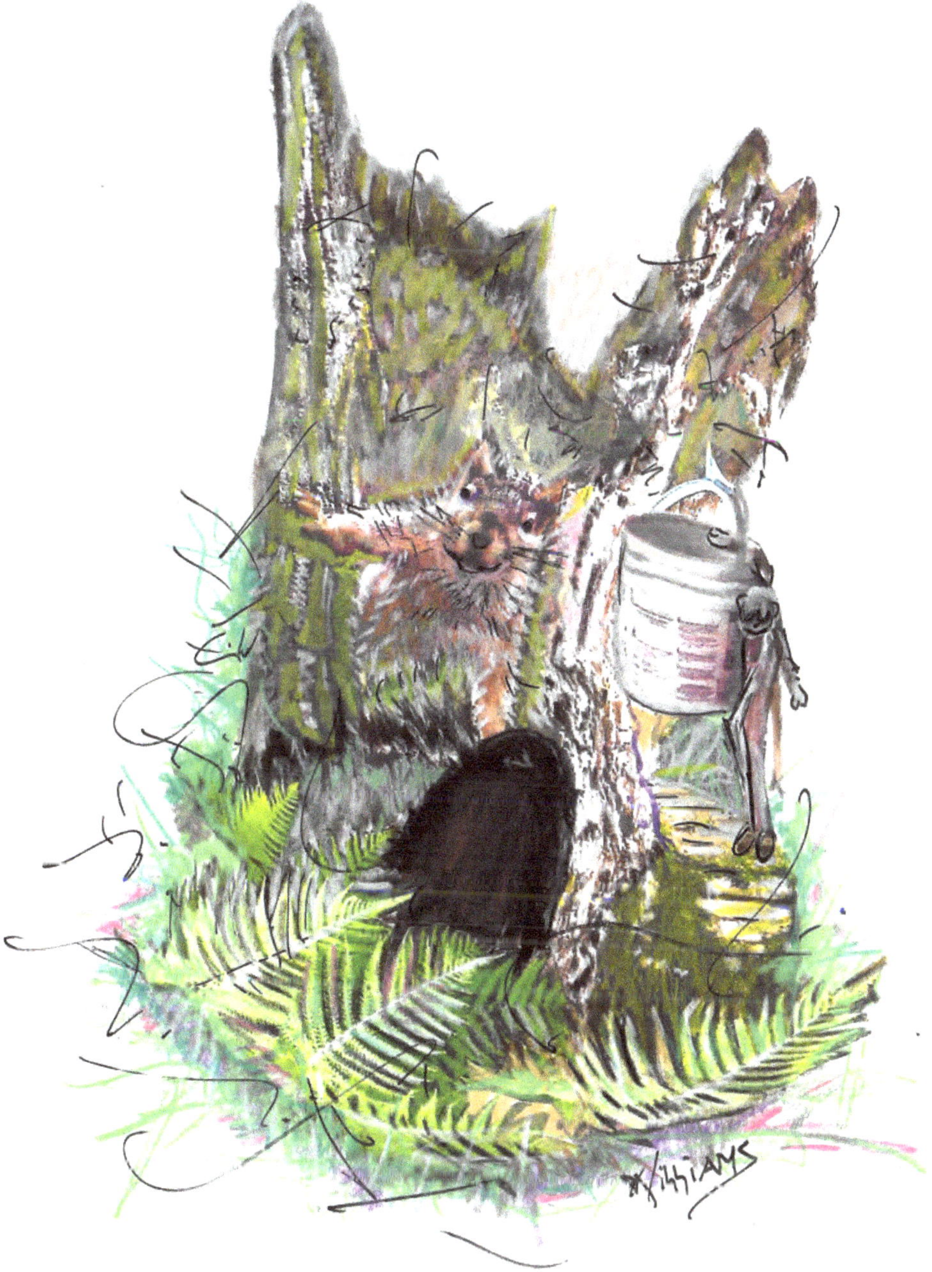
Williams

All the squirrels in the yard were
fast as fast could be,

They had to watch when crossing streets
and look for flying hawks;

Unlike their friend wise tortoise
who was really way too slow,

Up the trees they'd scamper quick to run
away from fox.

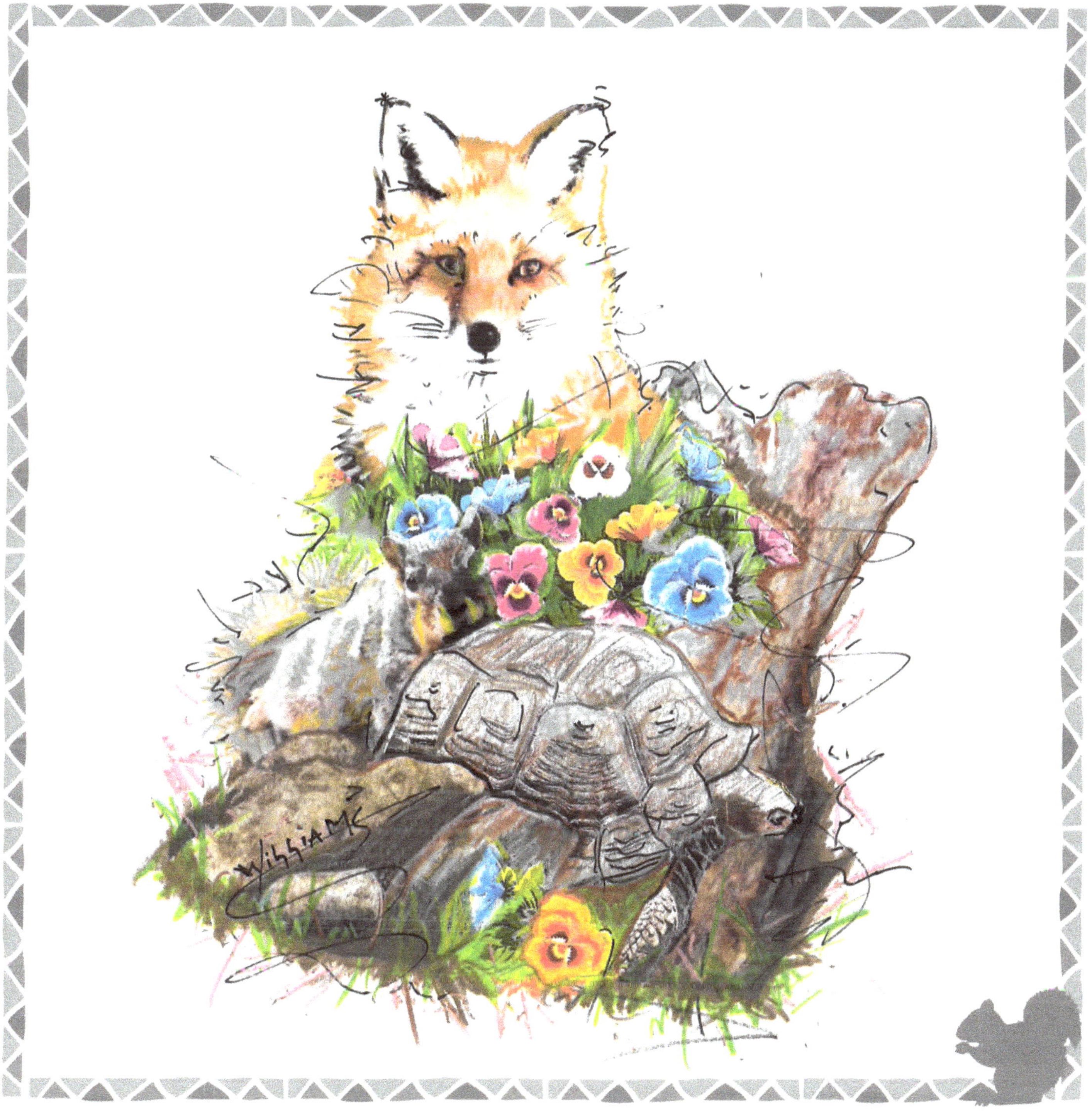

They loved to take a midday nap
inside their squirrel tree,

And just to keep them very safe
from hawks and foxes too~

Crafty, playful squirrels faked
that they were rattlesnakes,

By taking skin from one they found and
on it they would chew.

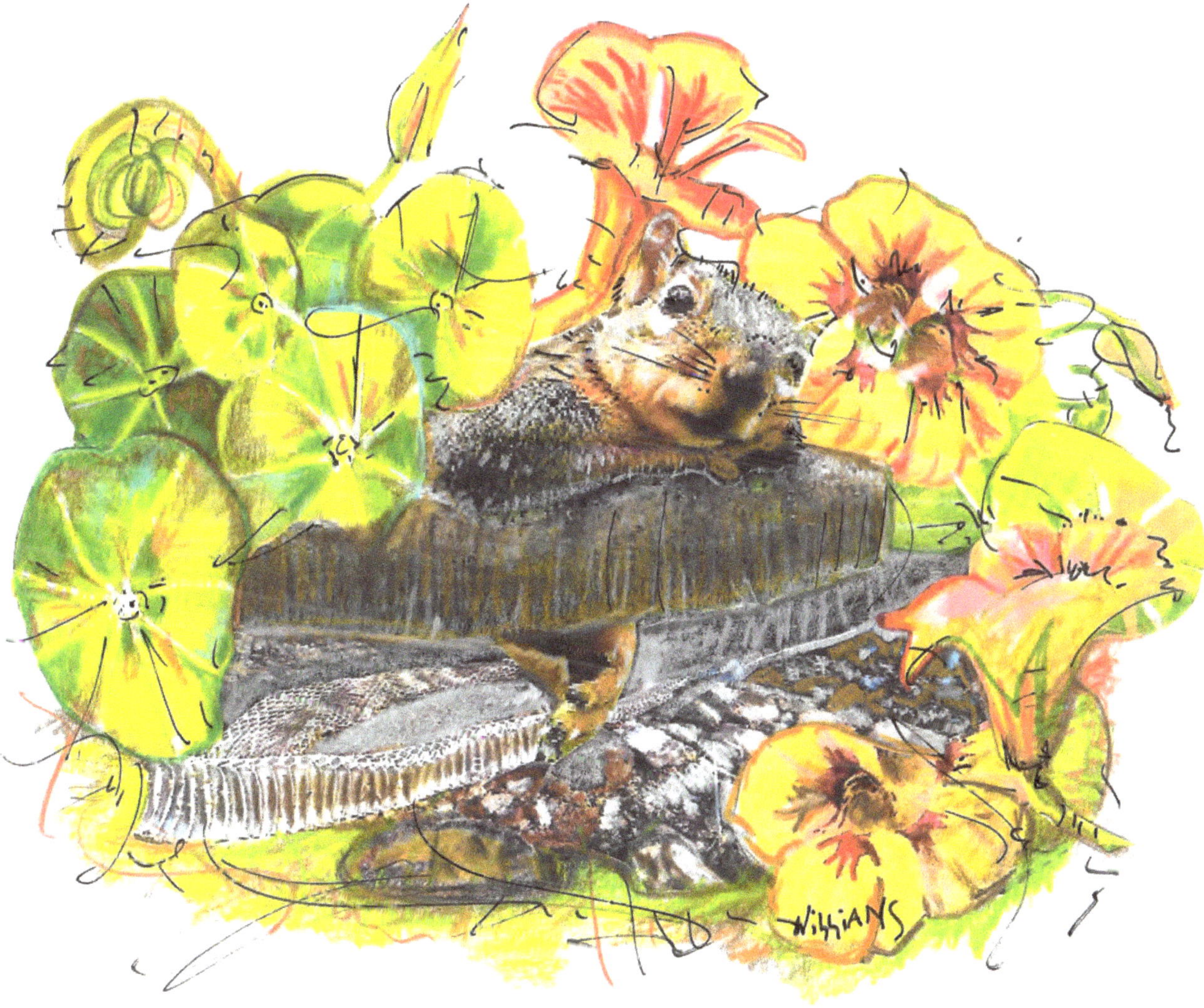
WILLIAMS

Lucky are the very few who
take the time to care,

Because their little squirrel friends will
love you even more;

The peanuts and the walnuts that you
share with them each day,

They steal from the birds that
wait outside the sliding door.

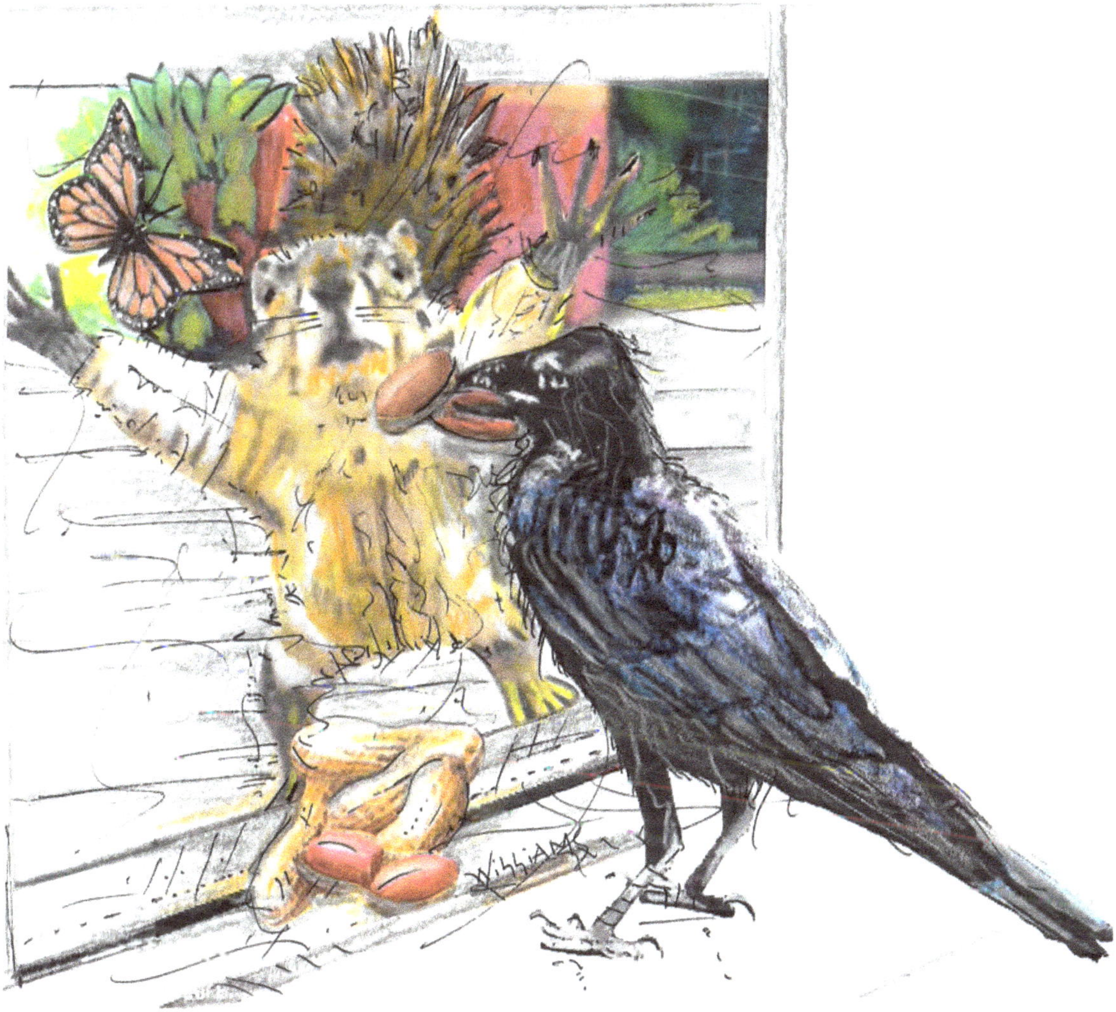
WilliAMS

Squirrels and their chipmunk cousins can have bushy tails,

And sometimes can be almost white which is a sight to see;

And while they are so very cute and take food from your hand~

Remember they are happiest when wild and born free.

The End

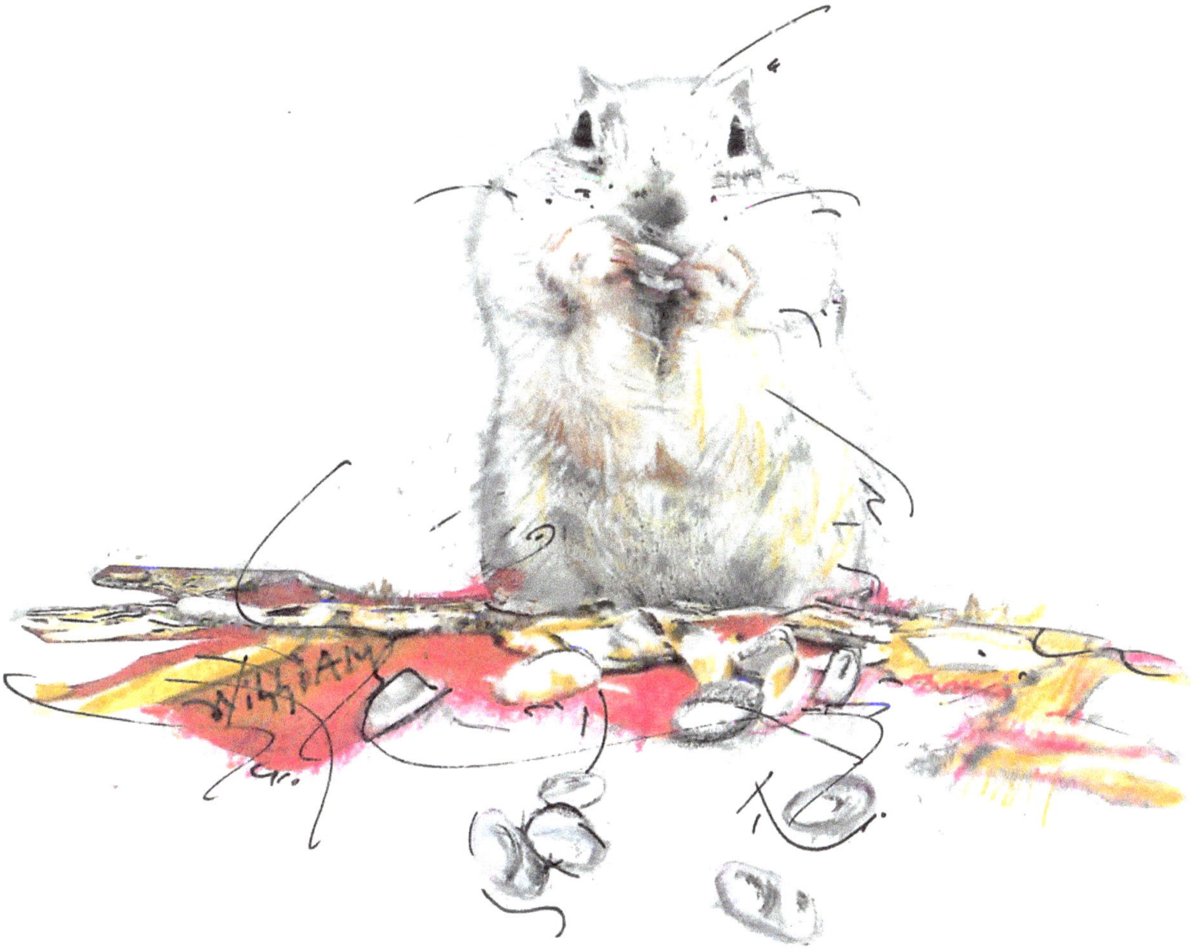

A "Catface" is a term used to describe an old wound on a tree trunk that can close over as it heals. There is a "Catface" sculpture by Reham Arti in Boise.

'Pooh' tree with Catface that houses squirrels, raccoons, wood ducks, birds, insects, and bees.

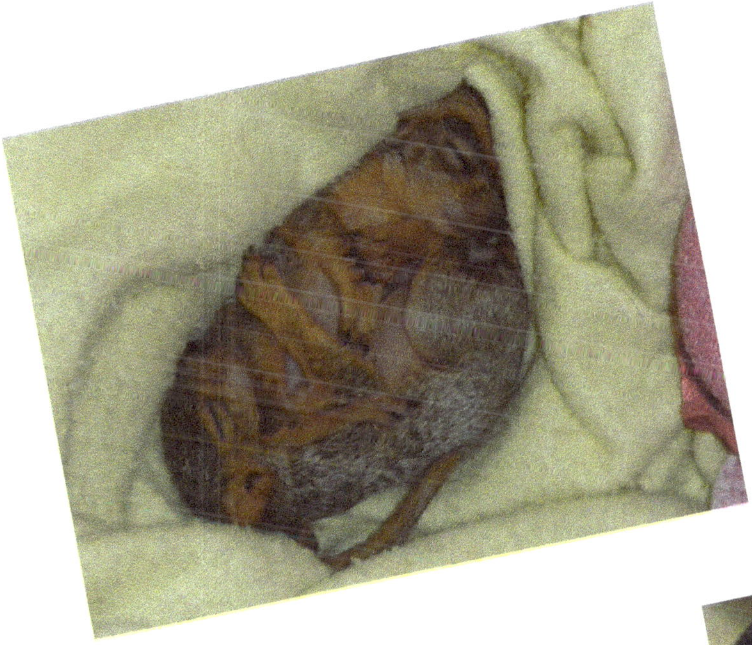

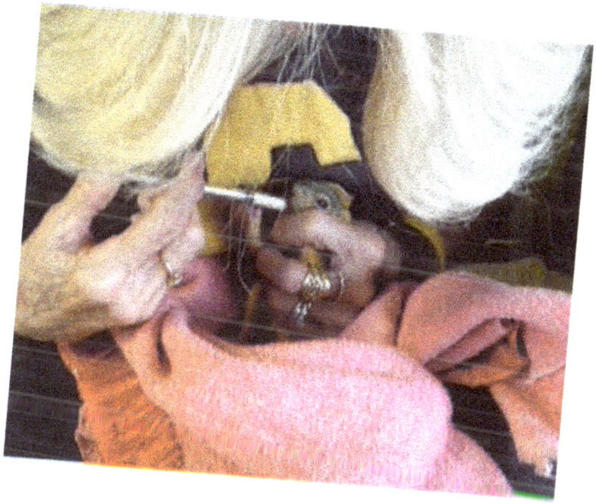

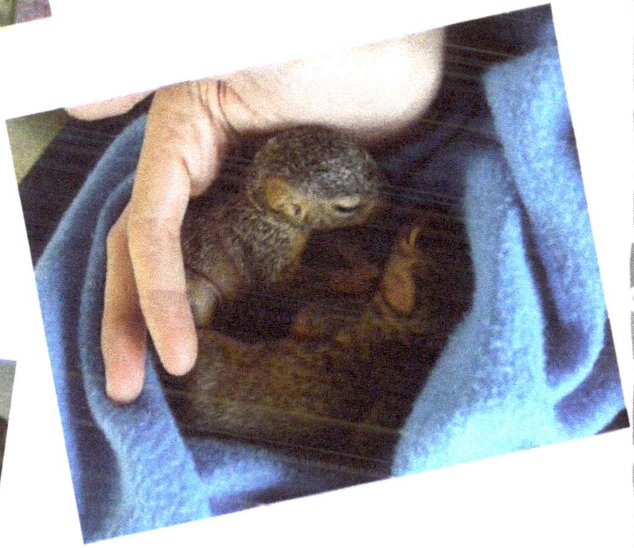

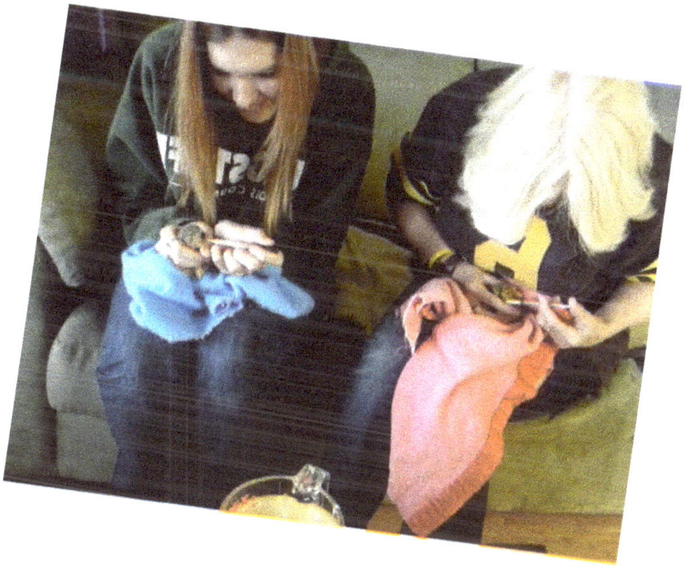

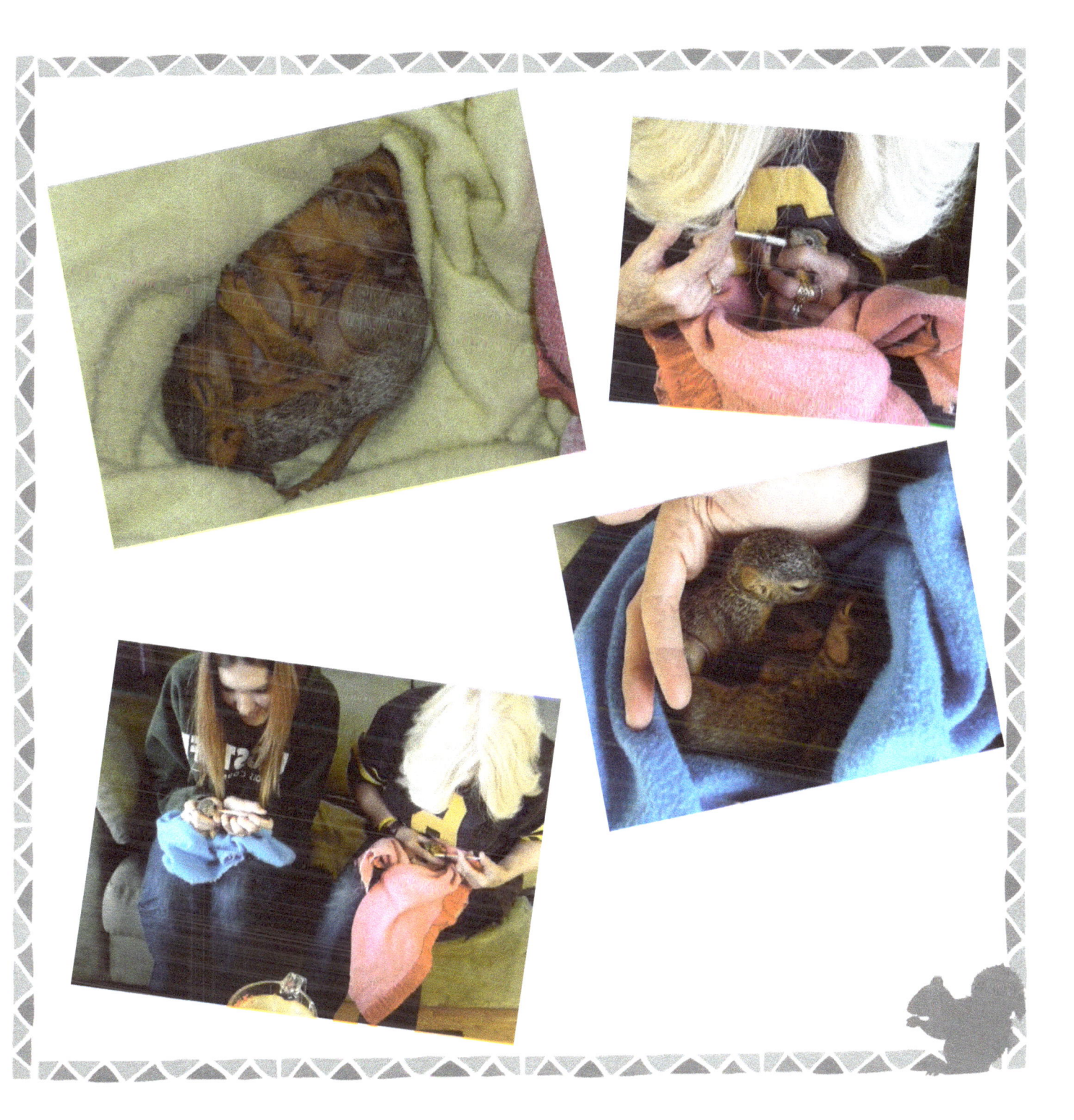

(Eastern) Fox Squirrel Facts:

1. Fox Squirrels like habitats with pine and mixed trees that are spaced out.

2. Fox Squirrels get their name because of their fur color that is like a yellowish-red fox with a tan or red-brown belly and orange-brown ears.

3. Fox Squirrels enjoy eating bulbs, tree buds, roots, pine seeds, almonds, acorns, pumpkin seeds, walnuts, peanuts, trees that begin to fruit in the spring, insects, bird eggs, and some agricultural crops such as wheat and corn. Dried fruit, raisins, and dates are not good for them, and moldy corn could even be fatal. They can get very bulky in the winter to stay warm.

4. Fox Squirrels can be hand fed, and lose their fear of humans. They may also scratch or nip by accident.

5. Fox Squirrels are not endangered, can be trapped anytime and without a permit, unfortunately.

6. Fox Squirrels can have multiple mates, and babies in the same litter can have different dads.

7. Fox Squirrels are very intelligent, and also little tricksters. Sometimes they will fool other squirrels by pretending to bury food. This act is done so other squirrels and birds think that they have found a cache of food.

8. Fox Squirrels are almost never found to be infected with rabies, or known to transport it to humans.

9. Fox Squirrels may occasionally be all white and considered to be albinos, or may have a rare white fur coloration (leucism) due to a recessive gene found in some eastern gray squirrels.

10. Fox Squirrels are both blind and deaf at birth.

11. Fox Squirrels can be raised by humans, and then may return for a visit. Some squirrels understand and remember a food source, and also that some humans are safe.

12. Fox Squirrels flick their tails for a number of reasons, including as a warning. They also use their tails to alert other squirrels about something dangerous, or to let predators know they've been seen.

13. Fox Squirrel babies stay in their nests until they are covered with fur and have the skills to survive on their own.

14. Fox Squirrel babies usually leave the nest in April or May, with a second litter leaving in September.

15. Fox Squirrels like to chase each other for

fun, and also show their dominance for mating purposes and food supply protection. They are territorial, and mother squirrels are very protective of their nests.

16. Fox Squirrels are mammals and experience limitless emotions like fear, happiness, frustration and anger. They feel pain and stamp their feet, growl, and grind their teeth to show emotion.

17. Fox Squirrels are problem solvers with memories. They can hide and scatter food, collecting some as needed. They may pretend to hide some food just to throw others off. They can figure out how to climb bird feeders to steal food or from each other, even recognizing people who will bring treats on a regular basis.

18. Fox Squirrels are omnivores, but mostly eat nuts, seeds, and fruit. They eat about a pound of food a week.

19. Fox Squirrels don't hibernate, but rely on the food they have stored and buried. Their sense of smell and memory help them recover most of the food, even in a foot of snow, where they might dig a tunnel to get to it. What they don't recover may just grow into trees.

20. Fox Squirrels can communicate with high pitched chirps and by the movement of their tails.

*A scurry or dray is a group of squirrels. Adults usually live alone, but may huddle as a group when it is cold.

*Squirrels are perhaps the most plentiful wildlife humans share their environment with, even though they can be quite mischievous.

*Squirrel Appreciation Day was founded January 21, 2001 in North Carolina, probably because they are so cute and versatile.

*Squirrels play important ecological roles year-round.

*The Sciuridae family (tree and flying squirrels, chipmunks, marmots) are worldwide (except Antarctica and Australia), ranging in size from five inches to three feet.

*Squirrels zig zag to escape predators, which helps them to elude prey (but not cars), and have even been known to chew rattlesnake skin and lick their fur to repel predators.

*Squirrels have teeth that continually grow (approximately six inches a year). They have been known to chew many a power line.

The Williams Family and Two Dogs

Loyalty and Love have no Conditions

Story and Artwork by
Jennifer Foreman de Grassi Williams

To Kirk~ Marry me again?

Tail-waggers who have left a paw print on
our hearts forever~
Buddy
Brandi, Rufus
Daisy, Butters
Tippytail, Bailey, Abaroo, Holly
Tbone, Mocha
Bummer
Gracie Bell
Nesbitt
Samantha, Bubbles
Snapper, Sugar, Pepper
Argus, Rosebud, Roscow
Arlo, Jeffrey, Seymour, Nana, Sadie, Honey
Rudy
Koko, Ginger
Sam, Scout, Lucy, MacDuff, MacTavish
Charlie, Barkley, Annie
Chelsie, Venus
Zoey, Zeek

Story number 7 is about two loyal and loveable dogs who were the catalyst that cemented the love of family.

Waikiki beach was a very cool place to live back in the 60's. Two blocks one way was the ocean, and two blocks another was the Honolulu Zoo. I spent hundreds of hours sitting on a bench outside of the gorilla cages, because I felt very drawn to their thoughtful demeanor as they watched me approach each day. One handsome and pensive male in particular, upon seeing me sitting, would kindly mimic me by sitting at the bars that separated us. He gazed my direction, sometimes, but also would look away or fiddle with something on other days, as if to ignore my gaze, or just to pretend I wasn't there peering into his soul. The eyes of this gorilla really spoke to me, so human and thoughtful, so seemingly understanding of life. To me, those eyes communicated many things I just could not put into words. I liked to believe that if the bars were removed, I could sit directly across from this sentient being, knee to knee, and not have to say a word, because we would understand just from a look. This is the way I feel about dogs. Though I've had few in my life because of all the other little beings that came into my life by accident, I have no doubt that dogs are the same communicators as the Great Apes. Dogs communicate so many things through their trusting and loving eyes. They say I trust you, and you can trust me to be loyal, kind, dutiful, uncomplicated, by your side always and forever, forgiving and loving. Even if 'by chance' a dog comes into your life, it is my belief that in some way they had a hand (paw) in ending up with you. Simply put, dogs choose us... It may be a wag of the tail as you approach, a whimper when you

walk by, a wiggle of the body, or maybe a wink you can't see. I'd say mostly, we end up with a dog that was meant to be for us all along. I'd also say the same about a four decades long relationship with someone you choose to be with forever. This story began with a mostly chance meeting between two teachers, a perfect kiss, two distinctly different dogs that came into our lives, and how we all fell in love with each other. Whether a dog comes from a friend, was given as a present, was adopted from a rescue center, a breeder, or just showed up, they are a gift. Given the choice I'd surely rescue a dog that needed a home, rather than purchase from a breeder, or a puppy mill. While a dog's life is short in comparison to ours, and the pain of losing a dog can be an unbelievably hard journey, I'd do it all over again just to feel that kind of loyalty and love given so freely by nearly all dogs. Somewhere I heard, "Don't cry because it's over, but smile because it happened". I don't ever want to let the pain of losing my friend to close off my heart to another dog that just wants to love you more than himself!

Love can surely happen when your heart's not even looking,

I saw it in her eyes and when she licked my gentle hand;

Her paw reached out and chose ME and for that I'm very blessed,

As the love we both could feel was amazing and unplanned.

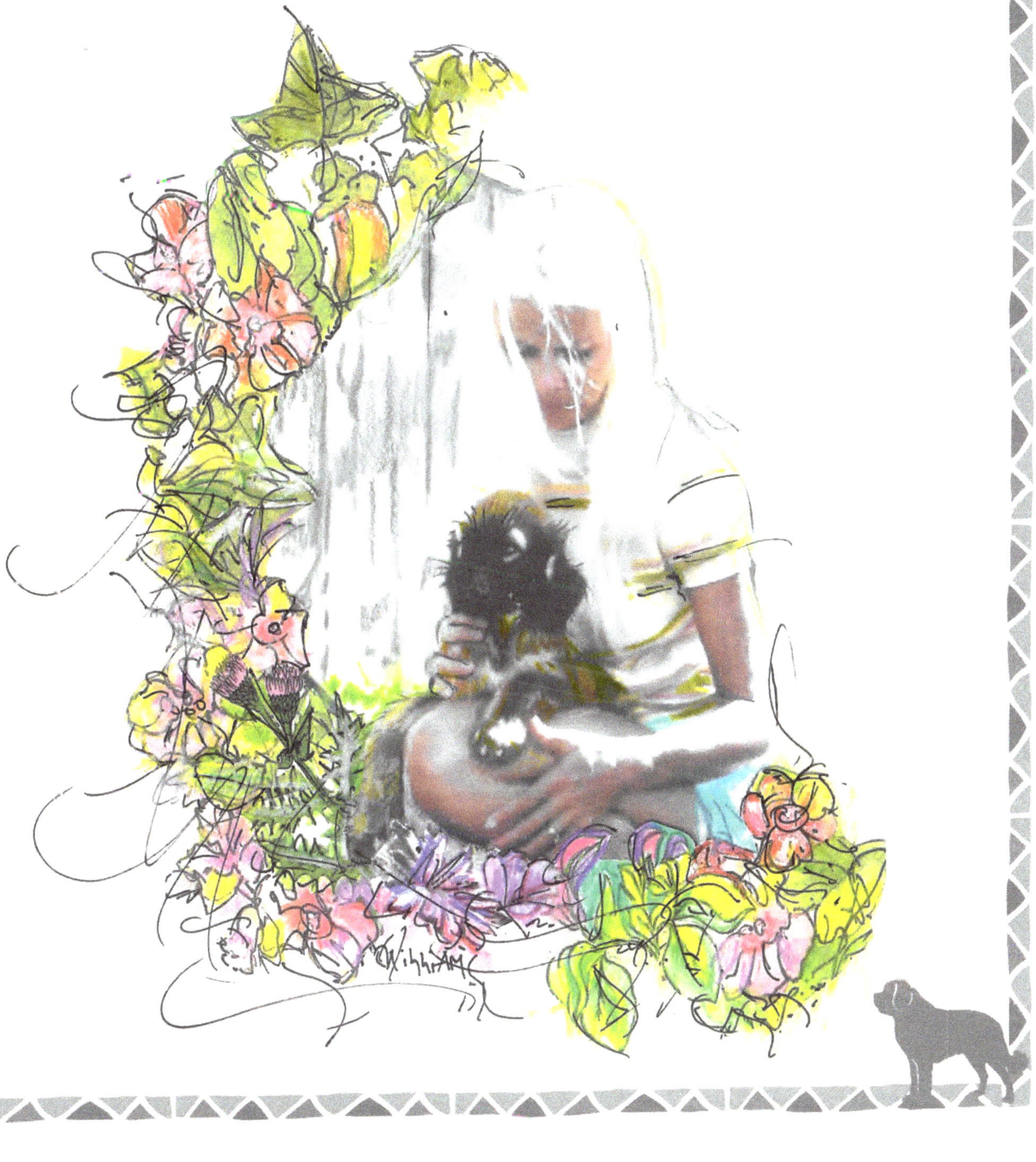

The many years we shared were filled
with hugs and doggie kisses,

As we played in ocean waves and drove
quite close to Heyburn peak;

We looked like twins together in a
sports car that was green,

And she could read my heart and soul,
though rarely did she 'speak'.

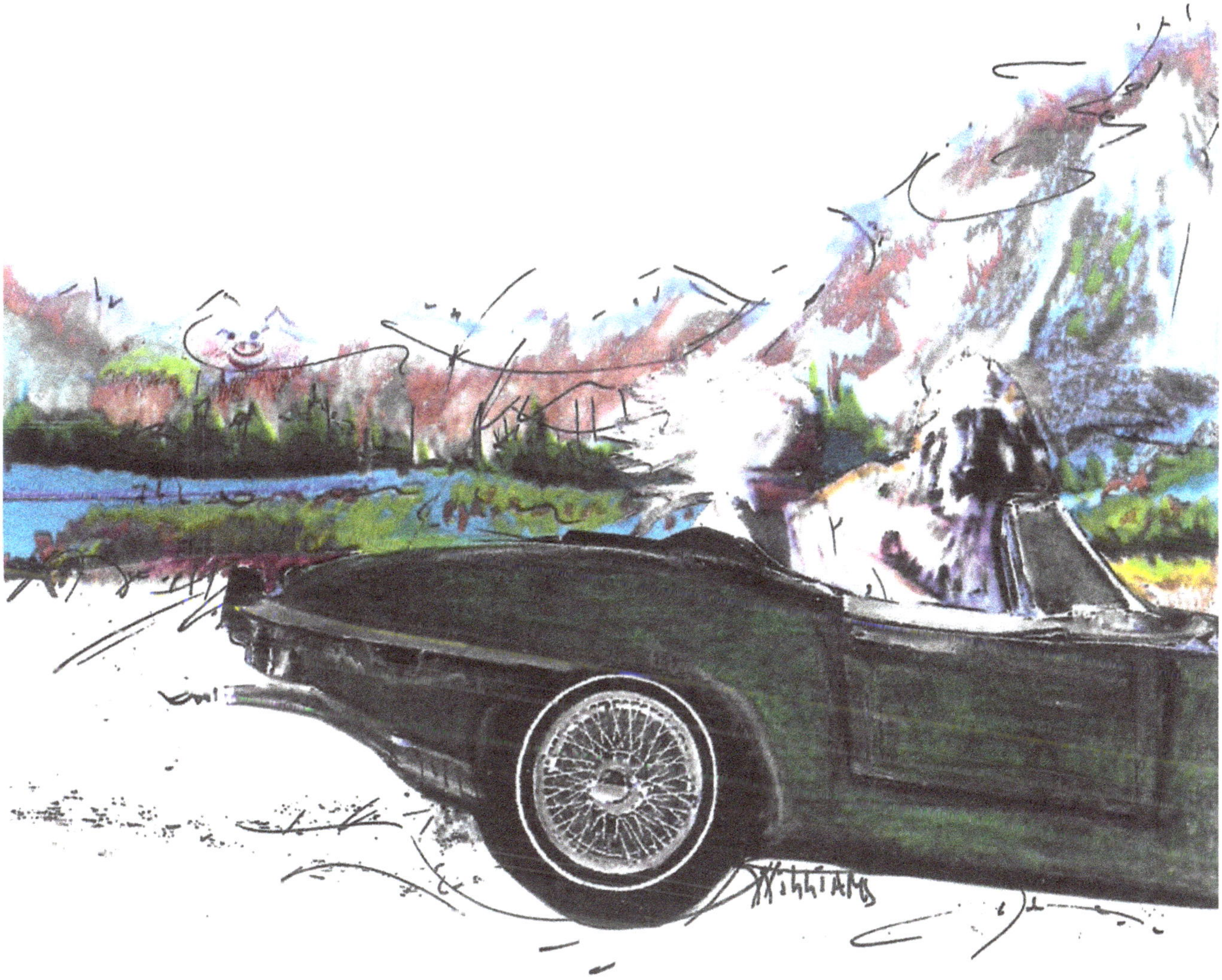
WILLIAMS

Many furry friends she had and
loved to tease for fun,

But next to me her tender heart
adored a good old boy;

Rufus was a giant fuzzy fluff
ball of a guy,

And when he looked at Brandi she
just filled his heart with joy.

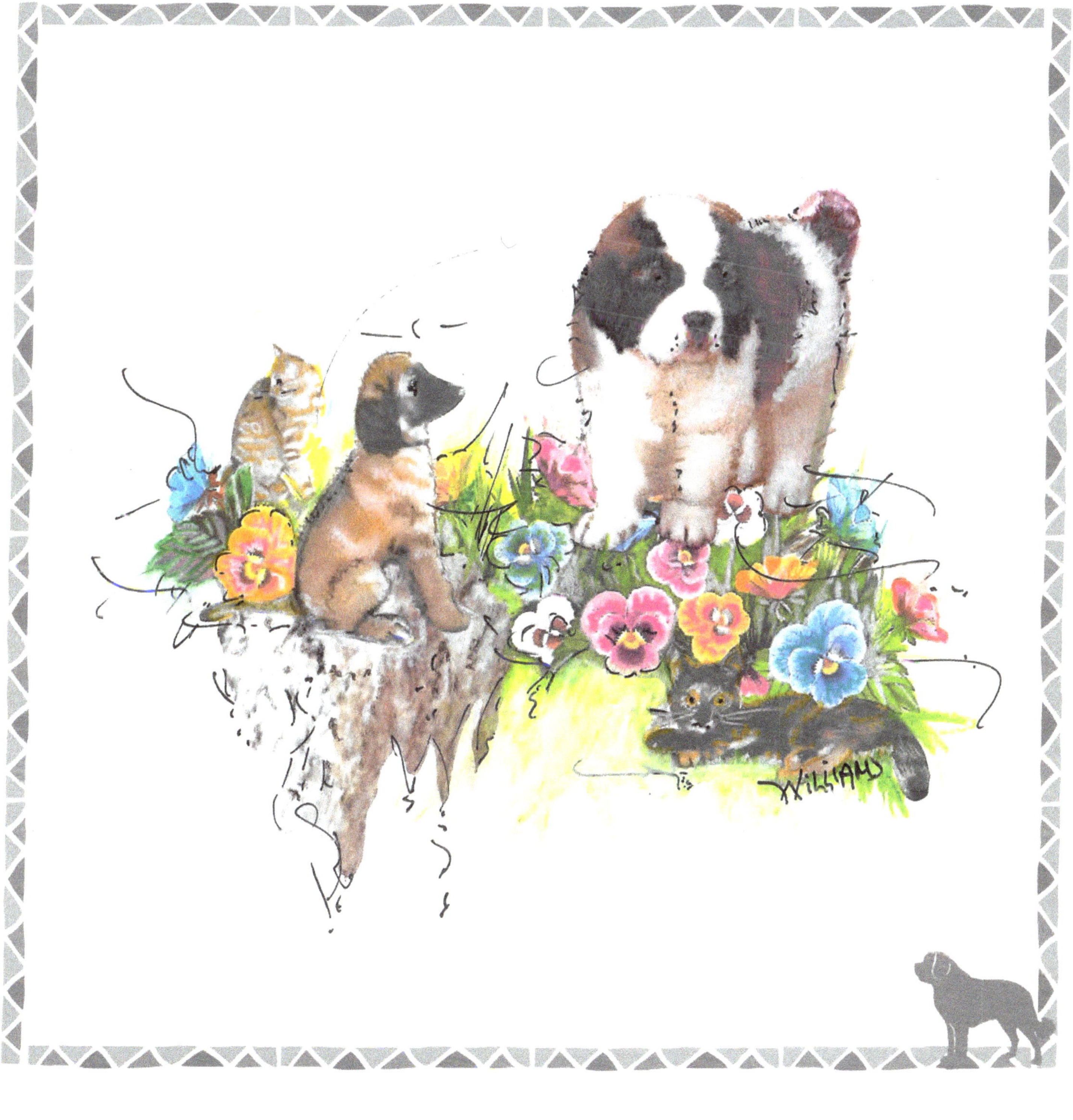
WILLIAMS

Rufus grew and grew so tall that
he could reach to shoulders,

And told his 'dad' he'd met a
dog as fast as any deer;

Brandi brought her 'mama' and sweet
Rufus brought his 'dad',

And in a yard where veggies grew
they played and romped all year.

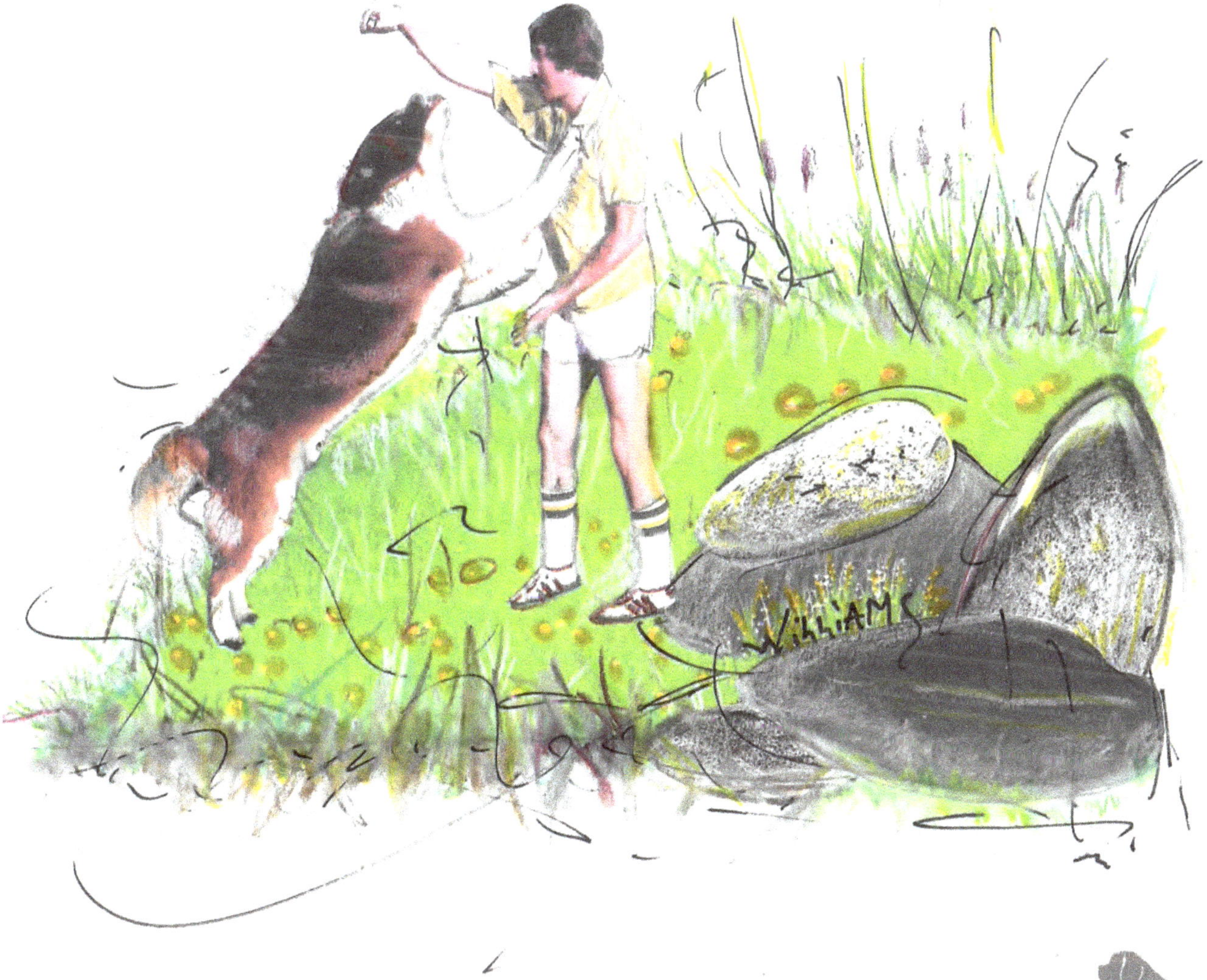
WilliAMS

Cats and turtles shared the yard
and little kids did too,

And in between the run and chase
the dogs drank from the hose;

And helped their 'mom' and 'dad' as they
picked corn and pretty flowers,

And shared a happy life forever
because of who they chose.

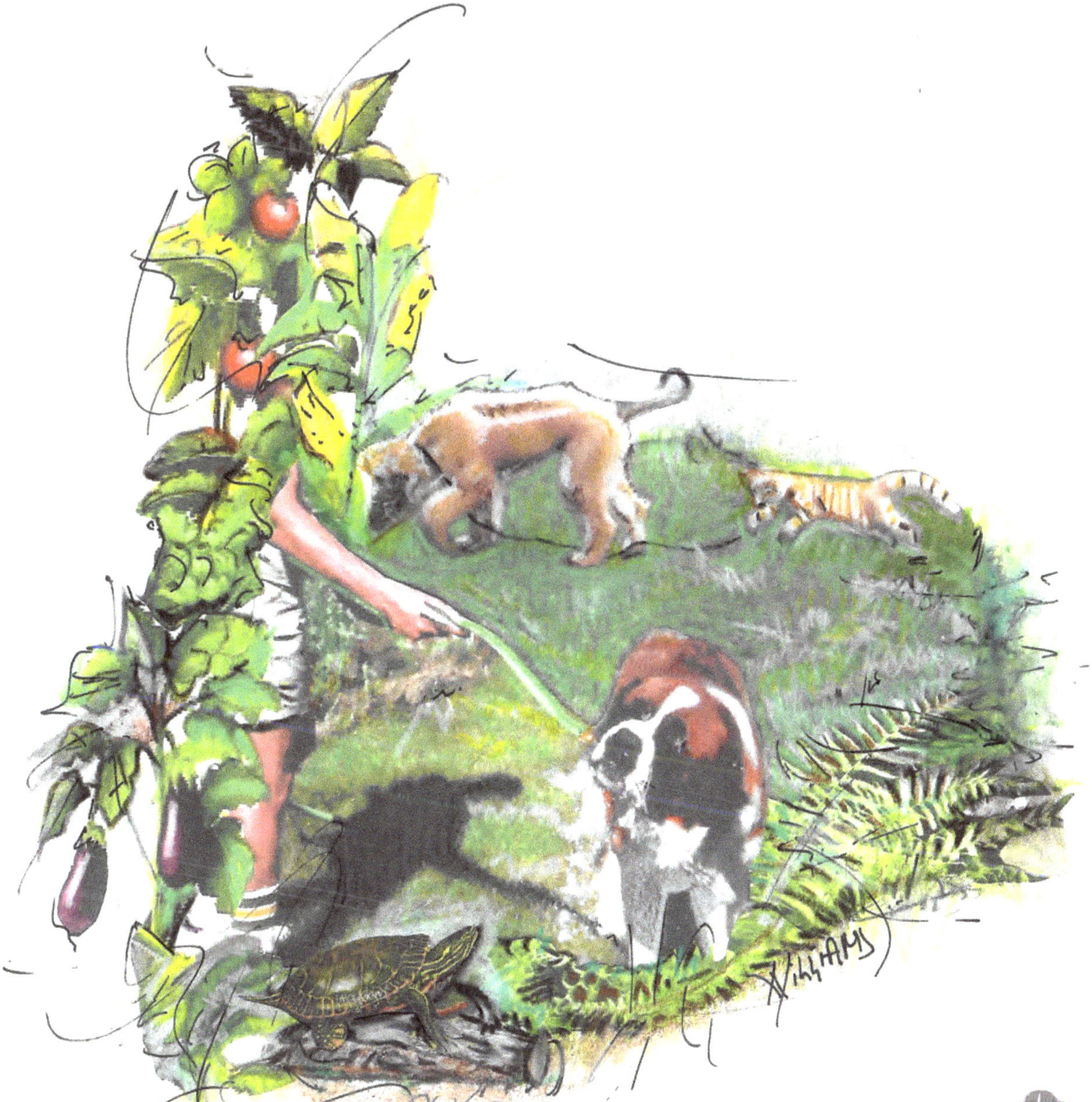

Rufus chased dear Brandi who was
fast as fast could be,

While all the Williams kids would laugh
and splash inside their pool;

And everyone would hug the dogs
but couldn't quite believe,

That Rufus had 12 inches hanging
down of doggie drool.

Williams

Sometimes when no one could see
these best of friends would try,

To hide inside the garden and then
plan to venture out;

Brandi would fly high and jump
right over a big rail,

And Rufus pushed the fence so
hard that all you'd see was SNOUT!

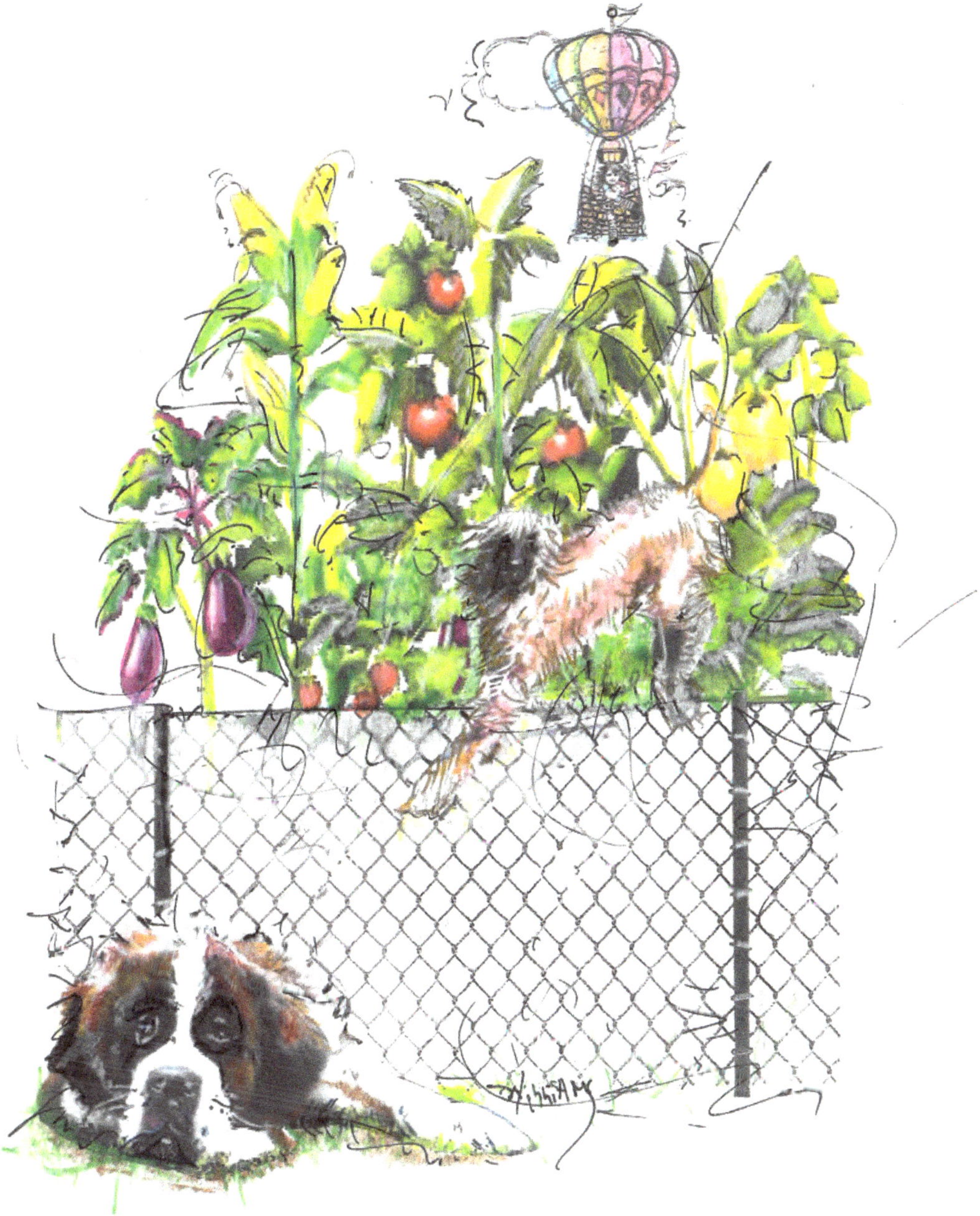

The friends loved great adventures
whether home or in the truck,

Especially if they got to go to
Chow Now for a treat;

Rufus put his great big head
inside the widow sill,

To eat in one big giant bite an
ice cream cone so sweet.

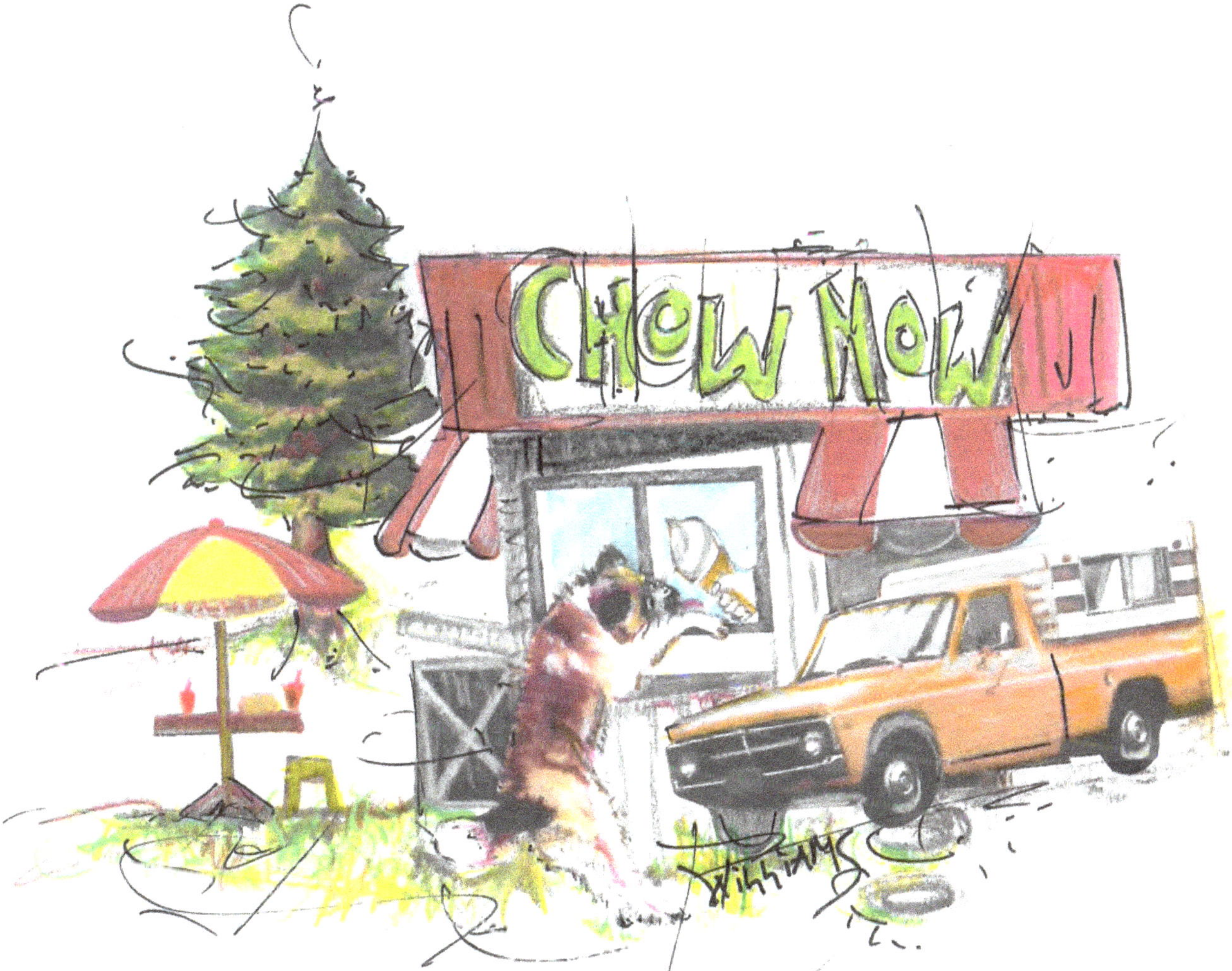
CHOW MOW
Williams

Winter found the kids outside all
covered in white snow,

And even both the dogs were only
bumps out in the yard;

Rufus poked his head up but his
body stayed quite buried,

And how the kids would laugh to
see this silly St. Bernard.

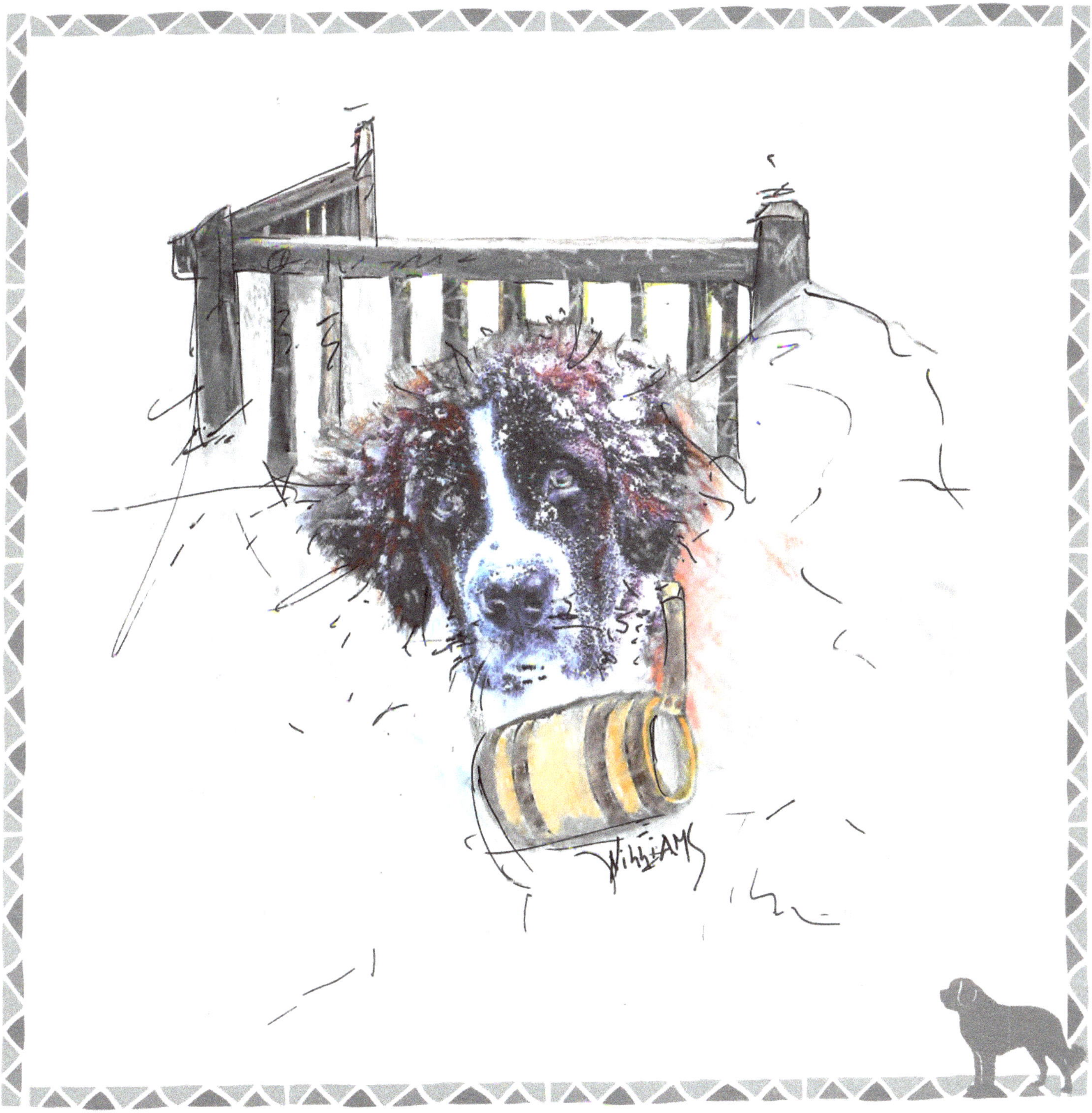
WILLIAMS

These two very different dogs shared
many things in common,

For they chose us 'mom' and 'dad'
cuz dogs are very clever;

Together their great loyalty blessed
us with so much joy,

And mostly all the love they gave
would be with us forever.

The End

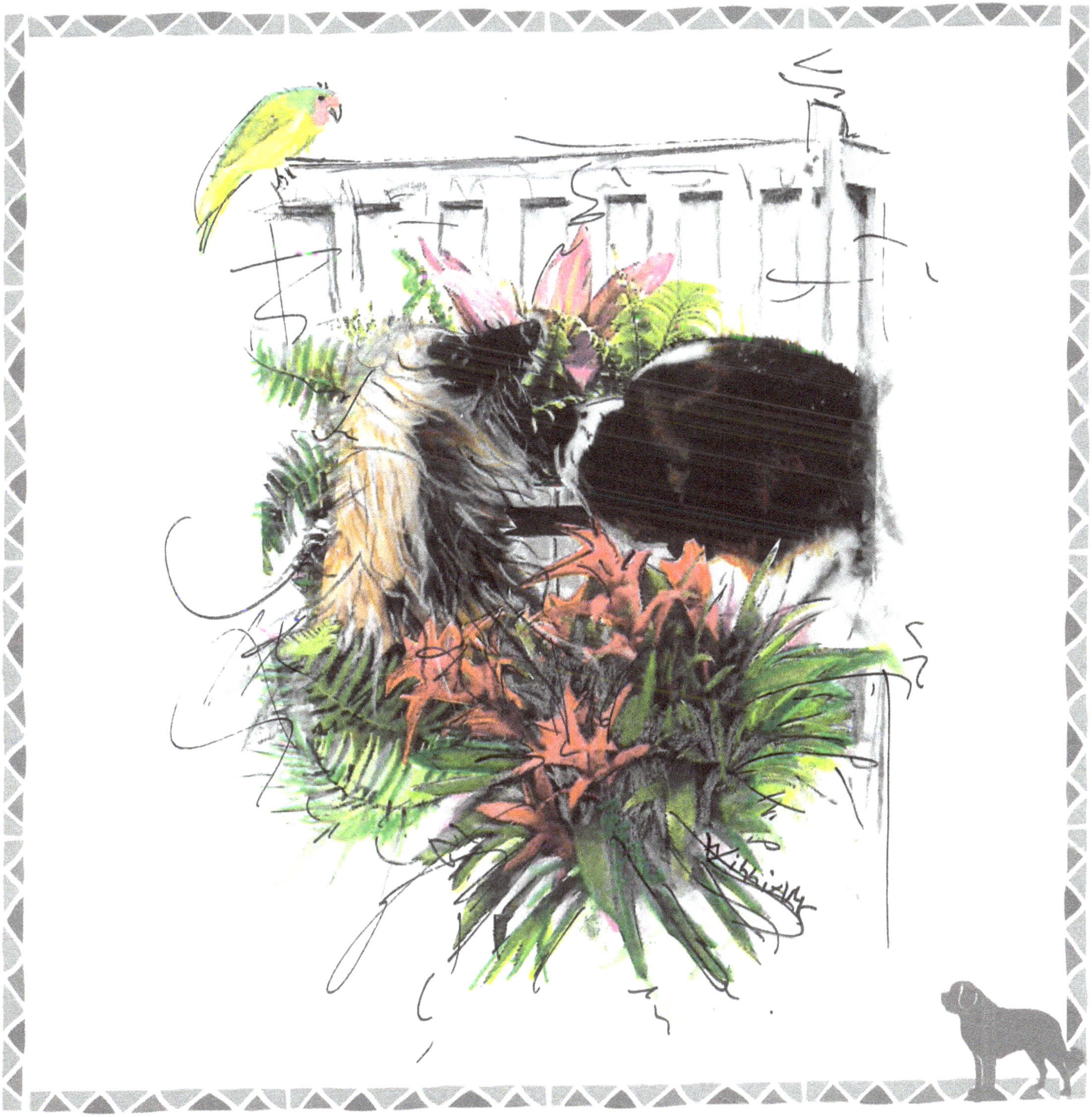

(Some) Dog Facts:

1. Dogs are direct descendants of wolves.

2. Dogs are nearly 100% accurate in detecting prostrate cancer by smelling urine samples, and other trained dogs can detect breast and lung cancer by smelling a person's breath.

3. Dogs (three) survived the sinking of the Titanic.

4. Dogs come in all sizes, but the tallest dog in the world is 44" and is a Great Dane. The Guinness book named Milly, a Chihuahua, as the "World's Smallest Dog". She is only 3.8 inches tall. Dogs have been known to influence some movie directors. George Lucas created the Ewoks in Star Wars after his family dog.

5. Dogs can have black tongues, like the Shar-Pei and the Chow Chow, and nobody knows why.

6. Dogs can run fast, but the Greyhound can outrun a cheetah in a distance race.

7. Dogs, and other sentient animals, still face painful and extremely cruel animal testing for things like cosmetics, food and toothpaste.

8. Dogs are the only ones who can hear a frequency that Paul McCartney added at the end of the Beatles song 'A day in the Life'.

9. Dogs dream.

10. Dogs noses are wet with a thin layer of mucous that absorbs scent. When they lick their noses they taste it in their mouth.

11. Dogs see in colors: blue, yellow, green-yellow, and even shades of gray.

12. Dogs do not age like humans, and do not age at a rate of 7 years (human) to 1 year of dog. Rather, the first year of a medium dog is closer to 15 years of a human, while the second year of a dog's life equals 9 years of a human's.

*The St. Bernard was called the "avalanche dog", named after the very dangerous St. Bernard pass in the Alps. They had the ability to find people covered in the mountains covered with snow, sometimes working in pairs with the male digging out a person, and the female warming the victim.

*A St. Bernard, named Mochi, is the record holder for the Guinness World Records because she has the longest tongue.

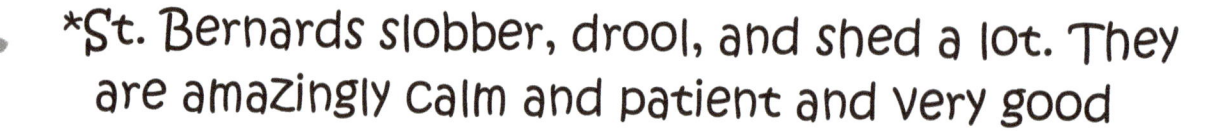

*St. Bernards slobber, drool, and shed a lot. They are amazingly calm and patient and very good with kids. They are eager to please, intelligent, and easy to train. Rufus learned spelled commands like LIE and SIT. In many pictures St. Bernards are depicted wearing a keg around their necks, which implies they would help cold travelers with some alcohol. However, these rescue dogs never actually wore these, but did carry packs with water and food. These 'gentle giants' make excellent family dogs, in spite of their size.

*Afghan hounds are one of the oldest dog breeds, which makes it difficult to know where they even originated, but legend says it was the dog on Noah's Ark. Possibly they were brought to Afghanistan with the army of Alexander the Great.

*Afghan hounds were used to hunt, and could corner animals, like leopards, because of their speed (up to 40 miles per hour), agility, cleverness, their independent thinking, and great eyesight. They have a field vision of 270 degrees.

*Afghan hounds are incredibly beautiful and have an elegant prance. Their flowing fur keeps them warm in the Afghani climate.

*Afghan hounds are sighthounds and love to run after things they want. It can be difficult to get them to come, and chasing one is nearly an impossibility.

*Afghan hounds have a low threshold for pain and will whimper quite easily if hurt.

*Picasso was inspired by many dogs, but the Afghan hound was a favorite. "Kabul" was in many of his paintings.

*Afghan hounds are an aloof dog, which might lead you to wonder what they are thinking. Their beautiful eyes will burn to your soul.

There are many dog rescue organizations locally, nationally, and worldwide, which take in a variety of other animals too. Many are non-profit, no-kill. Some take in senior animals, or animals from a shelter where they may be on a euthanasia list: Best Friends Animal Society (Utah), Petfinder (online North America), Hope for Paws (Los Angeles), National Mill Dog Rescue (Colorado), Old Dog Haven (Washington State), North Shore Animal League (New York), Dogs Without Borders (Los Angeles), The Gentle Barn (California), ARF (California), Humane Society of the United States (Washington, D.C.), American Society

'Old Buck' and Rufus

for the Prevention of Cruelty to Animals (ASPCA), and local organizations like humane societies or other pet shelters. There are also dog rescue and adoption organizations specific to breeds: Afghan Hound Club of America (AHCA), Afghan Hound Rescue of Southern California (AHRSC), Saint Bernard Rescue Group, Saint Bernard Rescue Foundation, Inc.

*The "Soi Dog Foundation was established in 2003 in Puket, Thailand, to help the street dogs and cats who had no-one else to care for them. Over 70,000 strays roamed the island, with the numbers growing alarmingly due to lack of spay and neuter programs to control the population. Soi Dog was created to provide a humane and sustainable solution to managing the stray population and to address their medical needs."

Rufus and Brandi

The Author

Jennifer Foreman de Grassi Williams

Jennifer was born and raised in Oakland, California, but came to Idaho in 1972 as the wife of an Air Force pilot. She began her teaching career at Mountain Home High School where she taught art for 25 years before teaching art at Skyview High School in Nampa. She earned her BFA in Art Education from Mississippi State University and her Master's degree in Art from Boise State University.

Jennifer lives in Idaho with her husband, Kirk (who still shoots his age in golf), where she has been an art educator for 45 years. Jennifer has been an adjunct professor at Boise State University, George Fox University and the College of Idaho. Jennifer has received numerous state and national awards in her teaching career, including the Governor's Award in Art Education, US West Teacher of the Year, Boise State's Distinguished Alumni Award and

Women Making History Award, ING's 1st Place National Unsung Heroes Award, the National Education Association's Teaching Excellence Award, Idaho's Art Teacher of the Year and was the 2002 Idaho Teacher of the Year. In 2016, Jennifer was one of only five teachers, nationwide, inducted into the NATIONAL TEACHERS HALL OF FAME in Emporia, Kansas, and is the first Idaho teacher to have ever been recognized by the President of the United States for this award. Jennifer is a published artist, having written two art textbooks and many articles. This is the volume 2 in a series of children's books she is writing, to share stories that are mostly factual, about the plethora of sentient beings that always seem to find their way into her life. Jennifer passionately advocates for all creatures. Her Volume 1 'Tails, Scales, Fur, Purr, Oink' is a hardback compilation of books 1-7. This is volume 2 hardback, which is a compilation of books 8-14.

    Jennifer has taken art to tiny one room school houses for over 40 years with her 'Project Van Go'. Four years ago she celebrated this milestone at the little red school house on the prairie in Prairie, Idaho. Her greatest work, she says, is that of

'WA' to her precious grandchildren, and Mother to four amazing children: Hillary an Investigator for Human Resources, Tyler (Lauren) a Doctor of Physical Therapy residing in Boise now with the rest of his family, exploring all things that present a physical challenge and tests limits, Jessica (Kyle) a high school Science teacher (and her high school's teacher of the year) in Idaho and amazing mother to our precious 'cheeky monkey' Norah, Harper 'peanut', and Emily (Jason) who is a School Counselor and stay at home Mommy to darling Sonja Hope and Reed William. In her free time, Jennifer rehabilitates wild and domesticated animals. At every opportunity she volunteers at the Makauwahi Cave Reserve on Kaua'i where her two giant sulcata tortoises, Shelly and Lily, are part of a project that promotes the propagation of native Hawaiian plants. Jennifer donates profits from her books to many organizations. Her greatest inspiration was her Mother who passed away 8 years ago. Jennifer smiles at the journey that is her life since she was Miss San Francisco Cable Car 1968.

The Watercolorist

Bobbi Kelly

Bobbi Kelly taught high school art in Mountain Home for many years before retiring and moving to Moscow, Idaho, where she resides with her daughter, Sandra, and their devoted dog, Holly. She is an active member of the Idaho Watercolor Society and the Palouse Watercolor Society, and teaches adult painting classes as well as doing volunteer art projects with elementary students. Bobbi enjoys painting local and regional scenes of interest, in a style she thinks of as "casual realism". "Illustrating Jennifer's children's books is definitely a change of pace from my usual watercolor subject matter," Bobbi says, "but one which is both creatively demanding and delightful."

Examples of her work can be viewed on the Palouse Watercolor Society website: www.palousewatercolorsocius.com

Books by Jennifer Foreman de Grassi Williams can also be purchased individually:

The Williams Family Adopts Tiki Turtle

The Williams Family and a Very Beloved Dolly

The Williams Family Bids Aloha to Shell and Lily

The Williams Family and Andy Cat

The Williams Family and a Curious Stinky Minky

The Williams Family Rescues a Piggy Named Otis

The Williams Family Shares a Rat "Tail"

Tails, Scales, Fur, Purr, Oink (Volume 1)

The Williams Family and an Iguana Named Diego

The Williams Family and MJ the Red Knee Tarantula

The Williams Family and Sunshine the Yellow-bellied Marmot

The Williams Family Saves Moose the Kangaroo Mouse

The Williams Family Fosters Rabbits, Parakeets, and Snails

The Williams Family Nurtures Squirrels

The Williams Family and Two Dogs

Introduction to Batik and Other Resists

Art 2 - Pottery, Sculpture, Batik and 3-D Design

For more information go to http://projectvango.org

* Located in each story is a small drawing of a pig. Did you find it?

Lightning Source UK Ltd.
Milton Keynes UK
UKHW021129181220
375433UK00002B/87

9 781087 929576